A JOE GUNTHER NOVEL

LOWER PROVIDENCE COMMUNITY LIBRARY
50 PARKLANE DRIVE
EAGLEVILLE, PA 19403-1171

W9-AAE-056

RED HERRING

ARCHER MAYOR

THORNDIKE PRESS
A part of Gale, Cengage Learning

GALE
CENGAGE Learning

Detroit • New York • San Francisco • New Haven, Conn • Waterville, Maine • London

GALE
CENGAGE Learning

Copyright © 2010 by Archer Mayor.
Thorndike Press, a part of Gale, Cengage Learning.

ALL RIGHTS RESERVED
This is a work of fiction. All of the characters, organizations and events portrayed in this novel are either products of the author's imagination or are used fictitiously.

Thorndike Press® Large Print Crime Scene.
The text of this Large Print edition is unabridged.
Other aspects of the book may vary from the original edition.
Set in 16 pt. Plantin.

LIBRARY OF CONGRESS CATALOGING-IN-PUBLICATION DATA

Mayor, Archer.
    Red herring : a Joe Gunther novel / by Archer Mayor.
        p. cm. — (Thorndike Press large print crime scene)
    ISBN-13: 978-1-4104-3268-1
    ISBN-10: 1-4104-3268-8
    1. Gunther, Joe (Fictitious character)—Fiction. 2. Police—Vermont—Fiction. 3. Serial murders—Fiction. 4. Serial murder investigation—Fiction. 5. Large type books. I. Title.
    PS3563.A965R43 2011
    813'.54—dc22   2010040362

Published in 2011 by arrangement with St. Martin's Press, LLC.

Printed in Mexico
1 2 3 4 5 6 7 15 14 13 12 11

To John Martin

You supplied me with several crucial plot
points in the writing of this story, revealing
a creative streak that has inspired me in
the past. You are a friend, an advisor, and
a sharp-eyed critic, and I thank you for all
three.

ACKNOWLEDGMENTS

It has become a convention to thank many and all for the results of a labor like this story. However, in some cases, the influence of advisors and sounding boards is more peripheral than in others. This effort, however, falls under the "others" category. Without the enthusiasm, assistance, time, and efforts of the kind and generous people listed below, this book would not have been written, quite literally. My thanks to you all:

Eric Buel
John Martin
Nancy Aichele
Paco Aumand
Steve Shapiro
Gaye Symington
Ray Walker
Castle Freeman, Jr.
Julie Lavorgna

Yael Cohn
Scott Casella

At the Brookhaven National Laboratory:

Elaine Lowenstein
Elaine DiMasi
Phil Sarcione
Kendra Snyder
Daniel Fischer
Mark Sakitt
Jeanne Marie Petchauer
Carl Anderson
Peter Guida
Garman Harbottle
Susan White-DePace
Andreana Leskovjan
John Dunn
Doon Gibbs
Jane Koropsak

And with very special and particular thanks
to Wally Mangel

Additionally:

The Brattleboro Police Department
The Vermont Forensic Lab
Vermont's Office of the Chief Medical
   Examiner

CHAPTER ONE

Doreen Ferenc slipped her nightgown over her head and let it fall the length of her body and gently settle onto her shoulders. This was the reward of every day, this threshold moment, when, as though dropping a heavy burden, she exchanged her regular clothing, complete with belts, buttons, zippers, and elastic, for the sensual, almost weightless comfort of a simple shift of light cotton.

Not that the day had been more onerous than usual. Her mom had been in good spirits, minimally judgmental of the nursing-home staff. They'd served Indian pudding for lunch, a perennial favorite. Her mother had once been an expert at the dessert, and it had led them both down a path of happy memories while they'd worked on the quilt for Doreen's new nephew. Doreen's brother, Mark, had recently married a much younger woman in Nevada, where they lived, and she'd just delivered their first child.

Doreen and Mark weren't particularly close, as siblings went, but they got along, and their mom loved them both. She preferred Mark, as Doreen well knew, but only because he was in a position to present her with a grandchild. Doreen had never found marriage appealing, and by and large didn't like kids, which, thank God, she was now safely beyond having anyway. The quilt had become a salutary talisman of good tidings to which Doreen could contribute guilt-free.

She left the bedroom in her bare feet and dropped her clothes into the laundry hamper in the darkened bathroom, pausing a moment to admire the unexpected snow falling from the night sky onto the enormous skylight she'd spent too much money having installed. The house was an almost tacky prefab ranch — virtually a trailer with pretensions — but she knew in her heart that it was also the house she'd most likely die in, so why not splurge a little, like on the skylight and the heat she poured on to make the whole house as toasty as in mid-July? She loved winters in Vermont, including flukily premature ones like this year's. She'd known them her whole life, and had, at various times, enjoyed skiing, snowball fights, and even shoveling the driveway. But no longer. Now she just wanted to watch the weather from the comfort of an evenly heated, boring modern house that was fussed over by a handyman complete with a snowplow — assuming he'd attached the plow to his pickup by now. She had started working full-time at seventeen, decades earlier, and now she was going to enjoy all the fruits of a slightly early retirement.

Entertaining such thoughts, she pursued the next step in her nightly routine, and entered the small kitchen. There, she dished out a single scoop of vanilla ice cream, splashed an appreciable quantity of brandy over its rounded top, and retired to the living-room couch, which was strategically angled so she could watch TV from a reclining position.

It was snowing — heavily, too — and only October. People hadn't switched to snow tires, sand deliveries were still being made to town road crews, and cars were going to be decorating ditches all over the state by morning. But Doreen didn't have to care about any of it. She was as snug as the proverbial bug.

Settled at last, she hit the remote, dialed in her favorite channel, and heard the doorbell ring.

"Damn," she murmured, glancing at the

digital clock on the set. It was just before ten P.M. "Who on earth?"

She placed her bowl on the coffee table, struggled up from her place of comfort, and sighed heavily as she crossed the room to the tiny mudroom and the front door beyond it.

Enclosing herself in the mudroom to preserve the heat, she slipped on an overcoat from the row of nearby pegs, hit the outside light, and called out, "Who is it?" She could see the outline of a man standing before the frosted glass of the door.

A weak voice answered, "You don't know me, ma'am. My name's Lyle Robinson. I've just wrecked my car about a half mile up. I was wondering if I could use your phone."

So much for keeping immune from the woes of poor weather. She then heard him cough and bend over as he clutched his chest.

"Are you all right?"

"I think so, ma'am. I wasn't wearing my seat belt, like a damn fool . . . Sorry. Don't mean to offend. I think I just bruised my chest, is all."

She hesitated.

"Ma'am?" he said next. "Not that it'll matter, but I'm a cousin of Jim and Clara Robinson. They used to live just outside

Saxtons River. I don't know if you know them."

"I do," she blurted out. "So, you're related to Sherry?"

"Yes, ma'am, although what she's doing way out west is beyond any of us."

Doreen threw open the door.

She was only aware of two things after that: the bare blade of an enormous knife, held just two inches before her eyes, and, behind it, a man disguised by a hooded sweatshirt worn backward, two holes cut in the fabric for his eyes. She now understood why his voice had sounded weak.

"Okay, Dory," he said. "Drop the coat and step back inside. You and I are gonna get acquainted."

CHAPTER TWO

He wasn't sure how it happened — he hadn't been paying attention — but Joe Gunther was now all alone in the room. Aside from the body, of course — one Doreen Ferenc, according to her driver's license, her neighbors, a computer check, and her mail. She herself was silent on the matter, not that he didn't think she had a few things left to tell him.

Joe sat gingerly on a wooden chair to take advantage of the sudden stillness, dressed in a white Tyvek suit that made him look more like a nuclear plant worker than a cop.

Crime scenes, especially homicides, were busy places — all bustle and talk, sketching and taking photographs, lifting prints and logging evidence. Along with a platoon of people — from cops to medics to funeral-home employees to state's attorneys and unwelcome official gawkers.

It left little room for quiet contemplation.

Gunther didn't worry about where everyone had gone. They'd be back too soon anyway. Instead, he sat motionless, studying both room and victim for what they might tell him.

It wasn't much. There was a single glistening drop of blood on her forehead, presumably from a scalp laceration above the hairline, and no obvious signs of disruption around her — a slightly displaced coffee table and a wrinkled doormat that could have been mere casual housekeeping. By all appearances, the entire house looked like what it had actually been: the home of a spinster of fifty-four who'd had a habit of lying on the couch every night to watch TV, accompanied by a plate of slightly spiked ice cream.

That was her version of the wild life, from what they'd been told by a nurse at her mother's nursing home, who'd also said that Dory came to visit every day for four hours, without fail, morning and afternoon, equally divided into two-hour increments — the best and most consistent relative or visitor the place had ever known.

Prior to Joe's arrival here, another cop had spoken to the nurse on the phone — not the usual place to discuss a death. Joe preferred to break such news face-to-face.

15

But a call had been made to the retirement home to make sure they'd have someone to speak with later, and the nurse — Brenda Small by name — had immediately blurted out, "I knew it. She's dead. That's the only way she'd miss visiting her mom." The cop had been too stunned to disagree. Joe didn't think it mattered. Small had vowed that she'd keep the death to herself, and volunteered what little they now had on Doreen, including the brandy garnish on the ice cream. She claimed that she and "Dory" had become virtual sisters over the years — unsurprising given that Doreen did little aside from staying at home and tending to her ailing and needy mother.

Joe had his doubts. He suspected Doreen got out more than Brenda imagined. In his experience, of which he had decades, people were quick to pigeonhole one another, reducing them to caricatures. As in using the word "spinster."

He imagined she had been that only literally. There was no evidence in the house stating otherwise — pictures or documents attesting to husbands or children, alive, dead, or estranged. But there were travel books and brochures, signs of a love of cooking, and a dozen albums and several cameras speaking to both an enthusiasm for and an ability in photography. This was a woman who, for whatever reasons, had chosen to hand over the majority of her time to accommodating her mother's needs, but who'd also managed to work in the basics of what appeared to be an enviable, if solitary, life.

Except for its last moments. Those had, by all appearances, been a waking nightmare.

Up to now, Joe had employed a favorite time-tested technique at death scenes — while acknowledging the body, he didn't start by focusing on it, choosing instead to work from the fringes inward. But he'd done that by this point. He'd wandered through the small, neat house, asked many of the preliminary questions, and gathered an overall sense of Doreen's daily rhythm.

Now he gazed at her, supine on the couch, her mouth agape, the blood shining on her forehead, her clouded eyes fixed on the ceiling as if she'd died wishing herself someplace else.

Joe didn't fault her there. The most compelling aspect of this entire scene, and which had transfixed every other investigator here, he feared, was the story suggested by her position. Her legs were apart, her nightgown pulled up to her waist and torn at the bodice, and her black underwear dangling from one foot.

By all appearances, Doreen Ferenc had been raped and murdered.

"Are you the one they told me to see?"

Joe glanced over to the door leading to the kitchen. A bearded man in his mid-thirties with longish hair was leaning over the threshold, hesitant to enter. Like everyone else, he was dressed all in protective white, but his self-consciousness about it was transparent.

Joe rose from his seat. This was no cop. "I don't know. Joe Gunther. VBI."

VBI stood for Vermont Bureau of Investigation, the state's major case squad. Joe was in fact its field force commander — a title that in more populated states would have guaranteed him a spot behind a desk. But not in Vermont.

Joe crossed the room, careful to stay on the floor's butcher paper travel lane — a crime-scene detail designed to curtail contamination.

He stuck out his gloved hand. "And you?"

The younger man flushed. "Oh, damn. I'm sorry. Jack Judge. I like John, to be honest, but everybody calls me Jack. Holdover from when I was a kid. I'm the new assistant medical examiner. Sorry I'm late. The snowstorm caught me by surprise."

Gunther smiled, amused by his self-deprecation. It was a nice break from the usual Type A behavior at such a setting.

"Welcome, John. You want to see the main attraction?"

Judge smiled back. "I guess that's why I'm here."

Joe led the way. The rule was that no one touched a body before the ME. This wasn't always observed, but it had been this time, Joe being in charge. Back in the day, AMEs, as they were now called, used to be volunteer local doctors, but as the world had become more litigious, violent, and complicated — even in this rural corner — they'd been replaced by trained investigators. Though not full-timers, they were often nurses or paramedics, used to responding to chaos in the middle of the night, working alongside cops, interpreting medication labels, and filing prompt paperwork.

"You just start?" Joe asked.

"Yes and no," Judge answered him. "I was a medic in the service."

Gunther looked at him more closely. "See any action?"

Judge nodded. "Iraq."

Joe, ex-army himself, nodded and circled the couch to introduce the AME to the reason he'd been called. "Tough," was all he said, before stating, "Doreen Ferenc; DOB 5/24/56, making her fifty-four."

Jack Judge squatted down, his forearms on his knees, and studied the body's face.

Joe kept speaking, knowing the drill. "Some of this is sketchy — it's still early — but we think she lived alone, led an orderly life centering mostly around her mother, who's in a nursing home. She had a regular doctor, whom she saw yearly, but had no medical problems and was only on an acid reflux med. I don't remember the name. One of the other guys has that."

Joe pointed at the small bowl of melted ice cream. "She supposedly had a little vanilla laced with brandy every night in front of the tube, so this looks like it happened last night."

Judge cast a glance at the darkened TV.

"We turned it off," Joe filled in, adding for no reason except to slightly humanize the victim, "It was on the Nature Channel. She had an ironclad routine, going to the nursing home every morning and afternoon to spend time with Mom, so when she didn't show up today, someone over there began calling. A neighbor finally saw this through the window and called 911."

"Who saw her alive last?" Judge asked.

"You're kidding, right?" came a voice from the doorway. "What the hell do you think we're all doing here?"

They looked up to see a scowling man with a withered left arm, the hand of which had been shoved into a pocket of his Tyvek suit to keep it from swinging around. This fellow, the arm notwithstanding, had cop stamped all over him.

Gunther said with a frown, "Willy Kunkle — John Judge, from the ME's office. Willy works for me, although nobody knows why."

Judge nodded, but Kunkle smirked. "They call you Jack, right? Jack Judge. Cute. Sounds like a cartoon."

Joe didn't say anything, recognizing the futility of educating Willy, but Judge, to his credit, simply answered, "Jack or John — doesn't matter. I heard of you, too."

Kunkle laughed. "I bet. You do her yet?"

"We were about to," Joe said.

Willy drew near, but had the courtesy to stay quiet. Joe didn't doubt that he'd give Judge more grief later. Hazing suited him, showcasing the least flattering of his many, often conflicting personality traits.

Jack Judge went back to studying Dory, finally rising enough to hover over her like a parent delivering a good-night kiss.

He spoke softly. "Nothing jumps out at

first glance. I see no signs of strangulation, or bruising around the face or shoulders." He reached out and deftly checked under the remnants of the torn nightgown before pressing against her sternum and along her collarbones and ribs, one by one, lifting each exposed breast gently to do so. Joe had seen several such exams, and even conducted a couple, but admired the man's sensitive touch, as if the patient were still alive.

"She's cold and in full rigor," Judge continued. "I'll check lividity in a bit, but I suspect that's fixed, too. That would fit your idea that this happened last night, right here."

He pulled a penlight from his outer pocket and moved to the scalp, where he parted her hair and began scanning the skin beneath. After a while, he straightened, frowning. "Can't find the source of that blood right off, but there's not much of it." He quickly shined the light into each nostril and raised her stiffened lips off her teeth, also peering into the mouth. "It's not castoff from there, so it may have come from whoever did this."

"You can call the guy an asshole, John," Willy chided him, emphasizing the name. "Nobody'll mind."

Judge had shifted to her hands, which he handled like porcelain, bending his body rather than manipulating them, so as to preserve their positioning, not to mention any trace evidence that might still be clinging there. Watching him, Joe suspected he'd done well as a medic, both highly competent and impervious to the likes of Willy.

"Nothing obvious here, either," the AME muttered. "Her nails are long enough to have done at least some damage, if she'd used them, but I don't see anything."

He took a step to the left, directly above her midriff. Again, from his pocket, he extracted something Joe couldn't at first identify, which turned out to be a small, powerful magnifying lens. Using both light and lens, Judge bent even closer to the body's exposed pubic hair.

Willy took a half pace backward. "You are shitting me."

Despite the circumstances, Joe smiled to himself. As unlikely as it seemed, cops were often squeamish around the dead, even tough guys like Kunkle. Joe wondered if Judge wasn't subtly wreaking a little vengeance with this show of interest; Doreen would be going upstate for an autopsy soon, encased and sealed in a body bag. That's where prints would be lifted, fingernails scraped, hair combed through, tissue samples collected. Not that Joe minded Judge's thoroughness here and now — it gave them all a better snapshot — but he sensed with satisfaction a little psychological warfare taking place.

Judge continued his close visual examination from her groin to her knees, paying close attention to the inner thighs, but looked disappointed when he finally straightened.

"Nothing," he stated. "No deposits, no stains, no signs of violence."

Willy scoffed. "Right. The expert. No offense, but I'll wait for the doc's vote on that."

"You've done this before," Joe suggested, both to clarify and, he hoped, to set Willy right.

Jack Judge nodded. "I was asked to investigate a few rape/homicides in Iraq."

Willy, also a combat vet, although carrying more baggage than most, looked away, pretending to be taking in the plate of melted ice cream, admonished but not willing to show it. "So, what do you think happened?" he asked as a peace offering.

Judge shrugged. "Maybe less than it seems? Why, I don't know." He looked at Joe. "You ready for me to roll her over?"

"Gently," Joe agreed. "Yeah."

She wasn't a large woman, and her stiffened state made it easy for Judge to simply lift an arm and a leg to pivot her onto her right side, just enough for the other two to bend down and examine the body's underside.

"Whoa," Willy exclaimed.

The cushions beneath were soaked with blood, which also covered the entirety of Ferenc's back.

Judge's position put him at a disadvantage. "Can you see what caused it?"

"Negative," Willy commented, reaching out toward a hole in the nightgown, at about mid-lumbar level.

"Hold it," Joe said, touching Judge on the shoulder to get him to set her back into position. "We'll let the ME give us that. I don't want to disturb any more than we have. Knife, gun, or ice pick, we know something was used, and we know for sure we have a murder. Let's just bag her hands carefully, wrap her up safe and sound, and do what we do best."

For once, Willy didn't argue, straightening up. He turned to Judge and asked with a tired, collegial half smile, "All right if we call the perp an asshole now?"

"Fine by me," Judge told him.

CHAPTER THREE

Joe sat in his unmarked car in the driveway of Doreen Ferenc's home, the engine running and the heater on, writing notes to himself on a legal pad. The vehicles were all on the Back Westminster Road, between Saxtons River and Bellows Falls. The road paralleled Interstate 91 — sometimes almost touching it — but otherwise remained hazy in most people's memories, leaving it to be used mostly by locals avoiding the geographical constraints of the faster road's widely spaced exits.

The passenger door suddenly opened, introducing a chilling wash of cold air and a tall, skinny man with angular features and a gentle, expressive face.

"Hey, boss," said Lester Spinney. "Looks like we got a live one this time, huh? So to speak."

Joe was used to this form of humor. Les had come to Joe's Brattleboro-based squad from years with the state police, where he'd finally found the bureaucracy and office politics too stifling — especially given the abrupt option of joining the VBI, which was then new, actively recruiting, and offering to match all benefits and pensions of qualified applicants.

"You could put it that way," Joe agreed. "You been inside yet?"

"Yeah. Willy gave me the nickel tour. He's calling it a rape/murder as if he was getting an argument."

"He is. The AME's claiming he doesn't see any obvious signs of rape."

Spinney removed his watch cap and peeled off his gloves, adjusting to the heat. "Condom?" he suggested simply.

Joe stared out the windshield. It had snowed overnight, a freak storm from nowhere, and then stopped almost as abruptly. By now, late morning, the sky was bright blue, ice-cold, and the frozen world below it so white, it pained the eye. The glare washed out the colors adorning a long row of cruisers, vans, and trucks and made them look like the discarded Christmas toys of some giant child. The problem was, Christmas wasn't for two months yet, and no one Joe knew was prepared for ten inches of snow on the ground.

He wasn't among the complainers, though, for mixed in with the snow-covered tree branches overhead were broad swatches of bright fall foliage, forming entire bouquets of orange, red, yellow, and mottled green leaves — a beautiful and rare New England postcard.

"Could be a condom, could be rough sex gone too far, could be a rape, or could be all three."

"Could've been staged, too."

Joe took his eyes off the scenery and blinked at him a couple of times. "Or could've been staged," he agreed.

"They find a weapon?" Spinney asked.

"Nope."

"So it's not a suicide or accident."

Joe smiled. "I doubt it."

It was a funny process, this preliminary stage. Everything was open to question, and everyone open to suggestion, to the level of the absurd. Except maybe Kunkle. Although Joe knew that Kunkle was asking himself questions; he just didn't like sharing them with others.

"The ME'll probably tell us more," Lester continued. "What're our marching orders till then?"

Joe glanced at his notes. "We better tell her mother first. Story so far is that Dory spent hours every day with her at the nursing home. Maybe they were the sisterly type, trading secrets. If so, assuming Mom survives the shock and talks with us, maybe she'll tell us about a boyfriend."

"Wouldn't that be handy," Spinney said.

"We've been told Dory worked her entire career as the executive secretary for McNaughton Trucking, first for the old man, then for his son, Chuck."

Lester whistled softly. "Nice."

McNaughton Trucking was the region's primary hauler, servicing most of the larger businesses in the tri-state corner of New Hampshire, Vermont, and Massachusetts. It was headquartered in West Chesterfield, across the river from Brattleboro, in tax-friendly New Hampshire, and was worth millions by anyone's guess. Guessing, however, was about where reality stopped, since McNaughton was a family-owned, private business, and closed to public scrutiny.

Lester turned in his seat to look anew at the modest house. "Sounds like she could've done better than this."

Joe tapped on the pad propped against his steering wheel. "Item three," he read. "Check finances."

Lester chuckled briefly. "Right; shoulda known. What else you got there?"

Joe was not enthusiastic. "Standard stuff — phone records, appointment calendars, answering machine, family interviews, neighborhood canvass — already under way — coworkers, personal files and records, whatever forensics might find and the ME coughs up. If precedent is any indicator, this poor woman pissed off somebody in her life."

"Single woman, nice-looking," Spinney mused. "You think she was passed along from father to son with the rest of the business?"

"Maybe," Joe agreed. "Looked like she was a photographer who liked to travel. Her mom's nurse claims she and Dory were bosom buddies."

"You believe that?"

"She does; she must have her reasons."

Spinney paused to think. "They find any tracks anywhere?"

Joe shook his head. "Only belonging to the neighbor who saw her through the window and called us." He suddenly added a note to his list.

"What?" Lester was watching him.

"Her doc," he said. "Probably nothing. He claims he hasn't seen her in ten months. Can't hurt to drop by, though."

"Should we go through her photographs?"

Lester asked.

"Sure. Starting with whatever's still in the camera."

Now they were both silent.

"It's not looking really good, is it?"

Joe cast him a look. "We haven't even started. Could be the first person we interview bursts into tears and fesses up. It happens."

"But your gut's saying not this time, right?"

Joe took in a long breath and let it out slowly.

"Not this time."

Doreen Ferenc's mother was named Margaret Agostini, or Maggie — at least by the nursing-home staff in Bellows Falls. Joe found her sitting by a bay window in the common room on the second floor of the century-old building, staring out at a small cluster of children throwing snowballs.

Joe had been met at the front door by Brenda Small, the nurse interviewed earlier on the phone, who'd hustled him upstairs, fawning and cooing and clucking about "the tragedy." It was only upon seeing the victim's mother staring out that window, however, that he'd clued in on one possible reason behind the nurse's focused attentions.

He stopped at the door and gently steered her back into the hallway by the upper arm.

She gave him a surprised look. "What's wrong?"

He played a reliable card. "Did I say anything was wrong?"

She blinked and wet her lips, broadcasting her discomfort. "No."

He sighed. "Brenda, it's over and done with now, so you can stop worrying. There won't be any repercussions. I just need to know: You already told her about Doreen, didn't you?"

Brenda's eyes widened, preparing him for the standard array of excuses he'd heard from others in similar circumstances. Her choice, however, was at least unique.

"She already knew," Brenda explained in a high whisper. "I could see it in her eyes. So sad. It would've been cruel not to share that pain."

She opened her mouth to continue, but Joe stopped her. "That's enough for the moment, Brenda. Thank you. Just leave us alone for a few minutes, okay? I'll wrap things up quickly and then you and I can talk. Deal?"

Brenda looked confused. "Okay."

Joe left her and softly approached the old woman, moving a low stool to the side of her chair and settling down next to her.

"Hi, Mrs. Agostini. My name's Joe. I'm a police officer, and I am so sorry to be meeting under these circumstances."

He left it there for a moment, gauging his audience. She acted as if he hadn't even entered the room.

He reached out and gently touched her forearm. "Is there anything I can do for you?"

It was never much of a one-liner, but it occasionally opened a minor portal.

Not this time.

"Mrs. Agostini," he tried again, "I would like to find out what happened to Doreen, and I sure could use your help. You two were so close. She may have told you something that would point me in the right direction, even if it didn't sound like much to you."

Still nothing. Joe sat there for a moment longer, and then finally reached into his pocket, extracted a business card, and left it in the old woman's lap, explaining, "That's how to reach me when you're ready, Mrs. Agostini. I know it's tough right now, so feel free to call, night or day."

He patted her arm again and got up, half hoping for one last chance. But she hadn't moved a muscle, and didn't start now.

He found Brenda Small still lingering in the hallway.

"Is she okay?"

"I doubt it," he told her. "Is there some-place you and I could chat?"

"Me?"

Joe considered a suitable comeback, as usual floating what Willy might say in the back of his mind, before merely saying, "Sure, why not? You and Doreen were close, right?"

Her face lit up. "Oh, yes." She crossed her fingers. "Like that."

She led the way down the dark hallway, still wood-paneled and stately from when it was built as a private home a century earlier, and turned into a small break room just beyond the back staircase.

There, she settled fussily into a chair at the table, folded her hands before her, and gave him her full attention.

He closed the door and sat opposite her. "Just so I can get a handle on Mrs. Agosti-ni's state of mind," he began gently, "could you tell me how you broke the news of her daughter's death?"

Her eyes grew sad for Doreen's mom. "It's like I told you. I didn't need to tell her. She knew. Like when a pet knows his master has died, you know?"

He knew of the folklore; he was less sure about comparing a dog and its master to this mother and daughter. Unless Brenda Small was subtly heading somewhere.

"So she said something?"

"It wasn't necessary. I saved her the heartbreak. I just wrapped my arms around her and said that it was all right, that Doreen had gone straight to Heaven and hadn't suffered at all, and that everybody has to die sooner or later, even if it seems unfair sometimes. That God's Plan was always right, no matter how mysterious."

Joe paused before opening his mouth, mostly to stifle his immediate reaction. "How did she take it?"

Brenda said simply, "She had to soak it in, didn't she?"

"That's what she's still doing? Soaking it in?"

"Sure."

He pursed his lips. "She hasn't said a word?"

"Not out loud. I'm sure she's talking with the Lord, though, seeking his comfort and guidance."

Joe nodded. "Understandable. She's a religious person?"

Brenda laughed. "Oh, no. Not Maggie.

She takes a tough line there, but I knew in her heart she didn't believe what she was saying. That's why I felt okay about bending your little rule and sharing her grief with her. I know one of God's chosen when I see them, and Maggie definitely fits the bill."

Joe was starting to sympathize with Maggie's choice to become catatonic. "What was she like normally, from day to day? Like when her daughter came to visit?"

"The life of the party. Laughing and making jokes. Sometimes I thought the two of them were like kids in a tree house, they had so much fun together."

"And you and Doreen?" he asked. "What kinds of things did you talk about?"

"Well, of course, her mother was Dory's first priority," Brenda explained. "So she wanted to make absolutely sure I knew how important that was to her."

"She paid you," Joe stated flatly, making it sound like the most natural and sisterly of acts.

Brenda flushed slightly and cast her gaze upon the tabletop. "Well, she did help me sometimes in taking extra care of Maggie."

Joe began to sense an inkling of revenge in Brenda's delivery of bad news this morning.

"I'm just trying to confirm something I

heard earlier," he lied. "That Doreen might've been a little stuck up sometimes. Not that she was a bad person, of course. But maybe a bit superior?"

Brenda smiled her forgiveness. "People can't be blamed for the way they were brought up," she said.

"That's very nice of you," Joe commented, feeling on more solid ground. "Most folks would've taken offense."

"That's not my way."

I bet, he thought. "Still," he suggested, "it's like what they say about apples not falling far from the tree. I guess Maggie had her moments when she could be a handful."

Brenda rolled her eyes, becoming ever more comfortable with this empathetic listener. "You can say that again. I sometimes felt like I was in one of those old movies, where the queen pushes all her servants around. And Dory and Maggie together were like double that."

She leaned forward and dropped her voice. "The two of them ganged up on me once, asking me what all Maggie's medicines were for, like I was trying to poison her or something."

"Something had gone wrong?" Joe asked.

She sat back and dismissed the notion

with a wave of the hand. "Probably something she ate. She had diarrhea and felt sick. But of course, it had to be me and how I was doing her meds."

"Was it?" he asked, figuring he had nothing to lose.

To his astonishment, she became angry. "It wasn't my fault. They work us too hard in here."

"How long ago was this?" he followed up.

"About six months. Not that they ever let it go. Doreen was always nagging — did I do this, did I do that? Like I was incompetent or something."

"And she stopped paying you extra?" Joe suggested.

She looked at him wide-eyed. "Why would she do that?"

He scratched his forehead and decided to move on. "Brenda, did you ever get any feeling for Doreen's personal life? Boyfriends? Problems with other people? Anything at all?"

"She used to travel before Maggie came here," she volunteered slowly. "It sounded like she always went alone, though, which I thought was a little strange. Sounds even stranger now."

So much for being bosom buddies, Joe

thought. "And how long has Maggie been here?"

"Three years."

"With Doreen coming every day?"

"Like clockwork, from day one. I thought it was sweet at first, before I found out what they were like."

"Did they treat everyone here like they did you?" Joe asked her, suddenly struck by a thought.

She looked disgusted. "Oh, noooo. Everybody thinks they walk on water around here. Doreen conned them good with all her doting on her mother."

Joe watched her for a few seconds, absorbing the transformation from cheerful best buddy to resentful malcontent.

"Do you know where Doreen lived?" he asked quietly.

"I was never invited there, if that's what you mean."

"But you did know."

"Sure, I knew. She even drew me a map, and always made sure I had her phone number on me. I was supposed to know the address in case I had to drive out there for some reason, like that would ever happen. That's the kind of thing I was talking about. She actually thought that because she gave me a handout now and then, it bought her special favors. I have a lot of residents to care for here. They run me ragged as it is, without me doing extra service just because Queen Maggie develops a need in the middle of the night."

Joe thought back, considering what he might have missed. "You said it sounded strange that Doreen went on her trips alone; actually, you said that it was even stranger now. What did you mean by that?"

Brenda looked nonplussed. "Well, she was raped, wasn't she?"

Joe tried to suppress his surprise. "Did the officer who called you tell you that?"

"Oh, no," she said. "He was a jerk, if that's all right to say. You're one of the nice ones, but most cops are like him. No, one of her neighbors called up right after to check on Maggie. I found out from her. They're all pretty upset — no surprise."

Joe suddenly studied her bland, flat face with new insight, a chilling thought evolving.

"Brenda," he asked slowly. "You told that to Maggie, didn't you? That her daughter had been raped?"

She became innocence personified. "Well, that's what happened, isn't it?"

He stared at her in silence for a moment, trying to imagine the moment, and the effect it must have had on the old lady.

"You really ended up hating them," he murmured.

Her face closed down. "That would be un-Christian. I have never hated anyone in my whole life."

A switch clicked in Joe's head. He'd had enough of this woman. He could always return, and if he did, he'd be far better informed about all the players in this sadness.

He got to his feet, just controlling his anger. "Thank you, Brenda. You've told me a lot — all of it useful."

"I do what I can," she said. "If people don't sacrifice a little for each other, what hope is there?"

Chapter Four

Lyn Silva slid into the small house's entryway quickly, snow from the trees outside
dusting the shoulders of her coat. As she
stamped her feet and brushed off her arms,
a few flakes broke free and shimmered in
the light from the lamp beside Joe's easy
chair. The weather had cleared and the
forecast was calling for warmer temperatures tomorrow, but for the moment, it was
still freezing, leaving all remnants of the
freak storm in place.

"I thought you'd be in bed," she exclaimed, crossing the living room to give
him a kiss. Her lips were cold and the night
air clung to her. It was after two in the
morning. Lyn owned a bar in Brattleboro
and worked several nights a week.

"I just got in a while ago myself," he
confessed. "We caught a murder in Westminster, up near Saxtons River. Been hard
at it all day."

She hung her coat on to a row of pegs opposite the door and pulled a face. "And in the middle of a snowstorm, of all days. I'm sorry. Was it bad?"

"Bad enough," he said. "We don't know who did it, which ruins the fun right off. It's not snowing again, is it?"

"No, no. It is beautiful, though. I always think I'll get used to it, like fall foliage, but it sneaks up on me every time."

"Well, you're allowed to be a little surprised this time. Plus, you get a bonus — foliage is still in the trees."

"I know," she beamed. "That, I'd never seen before, even after a lifetime of living up here."

She was younger than he, and originally from Gloucester, Massachusetts, where the ocean had a tempering effect on the winter weather. He doubted if even today they had snow in the trees down there. New Englanders could be snotty about their hardships — Vermonters, Mainers, and New Hampshirites were inclined to view southern New England as the Banana Belt.

She paused at the entrance of the kitchen area. "You want some chamomile?"

"With a good slug of maple syrup and a lot of that vanilla sweetener?" he countered. "You bet."

Lyn made a face and set to work, still visible across the counter separating the two rooms. "I saw your girlfriend on the news tonight," she said, her back turned. "Couldn't hear what she was saying over the noise, but she looked like she was getting ready to lead the nation. You think she has ambitions that big?"

Joe craned his neck to better study the set of her shoulders, but saw nothing obvious. The reference was to Gail Zigman, who had been Joe's lover for many years, some time ago. She'd been a state senator when they'd broken up, already living part-time in Montpelier, and was now running for governor, head-to-head against the incumbent, James Reynolds. By Vermont standards, which were pretty tame, it had been a bruising campaign, with a grueling primary race between the usual half-dozen disorganized Democrats, and now it seemed Jim Reynolds and the Republicans — unbloodied, fresh, and eager — were ready to hunt for bear.

"I don't know," he answered blandly. "We never discussed it. And she's my ex-girlfriend."

At that, Lyn turned and gave him a big smile. "I know. I'm just busting your chops. Can you talk about the case?"

He allowed the subject to pass, although he doubted she was as lighthearted as she pretended. He knew she was sensitive to being not only the replacement of a decades-long, erstwhile companion, but one who was currently the most talked about woman in the state.

"I can, but I don't have much more than the paper will tomorrow. Fifty-four-year-old woman found murdered in her own home, seemingly a rape/homicide. She lived alone, had no relationships going, and doted on her mother who's in a retirement home."

Lyn leaned on the countertop, having put the kettle on the stove. "That's horrible. Someone raped her?"

"Maybe," he conceded. "That's the way we're playing it for the moment. A neighbor called it in and had already begun spreading the word far and wide based on what he saw through the window, which suggested a rape, so there wasn't much left for us to put a lid on once we got there."

He shook his head in wonder. "I suppose I should be grateful that people call 911 at all, instead of just starting with the paper. We'd barely begun when the first reporter showed up, and by the time we planted a guard on the house for the night and headed out, there was already a TV truck from Burlington camped out on the lawn."

Lyn was looking confused. "So was she raped or not?"

"Maybe. It looks like it at first glance, but some relevant details are missing. The ME'll tell us for sure."

"What was her name?"

"Doreen Ferenc. Worked for McNaughton Trucking till recently. Lived on the Back Westminster Road."

Lyn snorted and set back to work. "Wherever that is. You woodchucks have the weirdest names for roads around here."

"Speaking of woodchucks," he asked, "how was work tonight?"

The bar was named Silva's, in honor of Lyn's late father, and was the current hot spot on Elliot Street, an honor it had held for over a year by now.

The kettle began whistling, so she killed the flame and began fixing two mugs of tea, not that there was much of that in Joe's mug by the end.

"Same ol', same ol'," she reported, entering the living room, handing over his milky-colored, sweetened concoction and sitting down opposite him. "We didn't have to call on any of Bratt's finest, which always works for me, and the band did a good job."

She took a sip, watching him over the rim

of her mug, and then asked, "No idea who did it?"

He shook his head. "Not a clue. That's what we've been doing most of the day, digging into her background, trying to find something to pin down, or someone. But all we've found so far is a completely regular human being who seems to have led a completely regular life — at least for her."

"What's that mean?"

He tapped the surface of the legal pad he'd been working on when she'd entered. "She made her choices — stuck with one job, seems to have opted for no sex life, dedicated herself to her mother's care, and spent her leisure time happily cooking, traveling, and taking pictures."

"No sex life?" Lyn asked. "That's unusual. Doesn't that make the way she died a little ironic?"

He stared into middle space, having heard that reaction before. "On the surface, unless it actually means something."

Lyn didn't respond. That was one of the qualities Joe liked about her: She knew when to ask questions and when to just let him think. She was a pragmatist generally, having handled her share of turmoil while still just shy of official middle age. Divorced, she had an adult daughter, one marginally functioning brother with a criminal record, and a mother who sat all day watching TV. Another brother and her father had been murdered by smugglers in Maine. Lyn Silva had earned her survivor merit badge.

For the moment, though, he was considering none of that. "We always tend to emphasize the who-what-where-when-how in these cases. I'm just wondering if 'why' isn't going to be carrying the most weight this time."

"Why the rape, or why the killing?"

"Yeah," he answered. "Course, I'm probably getting ahead of myself. The one person we haven't talked to yet is likely to shed some light." He raised his eyebrows at her. "Chuck McNaughton inherited Doreen when he inherited the business from his father. Certainly Willy's thinking there might be something interesting there, given that she was personal secretary to both of them."

Lyn made a face. She was no more fond of Willy than most people. "What do you want to bet it just proves he's a smart businessman, keeping the one person who really knows how the company works. You said it was a trucking firm?"

"Yup," he said. Lyn had only been in Brattleboro a little over a year, and was still so immersed in creating her own business that she barely knew who was who in town, much less the bigwigs operating just across the river.

"Why did you hold off on talking with Chuck?" Lyn asked. "He go AWOL?"

Joe smiled and checked his watch. "He's most likely in bed. He was out of town, due back tonight. I asked Sam to intercept him at the airport, hoping she'll get to him before he catches wind, although I doubt we'll get that lucky. She'll let us know in a few hours at the office."

"You going in early?" Lyn asked, already knowing the answer.

He smiled at her. "In four hours. You should've gone home tonight, instead of coming here."

She put her tea down, got up, and came over to give him a long, seductive, chamomile-scented kiss. "Not on your life. I'm here to make sure you go to sleep with pleasant dreams . . ."

In fact, Charles "Chuck" McNaughton was not in bed. His company's Falcon jet was taxiing off the Keene, New Hampshire, municipal runway, heading toward their private hangar.

Where, unbeknownst to him, Sammie

Martens, the fourth and last member of Joe's small Brattleboro team, was waiting for him.

Standing just inside the hangar's yawning open door, between the frozen black night and the heated, glaring cavern of metal trusses and walls behind her, she watched the jet roll toward the hangar's embrace. Unlike in Brattleboro, the falling snow had moved on, leaving behind an inky void overhead.

She'd spent the afternoon researching Chuck McNaughton, prepping for her interview of him, before discovering that he wasn't available. He'd been running the company for six years, about half of them with Doreen in the front office. That was a significant detail, given what Sam had heard of Doreen's prowess and Chuck's limitations. He was better on the back of a motorcycle, or at the controls of his boat, or his ATV, or his various snow machines, or simply flying around the country. Sometimes, if rarely, he even hung out with his wife and two kids.

He was not an idiot, she'd been told in discreet conversations, and perhaps even a chip off the old block. But he was untested so far, first overshadowed by his late powerhouse father, and then by Doreen's com-

50

plete if carefully muted competence.

He was also sleeping with Dory's replacement, according to the scuttlebutt, which had added that the girl had better be good in bed, because she sure wasn't much at a desk.

Did that mean that he'd enjoyed such an arrangement with Doreen? Interestingly, Sam's informant hadn't rejected the idea outright, but had conceded that if so, discretion had been absolute. Dory had been a good-looking woman, though, Sam had been told. Whatever that meant . . .

Like a sci-fi movie set designer's vision, the jet slid into the hangar, shimmering, clean, and muscular. Sam waited for it to coast to a stop, the enormous doors to rumble shut, and finally for the plane's side door to split away from its skin and metamorphose into a stairway. Only then did she push away from her station and stroll up to where she stood near the bottom step.

The hangar attendant, to whom she'd introduced herself an hour earlier, eyed her warily.

"You gonna arrest him?" he'd asked her at the time.

"Should I?" she'd countered.

He hadn't spoken to her since, preferring to sweep the floor until she thought the

concrete might start peeling. She'd understood the guy had been here for hours
already, waiting for the plane, which had
been delayed by the bad weather.

There was movement at the top of the
stairs, and Sam looked up to see a young
man in a blazer stick his head out the door
and ask the hangar man, "Car ready?"

"Yeah, but . . ." The man merely pointed
at Sam.

Blazer stared at her. "I help you?"

She showed him her badge. "Depends."

He scowled a moment, muttered, "Shit,"
and disappeared back inside.

A minute later a broad-shouldered,
athletic-looking man with the start of a
thickening waist and a toothpaste-ad smile
stepped onto the top step as if he'd just
been summoned onstage.

"Hey there, officer. I come in too fast?"

She waited for him to reach her level
before she showed the badge again and
asked, "Chuck McNaughton?"

The smile stayed in place. "I sure ain't the
pilot."

"Special Agent Samantha Martens —
Vermont Bureau of Investigation. I'd like to
have a few words with you."

He made a great show of flashing a Rolex
wristwatch and announced, "Three A.M. I

don't guess we're talking parking tickets."

"No, sir. Is there somewhere more private?"

"You can use the office," the hangar man volunteered, making them both turn toward him.

McNaughton laughed and raised a single eyebrow at Sam. "I don't think so. How 'bout back in the plane? I can throw everyone out. This won't take long, right?"

"Probably not," she conceded.

The plane's interior was just as she'd expected — both stylish and antiseptic, as if stuck between individual luxury and the practical knowledge that each owner might have to sell out to his successor at a moment's notice. In that way, she was reminded of a rented limo's air of nervous impermanence.

She even noticed that the company logo had been Velcro'd onto the fabric-covered bulkhead between the cabin and the cockpit.

McNaughton called out toward the front of the aircraft, "Hey, guys? We need a little privacy back here. Could you give us a few minutes?"

"Yes, sir," came the response, along with the metallic slap of the door.

Sam's host waved her to one of the cabin's leather chairs. "Sorry I can't offer you anything. They sort of button everything down after we land."

She sat down at the same time he did, opening her coat to the cabin's lingering heat. "Mr. McNaughton . . ."

"Chuck," he said, still smiling. "I insist."

"Mr. McNaughton," she repeated, "we were told you just came in from Oklahoma City, is that right?"

He did his thing with the one eyebrow again. "Yup. Is there something wrong with that?"

"We don't know," she answered. "What were you doing there?"

"Attending a trucking convention, which I'm pretty sure you know."

"You were alone?"

He gestured to their surroundings. "You know I wasn't." He checked the big watch again and stood back up. "You also seem to think you know some other things you're not telling me, in real Eliot Ness style. That's cute, by the way, and I guess it works for you most of the time, but it's late and I'm tired and I'm not nuts about your attitude . . ."

"Doreen Ferenc was found murdered in her home this morning," Sam interrupted him, adding, "I guess yesterday morning, actually. Did you know anything about that?"

McNaughton, his face suddenly drained of color, sank back down into his chair, his hands between his knees. "Fuck," he muttered.

"You hadn't heard?" she asked.

He shook his head, staring at her. "And that's one hell of a way to find out. You guys always this good? No wonder people hate cops."

"Miss Ferenc worked for you for a long time, and your father before you."

McNaughton sat back and studied her, shaking his head. "You're amazing, you know that? What did you say your name was?"

"Samantha Martens." Sam knew that she'd chosen the wrong approach, colored as it had been by her own prejudice. She considered the man a leech and a cheat, riding other people's coattails and abusing those around him. But she'd dealt with far worse more subtly before, and was kicking herself now for dropping the ball.

Still, she was headstrong by nature, and instead of trying to remedy the situation, merely stared at him now. Dealing one-on-one with self-confident men wasn't her strength, as a long string of failed relationships had established. And the fact that she was currently involved with Willy Kunkle, of all choices, seemed only to prove her shortcomings.

She stifled a frustrated sigh.

"Doreen Ferenc," McNaughton was saying, "was the best, most loyal employee our company has ever had, which includes me and my father." He now sat forward, his face reddening with growing anger. "And now that you've dropped out of the blue and done the worst job I've ever heard of breaking the news of her murder, I think you owe me an explanation."

For a split moment Sam weighed her options — a military-style "don't explain, don't say you're sorry," a simple cut-and-run retreat, or something more out of Joe Gunther's playbook. Joe had been her mentor for her entire career, using an ever-changing recipe of human emotions to open people up. He had more than once urged her to exchange her academy-taught, statistically supported, psychologist-vetted approach for something more dependent on the other guy's emotions, but she'd too often found it to be a no-man's-land of pitfalls and mistakes.

But that's what she opted for now.

"Mr. McNaughton," she confessed, leaning forward to complement his body language. "Let me start over."

"Good idea," he commented, instantly challenging her resolve.

"As hard-bitten as some of us probably seem to folks like you, starting the day seeing a woman's murdered body is no picnic. It hangs in your head and makes you madder and madder as the day goes on, and it's been a really long day."

He didn't respond, but she could see he was at least listening.

She held up her hand. "I'm not saying that's right, and I do apologize for hitting you so hard, but I'd sure appreciate another chance. I need all the help I can get to find out who did this."

She let him chew on just that, as tempted as she was to add to it. Joe had also taught her the value of silence, and of the influence of any suspect's inner debate.

And despite his having an alibi in Oklahoma City, along with no obvious motivation to have killed his erstwhile secretary, Chuck McNaughton was very much a suspect.

The man seemed to consider her request, pursing his lips, and then crossed his legs and placed both hands on the arms of his chair. "All right, fine. What do you want to know?"

Sam nodded and conjured up what she hoped was a conciliatory half smile. "Were you aware of anything happening in Doreen's life recently?"

"You mean her mother?" he asked in surprise. "It was sad she had to go into that nursing home, but Dory had it under control. That's why she retired early, as far as I know, to do unto her mom what the old girl had done for her as a kid."

"Tough upbringing?"

He lifted a shoulder. "I only know the Cliff Notes version, but tough enough, from what she told us. Single parent, no money, hand-to-mouth. Probably pretty typical nowadays — hell, my own father had worse in his day — but Dory appreciated her mom's sacrifices and effort, and wanted to make sure Maggie wasn't left wanting."

"She have much of a personal life as a result?"

"When?" McNaughton asked. "When she was younger, or after Maggie went into the home?"

"Both."

He stared at the ceiling a moment. "I guess she did all right in the old days," he said. "Good-looking girl, smart and outgoing. It wasn't my business, and she kept her private life private, but I always thought she knew how to have a good time."

"But no husband or regular boyfriends?"

"Nope. Unusual for a woman, especially in these sticks, but obviously possible. For all I know, she might've been a lesbian."

Sam widened her eyes. "Really? You basing that on anything you saw or know?"

He tossed the notion off. "Oh, for Christ's sake."

"You must've made a play for her," Sam pursued him, "back when you were in the game."

He smiled and tilted his head. "Well, she was older than me — not my style."

"How 'bout your dad?" Sam asked casually.

"Dad and Dory?" he exclaimed, laughing. "Wow. There's a picture."

Sam thought his eyes weren't reflecting the humor. "Wouldn't be the first time."

But he was waving both hands in the air. "No, no. Dad was all business. You wouldn't be thinking that way if you'd known him."

Sam made a mental note that Chuck had never actually denied that either he or his father had had a romance with the woman.

"Did the two of you keep in touch after she left?" she asked. "She must've been a huge resource during the transition."

"Yeah," he said, almost too easily. "We got on the phone now and then."

Sam had already studied Doreen's home and cell-phone records. She'd been in communication with Chuck a lot, right up to the end.

"Now and then?"

"Often enough," he conceded. "She knew the company inside and out."

Remembering their rough start, Sam let it be. "Did she ever express any worries about anything or anyone, let's say in the past month? An argument she might've had, or maybe something related to the nursing home?"

He shook his head. "I can't think of anything."

"How 'bout company business?" Sam persisted. "She must've known a few skeletons. Was there anything that came up recently that caused any ripples?"

He hadn't stopped shaking his head. "No, no. I don't think you'll find anything there. We just send trucks around; it's not that complicated."

Right, she thought, but resisted mentioning how the tangled history of the trucking business had proven to be anything but uncomplicated. "What about her replacement? Sue? That's her name, right?"

His voice gained a formality. "Yes. Susan Allgood. No Dory Ferenc, but highly qualified."

"Did they talk a lot? Passing the torch, so to speak? Maybe they exchanged a few private details, too."

McNaughton smiled indulgently. "Different kind of arrangement. Dory ended up being more like a company executive. Sue's just my secretary. They wouldn't have talked."

Sam took a stab. "Is Sue back from Oklahoma yet? I'll have to talk with her, too."

His expression froze, his eyes locked to hers, before he finally said slowly, "Right. I'll make sure she makes herself available to you."

At that, he stood up abruptly, crossed to a small closet, and extracted an overcoat. "Well, I hate to cut this short, but I have to get home and grab some shut-eye. Long day ahead."

He paused and gestured toward the exit. "Ladies first."

Sam rose slowly, refastening her coat. "You never asked me how Dory died."

He put on a surprised expression, painfully amateurish. "I assumed it was confidential. What happened?"

Sam gave him a thin smile before passing before him and leaving him ignorant, if only from spite. "You're right. We haven't released that yet."

She paused at the top of the stairs and looked back at him. "I'm surprised you didn't know Doreen had been killed, in this day of constant communication."

"I leave my cell phone off when I'm at these things," he answered blandly.

Right, she thought, and took her leave.

CHAPTER FIVE

"Mary Fish, I would normally call security and force you to take a vacation, or at least go home on time, but then the whole place would collapse and the trustees would kill me."

The school's headmaster was named Nicholas Raddlecup, as if he'd wound up here after being cut from a Dickens novel. He was cherubic, always wore a three-piece suit and a bad rug, believed himself to be a ladies' man, and had a brain as pristine as on the day he was born.

And Mary, as his assistant for the past ten years, was the one to know. She also knew he'd just now spoken the complete truth.

"Not to worry, Nicholas," she told him, seeing him in her office doorway. "I'll be wrapping up soon. Elise is at the fire department Bingo game anyway, so there's no rush for me to get home."

"You have an excuse like that every night,

Mary," he chastised her, but then immediately waggled his pudgy fingers at her in farewell and concluded, "But, to each his own. You are a saint. Have a good evening."

She waited until he'd retreated down the hallway before murmuring, "I will now."

Nevertheless, she did check the clock on the opposite wall — one of those dark, wooden framed monstrosities that looked like an antique but ran on batteries and was available at Wal-Mart. It was getting late and she wanted to be home when Elise returned. In fact, she did feel guilty about how little time she gave their relationship. They'd been together so long — over twenty-five years by now — that each of them had finally taken the other for granted. Or Mary had, according to Elise.

Mary paused in her paperwork, sighed, and sat back in her chair. In Vermont, a gay lifestyle, especially involving two white-haired "old ladies," was hardly worth a headline, much less any gossip at the country store. People respected your privacy, and your independence.

The irony was, of course, at least from her earlier experience of a twenty-year marriage to a man, that Mary was hard put to tell much difference between gay and straight housekeeping. She was happier with Elise

— no doubt about that — and more peaceful at heart. But the ups and downs remained largely the same. At least from her perspective.

She glanced at the paperwork before her, and the contents of the shimmering computer screen, before standing up and crossing to the window overlooking the snow-covered campus quadrangle. Ethan Allen Academy was a lower tier prep school, dangling between the lofty, well-heeled New England ocean liners like St. Paul's, Deerfield, and Exeter, and the best Vermont public high schools. It had nothing to be ashamed of, and yet spent much of its time scuffing its feet in embarrassment.

Mary touched the cold glass of the windowpane with her fingertips, wondering what had gotten into her. All this pondering of the psychological balance beam. She was happiest as a doer — a hands-on shaper of events. That's what made Raddlecup both so grateful and so useless: He didn't have to worry about Mary performing both of their jobs, leaving him to posture before the parents and the board.

Maybe it was this year's sneak attack snowstorm. She'd been brought up in this county. Her father had owned a farm in Putney. As a child, she'd helped do the milking before sunrise, her frigid fingers warming against the heat of the cows' teats. Snow and ice were as natural to her as sand was to a Bedouin. But she was tired of it now. It got into her bones, and the gray sky clouded her spirit.

It was time to pull the rug out from under that fat toad Raddlecup, make a gift to Elise, and go on vacation somewhere sunny. With the time she'd accrued over the years, she could probably get a month off or more.

Smiling at last, she switched off her computer, tidied up her desk, locked her office door, and headed for home.

Home used to be an apartment attached to one of the dorms, where she and Elise had doubled as surrogate mothers for an ever-revolving gaggle of self-focused teenage girls. But age and seniority had its perks in this environment, and a couple of years ago they'd been allowed to move into a small, highly coveted, school-owned cottage on the edge of campus.

It wasn't much larger than the old apartment, but hopelessly and endearingly cute. It was ancient and a school icon, featured in all the academy's literature and publicity — trim, neat, rustic; an erstwhile barn — the epitome of Vermont to all those foundations and out-of-state full-tuition parents with visions of cows, maple syrup, and bucolic mountains in their heads. Mary knew it also for its cold air leaks, floor creaks, cracked walls, and cranky plumbing, just as she knew Vermont for its poverty, bureaucratic inefficiencies, drug problems, and alcoholism. But every homeowner had such knowledge, just as every local knew of her neighborhood's aches and pains. None of it negated what met the eye, and Mary remained happy with the house, her relationship, her job, and the state in general.

She just needed a break.

She walked along the edge of the quad, its sidewalks meticulously cleared. Mary loved this time of night, halfway between the post-dinner bustling and the true darkness after lights out, when the kids were quiet and still. The moonlight and the old-style street lamps balanced each other appealingly, the snowbanks absorbed the sound of her footsteps, and even the cold gave her comfort, wrapped as she was in a heavy coat and scarf. She was beginning to anticipate breaking the news of her decision to Elise.

The cottage lay outside the quad, beside a field favored by the cross-country ski team. Elise had left the lights on for her, as usual, and with them a warming sense of home.

Mary opened the unlocked front door —

nobody locked doors around here — stepped into the tiny mudroom, and settled onto the bench by the wall to remove her boots and coat before crossing the threshold into the house proper. She had to admit to enjoying the ritual of the mudroom protocol — the shucking of armor against the cold for the coming comforts of the hearth.

Her slippers on her feet and her scarf discarded with her coat, Mary opened the inner door to the house and walked into the toasty embrace supplied by the woodstove, anticipating the preparation of a little soup and a glass of wine for dinner.

But there she stopped in midstep, staring ahead and frowning. Before her, looped over the living room's central, exposed wooden beam, was a heavy-duty electric cord. One end dangled just above the floor, the other ran off at an angle to her right and was attached to the cellar door.

She began to walk toward it, wondering what project Elise had going, when a gloved hand suddenly came up from behind her and clapped onto her mouth.

"Don't move, Mary, or Elise will die."

The voice was muffled, as if by a mask, and very soft, whispering into her ear. "Go forward," it ordered.

She did so, her mind fighting for a handhold — some starting point from which she could begin to comprehend, and perhaps to reason. What had happened to Elise? What did this person want?

She never found out. Before she could form a strategy, or choose where to start, she felt herself pushed forward slightly, so that she threw her hands out for balance, during which split second she saw a flash of red electrical cord pass before her eyes, and felt the slippery coldness of its coil around her neck. Then a violent jolt as she was simultaneously pulled back and up by the wire, her feet suddenly flailing in midair.

Mary felt her air cut off, saw the room turn red, and was only vaguely aware of her fingers faintly tapping at her throat before she lost consciousness, the last sound in her life being a terrifying rush, as from a train passing by two inches away.

CHAPTER SIX

"I heard you ate like a stray dog, but you come here for breakfast?"

A freshly wrapped bean burrito in hand, Joe turned around to face Paul Duffy, a Brattleboro fixture who owned several businesses, a former selectman with Gail Zigman for a couple of terms, and now a leader of the area's perpetually floundering Republican Party — a lonely minority in the most left-leaning town in a liberal-minded state.

Joe smiled. "I hate to be obvious, Paul, but you're standing in the same line."

Paul waved his arms wide. "Taco Bell? Or as Martha calls it, Tacky Bell? It's also Kentucky Fried Chicken, and I'm just here for the coffee. How've you been? Up to your neck in that murder, I bet. Terrible thing. I cannot believe how much we're turning into a Massachusetts doormat. If people around here won't face that reality and start giving guys like you more power and tougher laws, they better get used to it, right?"

Joe kept his expression neutral. Why was it all cops were assumed to be opinionated, right-wing extremists? For his part, Joe liked to avoid politics altogether, which had been all but impossible for the past six months, especially in this town.

Duffy, however, was on a roll. "I saw Gail on the tube last night. She's a real fire-breather. You hear that stuff about health insurance? Like we were Saudi Arabia or something? I give you high marks, putting up with that kind of talk all those years." He slapped Joe on the shoulder. "You're a better man than I am, Gunga Din."

Joe dropped his money on the counter and moved aside so Duffy could place his order. "She's a smart woman," he murmured.

The other man nodded, looking at the counter girl. "Of course you'd say that. I understand. Martha's as smart as they come, too."

He laughed and gave Joe a theatrical wink.

"Take it easy, Paul," Joe said, and sought out the fresh air. Win or lose, he didn't much care anymore. He just wanted the election to be over.

"Bad news, boss."

Joe paused while hanging up his coat by

71

the office's front door and looked over at Sammie Martens. She was wearing the same clothes she'd had on the day before.

"That you got no sleep last night?" he asked.

She laughed and shook her head. "Hardly. That's never a problem. Margaret Agostini was found dead this morning at the old folks home. Suicide. Looks like she locked herself in the bathroom last night around ten and put a trash liner bag over her head."

Joe walked farther into the room. So far, the two of them were alone. "Jesus," he said. "You check this out yourself?"

"Just got back. I heard the Bellows Falls PD put out a call for an ME while I was heading home from Keene, where I'd just interviewed Chuck McNaughton — there's a charmer. So, on impulse, I gave 'em a call and sure enough, it was the old lady. I figured I might as well keep driving. They've sent her up for an autopsy, but it looked straight-forward to me."

Joe busied himself at the coffeemaker, setting things up for the four of them, knowing he and Sam would be joined shortly.

"How so?" he asked, not bothering to face her.

"Door blocked from the inside with a wedge, mostly," she told him. "They had to break it down once they figured out someone was inside. She'd put a couple of pillows under her blankets to make it look like she was still in bed. That's how the midnight bed check missed her."

"What was Brenda Small up to during all this?" Joe asked mildly.

But Sam wasn't misled. "Think she whacked her?"

"No," he admitted. "But I'd be dumb not to ask."

"I did ask," Sam said. "Anything's possible, but let's just say it's pretty unlikely from what I found out. Everything's telling me this one's exactly what it looks like."

Joe finished setting up the machine and leaned against the counter. "An old, crippled, brokenhearted woman kills herself after her dearly loved daughter is raped and murdered. Can't argue with the logic."

"What logic?" Lester asked as he entered the room and draped his parka across the back of his chair. "Coffee ready yet? The heater in my car conked out. Colder'n a witch's tit."

"Margaret Agostini committed suicide during the night," Sam told him. "I checked it out and Joe was just saying that it made sense to him."

Lester froze in midmotion and stared at

them both.

"What?" Joe asked.

The other man shook his head in disbelief. "After we split up at Doreen's house, I got somebody from the Nevada State Police to break the news to her brother. I didn't want to call him direct till he'd heard. Anyhow, it was last night when we finally hooked up on the phone and I asked him a few questions. We're talking a hard-luck family here."

"How so?" Sammie asked.

Spinney crossed to the coffeemaker and bent over double so that he could monitor the slow dripping from the bottom of the filter. Willy entered while he was doing so and uncharacteristically sat at his desk without a word.

"Father was a drinker; abused everybody in the family, one way or the other, mostly by whaling on 'em," Lester explained, finally giving up and straightening again. "Hey, Willy."

"Hey yourself," Kunkle muttered.

Lester resumed. "Doreen, though, was a special case — Mom walked in on the old man raping her one day. That was the last straw. She threw him out, called the cops, and he was tossed in the can for a few years. The family pulled up stakes and left."

"Where was all this?" Joe asked.

74

"California somewhere. Mark — that's his name, Mark Ferenc — said he was too young to remember. Near LA was the best he could do — Claremont, Riverside, Corona. He said they moved around a lot."

Joe moved to the office's sole window, behind his own desk, and gazed out onto the narrow parking lot. They were housed on the second floor of Brattleboro's century-old municipal building, over the police department, and he had a view of their white cruisers lined up and dusted with snow.

"What'cha thinkin'?" Willy asked, well used to his body language.

Joe turned around. "That Lester just filled in the background to a lot of what we're dealing with — the closeness between mother and daughter; the reason Doreen never married and might've even been celibate; the impact that a rape especially must have had on Maggie. It all could go back to what happened in California."

"Meaning California might've come here?" Willy asked.

"The dad?" Sam asked, startled.

"That so unbelievable?" Willy challenged her.

"He's dead," Lester interrupted.

Joe was scrutinizing Willy. "You look like

you've been up all night, too. Find anything?"

"As long as you don't ask me how," Willy cautioned him with a smile.

Joe pursed his lips. Willy was the unit wild card. Committed and tenacious, he was also a recovering alcoholic, a crippled ex-military sniper, and a PTSD survivor who saw every rule as a suggestion. They had never lost a case because of his unorthodox methods, but most observers felt that was merely a matter of time.

His results were his saving grace. No matter how he did what he did — or how many people he pissed off in the process — Willy Kunkle brought home the goods, and he did it cleanly; or maybe just without ever being caught.

"Don't worry about that, Willy," Joe reassured him. "I don't want to know."

"Okay," Willy said, propping his feet up on his desk. "As far as I can tell so far, Doreen Ferenc was squeaky clean. She worked hard and steady, kept her nose clean and her skirts in place, devoted herself to the betterment of McNaughton Trucking as if it were the Red, White, and Blue, and took care of her mother like some kid out of a nursery rhyme."

"Nothing about any hanky-panky with

either father or son?" Joe asked.

"Nope. Nothing about any hanky-panky with anything or anybody. Most boring broad I ever looked into. Can't say the same about Chuck and/or Sue, though," he added with a leer.

Joe's brows furrowed.

"Susan Allgood is the younger McNaughton's secretary, slash lap pet," Sammie explained. "I interviewed him at the Keene airport, after he came in from spending the last few days in Oklahoma City, presumably with a bunch of witnesses."

"Including Sue," Willy said.

"For real?" she asked. "I didn't get him to actually spit that out."

Willy laughed. "Interesting choice of words."

"You're gross."

"You should know."

"Children," Joe stopped them. "Enough." The other wrinkle to Willy Kunkle's complicated profile was his relationship with Sam — a now years-long pairing that no one had thought would last more than an explosive two minutes. But despite their volatility with each other, they seemed to make it work, much to everyone's relief.

"I talked to Sue," Willy conceded. "She got in a little earlier than her boss, since he put her on a commercial plane, but she was half drunk and totally sleep-deprived when I found her, so she didn't offer much resistance. She pretty much copped to screwing the boss on one hand, and knowing he was puttin' it to the company on the other."

"He's ripping off the firm?" Lester asked.

"According to her," Willy told him, waggling his open hand from side to side. "Might make for a good way to get at him when the time comes. The man does stink. I know he's crookeder than a dog's hind leg."

Joe scratched his forehead. "One thing at a time, Willy. Let's stick with the homicide."

"He didn't do it," Willy said flatly. "At least not with his own bare hands. That what you wanted?"

"But he could have had it done," Lester suggested. "If Doreen knew what he was up to, it wouldn't matter if she was blackmailing him or just could've if she wanted to. She'd be a threat either way."

The phone rang. Joe glanced at the readout on the device's small screen, held up his finger for silence, murmured, "Medical examiner's office," and answered.

"Joe? It's Beverly."

Joe smiled instinctively. In the far-flung

78

professional community he'd inhabited for decades, there were certain people who'd earned his highest esteem. Beverly Hillstrom, the state's chief ME for over twenty years, rated above even them. The two were colleagues, confidants, advisors, true friends, and — on the basis of a single night years ago — even lovers. Beverly Hillstrom had a passion for investigation and the integrity to keep it perpetually fueled. In that, he'd proven she had a soul mate in Joe Gunther.

"Good timing, Beverly," he told her — virtually the only person in law enforcement permitted to address her by her first name. "You caught all four of us in a morning briefing."

"Excellent," she said, her voice crisper and more authoritative. "Would you like to put me on speaker?"

"Absolutely," he reacted and hit the appropriate button.

"Good morning," she began. "I have conducted the autopsy on Doreen Ferenc and merely wished to confirm what I assume is the obvious — she is now officially a homicide, death due to the severing of her aortic artery, accessed through her back at about the T-12 level with what appears to be a pointed, narrow, double-edged, blade-like object."

"A stiletto," Willy said softly.

Hillstrom surprised them all by saying, "Quite possibly, Mr. Kunkle."

She added, "I will be sending you the full report, of course, but I thought you'd like to hear at least that much, along with the possibly pertinent addition that I agree with my field investigator, Mr. Judge, in his opinion that no signs of physical rape were evident. I take it that I don't need to emphasize that I am not saying no rape took place — merely that there is no evidence of it."

"Got it, Doctor," Joe said, addressing her formally but with a smile for the rest of them. Her scholarly manner and matching syntax were famous — and often mimicked — across the state.

"Do not mock, Joe," she cautioned him. "You know how these things get misconstrued."

"No mocking from me, Beverly," he told her. "Point taken. Did you find anything else on her, like signs of a struggle?"

"I'm sorry to say no," she answered him. "I checked her throat, wrists, chest, and thighs literally microscopically, but other than the usual minor scrapes and bruises that we can all pick up in the course of a day, I found nothing of note."

The squad-room audience was stumped.

"One detail I might mention," she continued, Joe thought almost to make them feel better. "It concerns her black underwear. When found, they were hanging off of one foot, as if placed there during the course of a rape, or certainly during some sort of sexual activity. Curiously, however, I found them to be stained with blood, faint traces of which I also found along the backs of her legs."

"What did that tell you?" Joe asked, following a telling pause.

"That she was stabbed before the item was removed," she said, sounding faintly dismayed at his denseness. "It suggests either some postmortem paraphilia, or that the body was arranged to make an initial impression."

"The rape was staged," Willy stated.

"What's paraphilia?" Lester asked.

"A sexual response to an abnormal stimulus," Joe told him.

Lester stared at him.

"Getting your rocks off while wearing your kid's dirty diapers on your head," Willy drove home.

"Thank you for that image, Mr. Kunkle," said Hillstrom. "Was there anything else at the scene that might suggest a sexual abnormality?"

Again, no one said anything for a couple of seconds. "Not noticeably," Joe finally answered.

"Then judging from the blood drop and the body's overall presentation, I, too, would suspect staging," Hillstrom went on. "In fact, I and my diener tried reenacting what might have happened, based on the scene photos we received. We concluded, consistent with the angle and placement of the wound and the distribution of blood on the couch, that the killer possibly sat behind the victim on the edge of the couch, stabbed her in the back — most likely controlling her with his other hand — and then let her collapse supine. That would have perfectly positioned her for the removal of the underwear and the spreading of her legs. That is, however," she added with emphasis, "no more than educated conjecture."

"What did you mean by the blood drop being staged?" Joe asked, returning to the beginning of her statement.

"The deposit on her forehead, unrelated to any wound. It might have ended up there by circumstance, but it seemed carefully placed to me. Nowhere else was there any blood appearing out of context."

"Couldn't it have come from the killer?" Lester asked.

"Absolutely, which is why it is being analyzed," she said. "But if you combine the rape-suggestive position and the carefully arranged underwear, and then add some attention-getting blood, I query if the last appeared accidentally. It seems more of an overall pattern."

She paused and then added, clearly as an afterthought, "Of course, my own objectivity may have been tainted by repetition. One has to be careful of cross-influence between cases."

"Jesus, Doc," Willy protested. "What the hell's that mean?"

"Willy," Joe snapped, but was interrupted.

"No, no. He's quite right. I get a little too wrapped up in my own thoughts on occasion. I don't make myself clear. My apologies, Mr. Kunkle."

Willy rolled his eyes, but Joe stabbed his finger at him, his meaning clear.

"No problem, Doc," Willy reluctantly complied.

"What I meant," she continued, unaware of all the pantomime, "was that this is the second case in two days where a deposit of blood appeared out of context."

Joe leaned forward, his attention seized.

"What?"

"A suicide," she said airily. "It came in last night, from north of you — Ethan Allen Academy. An elderly woman found hanging from a beam by her companion. Left a note; no one seems to think it's anything else. But there was a small deposit of blood on her foot, with no clear source. I thought I should mention it."

Joe studied his companions, seasoned investigators all, who were facing a blank wall in one case and had just now heard a distinct echo bouncing off from another.

"Hold on to that old lady, Beverly," Joe requested. "I think we'll want to take a look at her."

CHAPTER SEVEN

"That's where she was hanging. Here's the photograph." The Vermont state police detective handed Joe a computer printout. "Sorry about the quality. We have a crummy printer at the barracks."

His name was David Nelson. He was dressed in a suit, with a completely shaved head — square-shouldered, flat-bellied, and monotoned in voice. A poster boy for the state's largest, best-trained, best-equipped — if occasionally too highly self-regarding — law enforcement agency. The VSP's oft-quoted in-house sobriquet was "the Green and the Gold," which, while literally representing their uniform colors, unfortunately also smacked of the very pride that irritated so many of their law enforcement colleagues.

Not that Joe was one to complain. Most of his own elite VBI ranks were filled with former troopers, who, pride aside, were in fact damned good at their jobs.

Willy Kunkle sidled closer to peer at the photograph. "Fat," he murmured. "Couldn't have taken her long once she had that strain on her neck."

Nelson looked at him, faintly shocked. He was brand-new to plainclothes, as he'd admitted during introductions, and a transplant from near the Canadian border. Surprisingly, in a state this small and thinly populated — certainly by full-time cops, of which there were barely a thousand — neither Willy nor Joe had ever met the man.

"A power cord," Joe said softly, tapping the photo with his fingertip. "That's unique. It's usually clotheslines or lamp wires."

"And a woman," Willy added. "Not their favorite method."

"She was a lesbian," Nelson suggested.

Both VBI men looked up from the photograph to peer at him.

Nelson blinked in return, sensing that he'd misstepped. "Well, you know . . ."

"Right," Willy agreed with him. "Amazing she didn't cut her head off with a chain saw."

Joe sighed inwardly. Nelson's comment had been legitimate, if poorly presented, but Willy was never one to show mercy for an easy kill.

Willy pointed to a stool sitting in the

corner, looking out of place. "That what she used?"

In the picture, Mary Fish's feet dangled several feet off the floor, the stool lying toppled beneath her.

"Yeah," Nelson conceded, his voice tighter. Joe suspected the poor guy had already been ribbed about meeting up with two VBI cops. By gubernatorial decree, the Bureau had been born largely to replace the VSP's plainclothes branch — the BCI — as investigators of statewide major crimes. A black eye of major proportions, an unusual setback for Vermont's most influential law enforcement agency, and a partial explanation of why someone of Nelson's relative lack of experience was even here. The BCI detectives were still alive and functioning as second-rank investigators, but without their sharpest members, who'd fled to the VBI, and minus the prior presumption that they were the best and the brightest.

Joe sympathized. Once chief of detectives for the Brattleboro PD, he wouldn't have liked the VBI hovering overhead either, waiting to pounce on the choicest cases. For that very reason, he had urged the architects of the new outfit to make sure that the Bureau could only enter if invited by the host agency. Nevertheless, resentments festered, in large part because while other agency bosses were only too happy to call for help in traditionally budget-busting major cases, their own rank and file lived for the glory of a good headline-grabbing showstopper.

"Could you do me a favor, Dave?" he asked the trooper now, hoping to coax him in from the cold. "Could you put that stool where she must have had it to climb on?"

Nelson shrugged and complied, while Willy and Joe stood back, approximately in the same spot from where the photo had been taken.

"Huh," Joe grunted. "You see that?"

Willy was similarly struck. "Might be what they call a clue."

"What?" Nelson asked, returning with genuine interest.

Joe handed him the picture. "Hold it in front of you and line everything up. You can see how the stool is sitting now, where it had to have been for her to use it, and you can see how she's hanging in the shot."

Nelson stood motionless for a few seconds, his eyes flipping from the image to the reality before them, mentally trying to put Mary back where they had found her hours earlier, before taking her down for her rendezvous with Beverly Hillstrom.

Willy sighed after a few seconds and wandered off, not sharing Joe's teaching propensity. Nelson's face reddened slightly as he almost stammered, "It looks like her feet ended up higher than the top of the stool. Isn't that impossible?"

Willy laughed, not turning around.

Nelson's astonishment overrode any embarrassment. He stared at the picture again. "But there was a note."

"That, I'd like to see," Willy commented.

Nelson walked over to a briefcase he'd placed on the counter dividing the living room and kitchen areas. He snapped it open and extracted a sealed plastic evidence bag with a single sheet of paper inside it. Joe and Willy gathered around him to read.

"Typed," Willy cracked. "How convenient."

Joe read aloud, " 'I'm sorry, Elise. I can't live with you and I can't live without you. I love you, but you've made my life a living hell.' "

It was signed with a capital letter M.

"A guy wrote that," Willy said flatly.

Nelson opened his mouth, Joe suspected in order to restate his earlier comment about Mary's sexual orientation, but then closed it.

"We heard her companion found her," Joe

commented, moving along.

Nelson took one last look at the note before gazing at the older man. "Yeah. Elise Howard. They'd been an item forever, supposedly. She was at Bingo, came home, found Mary, and called the headmaster — some guy in hysterics named Nicholas Raddlecup, if you can believe that. He's the one who called 911 — of course after he came over to see for himself. From discovery to phone call was maybe twenty minutes, from what we put together."

"You were among the first on scene?"

"Close enough."

"How was Elise?"

"Hysterical," he said flatly. "She's in the hospital right now, sedated."

"Place was unlocked?" Willy asked, wandering around once more.

"No one's even sure where the key is," Nelson told him. "The whole campus is wide open, except for the administrative offices, the lab classrooms, places like that. They like to consider the school a big happy family."

"It may be," Joe said quietly, taking in the place as a whole — the way it was decorated and accessorized; the homey touches reflective of an old couple with a lot of shared history.

"And the electric cord belonged here?" Willy asked.

"Yeah," Nelson answered. "It usually hung from a hook at the top of the cellar stairs." He pointed to a slightly open door off on the side wall. "They'd just bought it to replace a ratty one Elise had been complaining about."

Joe noticed a movement through the window by the front door and caught sight of a short, round man with a red face, dressed in a long, virulently green coat with blue trim. He was approaching across the snowy yard — an elf on the run.

A hurried knock was followed by the door being flung open.

"Who are you?" the elf demanded.

Willy bristled. "We're the police, dipwad, and you're not invited."

"That's Nicholas Raddlecup," David Nelson said, his distaste audible. "The school headmaster."

"We're conducting an investigation here, Mr. Raddlecup," Joe told him. "I'd like to speak with you at some point, but not right now, if that's all right." He pulled out a document and handed it to Raddlecup. "That's a search warrant making this all nice and legal."

The headmaster distractedly took the

folded sheet of paper. "Investigation?" he burst out. "What's to investigate? The woman strung herself up without so much as a how-do-you-do. She broke Elise's heart, abandoned her responsibilities; she left me totally in the lurch." He paused to shake his head before adding, "Suicide is such a selfish act."

"Takes one to know one," Nelson muttered mostly to himself before retreating deeper into the house.

Joe began closing the door. He had a northerner's aversion to heating the outdoors. "I'll be happy to hear all that in a bit. We shouldn't be too long. I take it Detective Nelson knows how to contact you?"

Raddlecup put his hand on the door to stop it. "Wait."

"Why?" Joe asked, his tone no longer inviting.

"What are you people doing? Isn't this over?"

Joe considered saying something diplomatic, but he'd found that his reaction to this man was no better than Nelson's.

"No," he said, slamming the door.

"What an asshole," Willy said.

Joe stared at the floor for a second, before looking up at Dave Nelson. "Okay, let's kick this around from a different angle."

"As a murder?" Nelson asked.

"You think?" Willy grumbled.

Joe ignored him and kept addressing their colleague. "We are told to approach every death as a homicide, and maybe we do at first, but it doesn't take long to start seeing a duck as a duck and ruling it out as anything else." He waved his hand to encompass the room. "This may be a perfect example — it *looked* like a suicide . . ."

"But it might've been a homicide," Nelson finished.

Joe smiled. "Right. Do you have more photographs of the scene?"

Dave returned to his briefcase and extracted a thin sheaf. "I thought you might ask, when I heard you were coming here." He laid out a row of pictures on the countertop. Willy and Joe stood side by side, studying them closely.

"There's the blood," Willy commented, pointing.

Joe indicated the body's bare foot, and the red drop upon it. "You see that at the time?"

"Sure," Nelson told him, sliding another shot to the front. "That's why I took a close-up. But I assumed it came from up her dress someplace — that the ME would find out where."

"You didn't check it out yourself?" Willy asked.

Joe thought that was unnecessarily judgmental; he had serious doubts Willy would have stuck a flashlight up there himself.

"Reasonable assumption," he therefore said. "The ME prefers it when we don't mess with her bodies, so you get my thumbs-up on that one. Besides, that's exactly what Hillstrom did. Except she *didn't* find a source for it."

Nelson stared at him. "Where did it come from, then?" He paused before rubbing his forehead, adding, "Oh, shit. Did they get a sample, or was it wiped off inside the body bag?"

"They got it," Willy grumbled.

"So it's the killer's."

Joe shook his head. "We're not sure it isn't hers," he stressed. "We'll get that in a week or less, depending. In the meantime, we proceed as if you're right."

Nelson seemed stuck on his earlier statement. "Where else could it have come from?"

"You sure it wasn't the girlfriend's?" Willy asked.

Nelson had thought of that. "I asked. It didn't appear to be."

"What feeling did you get about them as a

couple?" Joe asked. "Happy? Unhappy? Did you pick up any rumors last night, when all this was fresh?"

"Everybody was stunned," Nelson admitted. "Raddlecup said they were just like Ozzie and Harriet, whatever that means."

"Old TV show," Joe told him. "No troubles in paradise? The note sounds like there were."

"That's what hit Elise the hardest," Nelson said. "She kept holding on to the note and saying it didn't make sense. She said, 'We were happy, we were happy,' again and again until they took her away. To be honest, I was glad to hear you had doubts about the note, too."

"How many people did you interview?"

"Not many," he conceded. "It was a suicide, as far as we were concerned — no signs of violence, no forced entry, the note. I asked Raddlecup if she'd been under any pressure and he said she was a workaholic and that he was always telling her to go home to Elise. He sounds like a phony every time he opens his mouth, so it's hard to tell, but he said there was no way he could put in the hours she did and remain sane. She virtually ran the whole school."

"Doesn't say much for him," Joe said quietly.

Nelson smiled. "I'll give him that much. He seems to know he's a lightweight. Anyhow, given what we thought we had, we didn't push too hard. I did call her doc. She was on meds for cholesterol and high blood pressure. The doc said he was surprised — called her a real trouper — but that she'd been tired and overworked the last time he saw her and seemed a little depressed. So even there . . ."

He left the sentence unfinished.

Joe got the idea. "They have a computer here?"

Nelson appeared to be gaining self-confidence. "For the suicide note? Yeah. In the upstairs office."

Bringing the note, he led the way to a steep and narrow staircase and took them up to a virtual cubbyhole across from a bedroom. The entire house was beginning to feel like the set of a Disney movie about anthropomorphized mice. Stooping under the low ceiling and huddled together like conspirators, the three of them compared what they had in the evidence bag to the top sheet in the printer's outfeed tray — a grocery list.

"Not even close," Willy commented.

"I did notice that," Nelson said. "But I also figured that the two women might've liked different typefaces."

Willy chuckled for the first time. "Good point," he allowed. "You'll be yanking out the hard drive anyway, though."

Joe straightened and pointed at the computer. "Yeah. Someone better get a warrant for that."

Nelson gave him a sideways glance. "You people taking the case?"

But Joe shook his head. "If we're invited. The reason we're here now is because of something the ME said. That's why I asked you on the phone if meeting us would be okay. I'm not big on stepping on people's toes."

"Not to worry," Nelson said. "You saved me from dropping the ball."

Joe hoped Willy wouldn't jump in for a cheap crack, and as usual, Kunkle surprised him.

"How long exactly you been in a suit?" Willy asked.

"One week," the trooper admitted.

"Don't beat yourself up, then. You were supposed to think what you did."

Nelson pulled out his cell phone. "I'm telling my lieutenant you should get this."

But Joe laid his hand on his arm. "You check out her office computer?"

This time, Nelson looked at Willy when

he said, "Jesus. Just when I was feeling good."

Willy laughed as he headed down the precarious stairs, talking as he went. "Hey! If it matches, then *we'll* look like jerks, not that you weren't thinking that anyhow."

CHAPTER EIGHT

"What did you guys find out?" Sam asked as Joe and Willy entered the office, removing their overcoats.

"A suicide, it's not," the latter said, heading for the coffee.

"Where's Les?" Joe asked her, settling behind his desk and checking his computer for messages.

"Doing homework on Doreen at McNaughton Trucking," she said. "So this woman was murdered, after all?"

"It wasn't natural causes," Willy continued.

Sammie sighed and looked to Joe.

"She may have *been* hanged, instead of doing it herself," he told her. "The suicide note looks bogus — it wasn't printed from either her office machine or the home's — and we can't figure out how she could've climbed the stool and kicked it over, and ended up with her feet higher than the stool when it's upright."

"Ouch," she said. "There's a goof."

Willy turned away from the machine, a mug in his good hand. "Which makes you wonder," he said, "what the hell's going on?"

This, thought Joe, noticing Willy's leading tone of voice, was the primary reason he kept this quasi-sociopath employed. "Meaning what?" he asked him.

"Maybe it's a stretch," Willy said, pausing to sip. "But it looks like we got a rape that's not a rape and a suicide that's not a suicide. Both victims are older women; both have a drop of blood on 'em we can't track to an obvious source; neither case showed forced entry or peripheral violence. They both look carefully planned and carried out, and they both turn into something else as soon as you barely scratch the surface."

"As if that was planned, too," Sammie suggested.

"Right," he agreed. "So — no goof with the fake suicide."

"Like a calling card," Sam barely murmured.

"Along with the drop of blood," he added.

"But," Joe challenged them both, "then what? Why go to all the trouble? Why the misdirection?"

"Find the connection," Sam said, "and you find the answer."

"Between Mary and Doreen?" Willy asked.

"Yeah," she continued. "Standard, old-fashioned link analysis. I don't know why, but the blood we keep finding has to mean as much as the bogus setups. Sure as shit, the same guy must've done both women. It stands to reason both of them pissed him off somehow, and that maybe part of the explanation is in the theatrics."

Joe was nodding and writing on a legal pad. "I'll get the lab to put a rush on the blood tests. Also, let's see what overlaps might exist between McNaughton Trucking and Ethan Allen Academy. Both women were key to their organizations — invisible number two people. There could be a psycho-sexual angle tying them together — some guy who worked at both places and resented strong women pushing him around."

"The link could also be between the women," Willy suggested. "Mary might've once been a teacher, Doreen her student — there's about a twenty-year gap between 'em — so maybe the guy fits in there."

Joe sat back from his pad. "Okay. Well, Christ knows at this point. We need to do some serious digging — put a foundation under the theory. Connect the dots, like Sam said." He pointed to her and suggested, "Call Lester and tell him what we're after. He's already at McNaughton; he can broaden his questions and see if Mary Fish pops up. As for the rest of us, it's time to find out more about these two ladies than their mothers ever knew."

He paused a moment then, watching Sam reach for the phone and Willy head for his desk. For all the drudgery and headaches this job could involve — the lousy hours, minimal pay, exposure to bureaucrats above and dirtbags below, and politics from everywhere — there were just enough moments like this one, when the first faint glimmerings of an idea began forming, that made it all a pure joy.

Until the phones began to ring, of course. Which his did at that precise moment.

"Gunther — Vermont Bureau of Investigation."

"Joseph, my old pal. You've been trying to avoid me."

Joe felt a small shot of adrenaline. He not only recognized the local paper's editor-in-chief, Stanley Katz — an old and respected sparring partner — but suddenly realized that only the four people in this room knew Doreen to be probably just the first half of any news story about homicide. Little did Katz know what he was actually poking into.

"Stanley," Joe responded in a jocular voice, loud enough for the rest of them to know who was on the line. "I'm surprised you took so long. You're losing your touch. Nice article this morning, though."

Katz laughed. "Yeah, right. As if you're going to tell me a ton more now than you would've if I'd called you in the middle of the night, which is nothing."

"That wouldn't have stopped you in the old days."

"In the old days, I didn't need all the drugs I take now. I'm in a fucking coma every night with the shit they have me on."

Joe laughed outright. Trust Stan Katz to reduce the general state of geriatric suffering to a one-liner. "You shouldn't have lived the way you did way back when. I told you that more than once."

"You fairy," Katz retorted. "You'll get to dance on my grave — I'll give you that — but I'll still have the bigger smile on my face. Give me what you've got on this Ferenc lady. Raped, too, was she?"

Katz and Gunther went back years. In more ways than one, it seemed a very long time.

"You clearly received the press release,"

Joe answered him.

"Worthless piece of crap. Tell me about the rape."

"Nothing to tell yet."

"Tell me about the rapist."

Joe knew better than to react.

"You got anything at all?"

"We're working on it right now," Joe told him.

"Ooh. There's a headline: 'Cops Working on Homicide.' Better than the opposite, I suppose. Come on, Joe. You're busting my balls here."

"I haven't even started, Stanley. And you of all people know I'll call when we get something we can make public."

"God, you're a prince."

The phone went dead and Joe slowly hung it up. Stanley Katz's casualness notwithstanding, this had been a warning shot, if not precisely from the *Brattleboro Reformer*, then from the industry it represented.

It wouldn't take long for the press in general to crank up its interest, especially as things got more complicated.

Bob Clarke looked balefully out the window as he slipped his much patched winter parka over his Taco Bell uniform.

"Great," he muttered, watching the snow

drifting from the night sky into the parking lot lights, and there coming to life like excited fireflies.

"It's not supposed to be bad," a female voice said behind him. "They said a dusting, maybe."

He turned to see his coworker also getting ready for the cold, pulling a knit cap over her blond hair and tucking in the loose strands.

"Easy for you to say," he told her. "You got snow tires."

"You don't?" she asked.

He grimaced, glanced one last time out the window, and began heading for the front door. "I don't even have tread."

Bob braced himself and pushed open the glass door, exchanging the fast food–scented warmth for the shock of winter chill. He hated the cold. Born and bred in Post Mills, he'd still never gotten used to it.

He pulled his keys out as he approached his Toyota pickup, parked near the Dumpsters, as required by management. It was a rusty, springshot, oil-leaking heap, and every time he saw it, it reminded him of his overall fate — stuck in the boonies, living with his grandmother, his father in jail and his mother God-knows-where. He was all of nineteen and felt like an old man. Even the manager of the Taco Bell considered him a loser, and that Bozo could barely tie his own shoes.

Which didn't mean he wasn't right.

Bob unlocked the truck's door and hitched himself in behind the wheel, struck by how, even in below zero temperature, the cab smelled of mildew and general decomposition.

He went through the painful ritual of bringing the engine to life, using the starter as a defibrillator.

He'd gotten the truck for a hundred bucks and had put that much into keeping it running. If he hadn't been friends with the mechanic who issued the inspection sticker every year, even that much wouldn't have done the trick.

Running at last, he nosed out of the parking lot, his headlights dim, his windshield scratched, and his ineffective heater not even on. At least he had his iPod, which he'd stuck into his ears first off, making the lack of a radio the one aggravation he could overlook.

Traffic in West Lebanon, New Hampshire, where Bob worked in the entrails of a long commercial strip next to the interstate, was down to a trickle. It was midweek, very late, and most people had sense enough to stay indoors when the weather reports were bad.

At least, most people who had a choice.

His head bobbing slightly to the music, he aimed north toward home, on the other side of the Connecticut River, above Thetford Hill, Vermont. It would take him about forty minutes, avoiding the freeway, which he wasn't fast enough for anyway — assuming the snow didn't get more ambitious than the flurries dusting his hood.

And, he added to himself with pressed lips, assuming his tires held out, the engine didn't quit, the tranny kept hold, and the creek don't rise.

The irony was, while he was pretty depressed by his present state, he also knew he had it better than a lot of his friends. Marginalized rural Vermont kids over sixteen could easily screw themselves up, and so far, Bob Clarke had managed to stay sober, avoid drugs, keep out of trouble, and hold a job. The fact that he was occasionally either tempted or frustrated didn't stall the stamina that his grandmother kept stoking through her gentle support. As embarrassing as it was to be living with an old lady in her ramshackle farmhouse, Bob had to admit that the good outweighed the bad. As old ladies went, she was cool, and you couldn't knock the lack of overhead.

He was in Vermont by now, having crossed the river, and had been daydreaming long enough to have covered two-thirds of the journey home, when he saw a glowing aberration in the featureless darkness before him.

There was a red flare in the road ahead, and the vague shape of someone waving him down behind it.

Bob crawled past the flare to see better what had happened. A car was pulled over to the side of the road, and a man dressed in new insulated coveralls was standing next to it.

"Trouble?" Bob asked.

"Damn, yeah," the man said, pulling his watch cap low. "My engine quit, and I thought I was gonna freeze to death out here before anybody came by. This road is, like, never used."

"Not too popular," Bob agreed, wondering who this might be. He'd forgotten to check the license plate, and now he'd pulled ahead of where he could see it.

"Where you headed?" he asked.

"Well, that's the worst of it. It's only a few miles, but no cell phone, no passing cars, and no luck — until you came along."

Bob was assuaged by the local reference. "You want me to see what I can do?"

The man's eyes widened. "Could you? I know nothing about engines. They either work or they don't. This might be super simple, for all I know."

Bob pulled ahead of the car and swung out of his truck, noticing as he did so the sound of rushing water far below. A year-round stream ran alongside the steep bank here — a locally known bad spot, complained about for its lack of a guardrail and propensity for swallowing up vehicles surprised by the tight curve.

He sidestepped between the truck and the top of the bank, and met the man around back.

The man proffered an open bottle of Scotch. "You want some?"

Bob stopped dead in his tracks, staring. "What?"

"You want a swig?" he repeated.

Before Bob could answer, a large hunting knife appeared in the man's other gloved hand, its blade pointed to right under Bob's left eye.

"Trust me," he said, his voice low and steady. "You do want a drink."

Bob didn't move, his heart pounding as if it wanted out of his chest.

"Take the bottle, Bob."

"You know me?"

"And Candice, your grandma. Take the bottle."

"Who are you?"

The tip of the blade came to rest against Bob's cheek, making him wince. He took the bottle in his bare hand.

"Drink."

"I don't drink. I mean, maybe a beer, sometimes."

He felt a light sting just under his eye. Slowly, he lifted the bottle to his lips and poured a little in. Just as he reacted to the harshness of the liquor, the man pulled the knife away, letting the boy half retch without being cut.

But the blade returned immediately after.

"Again," he was ordered.

"Why?"

The man's eyes narrowed. He grabbed the bottle back with his free hand, pushed Bob against his truck, and held the knife high and flat. Behind him, the red from the flare cast a devilish halo.

"I do have a cell phone, Bob, and a buddy holding a knife just like this to your grandma's throat. You either drink up or she gets to swallow her tongue like a ham sandwich. And I'll make sure she finds out why, you little shit."

Bob tentatively took the bottle and tried

again, swallowing a larger amount this time.

"Again."

He repeated the process five times before the man finally stepped back, taking the bottle and quickly placing it on the ground. The knife, he tucked inside his belt, freeing his hands.

"That wasn't so tough."

Bob wiped his mouth with the back of his hand, hating the taste both of booze and fear.

"Now what?"

The man shrugged. "Nothing. You get back in your truck."

Bob studied him incredulously. "That's it? You want me to drive drunk?"

"Yeah. I busted your cherry. Look at it that way."

Bob scowled. "You're an asshole, man."

"Remember Grandma," was the response.

Bob couldn't see much choice, or the point to any of it. Angrily, he shook his head and turned away to negotiate the narrow gap between the truck and the clifflike bank.

He didn't see the man extract a heavy iron truncheon from his back pocket and couldn't avoid the lethal club landing high on the nape of his neck.

CHAPTER NINE

"Joey? You sound like shit. What's wrong?"

Joe's initial groan at the phone ringing by his bedside instantly became a low chuckle at the sound of his younger brother's irrepressible voice. "Hey, Leo. Not that it matters to you, but it's five-thirty."

There was a pause on the other end. "So?"

Joe began laughing. "So, nothing. I was roofing the house is all, and I had to get off the ladder to reach the phone. You heading off to work?"

Leo was a butcher in Thetford, about ninety minutes north of Brattleboro by interstate. A bachelor extrovert who still lived at home with their widowed mother, on the remnants of the farm their father had worked for his entire life, Leo was now a local celebrity because of his market, to which shoppers flocked over sometimes enormous distances as much to bask in his upbeat aura as to partake of his excellent cuts of reasonably priced meat.

"You are full of it, Joey. Bet you were still sleeping. Helloooooo, Lyn," he suddenly screamed, making Joe wince and violently pull the phone away.

Lyn merely dragged a pillow over her head.

"She says hi," Joe said.

"Liar. Hey. I was wondering if you could do me a favor."

"Sure. Shoot."

"There was an accident up here last night. Kid got killed driving drunk — went off the road. Robert Clarke. Bob. That ring a bell?"

Joe stared at the ceiling a moment. "Nope."

"Nice boy. Good manners and lived right. Most of that due to Candice Clarke."

Joe interrupted. "Well, her I know. Mom and she are like Butch and Sundance. At least they used to be."

"Yeah, yeah," Leo was saying. "Still are. That's why I'm calling. The kid was Candice's grandson. After Bob's fuckup parents fell out of the picture, Candice took him in and brought him up."

"Ouch," Joe said.

"Right. So now Candice is totally destroyed and Mom's a basket case, and I gotta go to work."

Joe became wider awake. "Leo, I'm in the middle of a case . . ."

"No, no, no, no. That's not what I meant. I just want you to call her. Maybe a couple of times today. She wouldn't want you around anyhow, since she's already at Candice's, holding her hand. I'll give you the number there and you can let her know you care. Lie your ass off."

He was laughing as he recited the phone number. Joe fumbled for a pen on the night table and wrote on his palm.

"Jesus, Leo. You are a pain in the butt. But this is terrible. Didn't Candice's husband die in a car crash?"

"Yeah. That's irony for you, right? He was a drunk, too. That was a thousand years ago, though."

"Still," Joe mused, the cop in him stirring, "I thought you said Bob was a straight shooter. He go on a bender for some reason?"

"Nobody knows. He left his Taco Bell job on time, headed home like always, and was never seen again. Somebody noticed faint tire marks by the side of the road about an hour ago and looked over the edge. The truck was smashed into the creek and Bob was dead and stinking of booze. An empty bottle was in the cab. Beats me what hap-

pened — probably a girl. Poor bastard just
went off the tracks or something. Christ
knows how many times I nearly killed
myself in the old days."

Leo had a huge fondness for cars from
the sixties and younger women with com-
mitment phobias. He was no longer as wild
as he used to be, but he'd just now told no
lie.

"I gotta go, Joey. Will you do that for me?"

"Course I will."

"Cool." He screamed again, "Bye, Lyn.
Love youuuuuuu."

The phone went dead, leaving only a faint
ringing in Joe's head.

Curious, he thought, and maybe deserv-
ing of more than a phone call.

Deputy Rob Barrows walked into the café
in Thetford Center and gave Joe a wide grin.
"Isn't this what they call déjà vu all over
again?"

Joe rose to shake his hand and waved to
the waitress to bring a second cup. A couple
of years ago, Barrows had helped him
investigate a car crash that had landed both
his mother and Leo in the hospital.

"Not so good an outcome this time, of
course," Rob added, as if hearing Joe's
thoughts.

115

"True," Joe agreed, "and maybe even more complicated, from what you told me on the phone."

Rob pulled a sheaf of several pages from the inside of his insulated uniform jacket and laid them on the table. "I kinda noticed your sudden interest. That's the printout from my narrative, complete with some pictures. I'm still a little fuzzy on what got you so excited."

Joe glanced up from the paperwork. "You said you found a single drop of blood on the dash but that the driver didn't have a scratch on him."

"Not obviously," Rob agreed. "It might've come from his nose or something. It's not like I pried his mouth open, either. Maybe he busted a tooth."

Joe studied the full facial shot before him. The young man's slack features revealed nothing. He moved through several more pictures of the truck, its nose in the water, and of the driver, wedged behind the steering wheel, until he reached what had truly brought him up here.

"There," he said, displaying an image of a circular disk of glistening blood on the dashboard, about the size of a silver dollar.

Many cops, confronted with evidence of one of their own investigations, verbally circle their wagons with rationalizations, surplus explanations, or excuses, even before being challenged. Rob Barrows, to his credit, merely studied the picture more carefully, trying to see it in a different light.

"It's a lot of blood to have come from a tooth or an invisible nose bleed," he conceded.

"What else?" Joe prompted him. "I want to make sure I'm not reading into it."

Rob nodded, understanding. "I see what you're saying," he finally said. "It's perfect. There's no direction to it; no spatter. It looks poured in place, and from an angle the kid couldn't have reached with his head."

Joe's enthusiasm was growing. He returned to an earlier photo and tapped on it with his finger. "Look at the way his feet are slightly twisted; and the pants material — the way it folds toward the door along the length of both thighs. What's that suggest to you?"

Again, Barrows took his time before saying at last, "He almost looks slid in, like when an old person is shifted onto a hospital bed or a wheelchair."

Joe laughed. "Exactly what I thought. My mom's in a wheelchair. My brother and I move her in and out of it all the time, and her pants always look that way — kind of bunched up because of the friction between her legs and the surface she's being put on."

"Meaning Bob Clarke might've been positioned behind the wheel after he died," Rob concluded for the both of them.

"Could be," Joe agreed. "Looks possible, anyway. Did you collect that blood?"

The deputy looked apologetic. "Didn't see the point. But I still have the truck."

Joe was back to the sheaf of photographs. "Well, hang on to it for a while. The body went north, right?"

"For autopsy? Yeah — barely."

Gunther stared at him. "What?"

"I don't know about you guys," Barrows explained, "but our local SA gets huffy about who gets cut and who doesn't. I think she gets a kick out of pissing off Hillstrom. Why, I don't know. Anyhow, she wasn't interested here — you know, the drunk son of a drunk father. I sort of made an issue out of it, and got Clarke's grandma to weigh in. A voter will get this woman's attention, even if a cop can't."

"So Candice was interested?"

"You know her?"

"She and my mom are best buddies."

"Nice lady," Rob said, frowning. "This really knocked her for a loop. Her husband died the same way."

"Yeah." Joe dragged the word out and gazed at his companion.

"What?" Rob asked.

But Joe merely shook his head. "Nothing. Kind of like a theme song I can't pin down. Keep going."

Barrows nodded. "None of this makes any sense to her, which is partly what got me thinking about it, too. I mean, everybody's kid is a virgin or a choir boy, even when you hit them with the evidence, but Candice is like a rock, and I believe her when she said she brought him up right. So Bob went north. Oh," he added, "and the truck's in the wrecker's garage until Candice decides what to do with it."

"You got a place we can lock it up as evidence?"

"Sure. You really think something happened here, don't you?"

Joe was about to downplay the notion, perhaps by stressing how they should all wait for clearer results. But he ended up admitting, "Yeah. I do."

The Clarke farm outside Post Mills reminded Joe of the house he'd grown up in — planted in the middle of a field and bordered by a thin grove of trees. It was modest, slightly peeling, very old, had clearly been inhabited through several generations of farmers, and yet was just now starting to appear vaguely imperiled. It was reminiscent of a very old relative, usually taken for granted, who suddenly looked as if he had one foot in the grave.

Joe drove up the long, plowed driveway, not surprised to see his brother's car parked near the front door. Leo habitually delivered their mother to her friends' homes in his car — customized to carry a wheelchair and its occupant — and simply exchanged it for whatever he found there to continue on to work. Presumably, Candice Clarke's car was therefore now parked outside the butcher shop. That was life in a small, tightly knit community, and spoke well to Joe of Post Mills, Thetford, and their neighbors. There was erosion at the edges, in the form of urbanites transplanting to the boonies and unintentionally disturbing the social currents and eddies, but here — still — a tenuous core had been maintained, if only by a group of ancient widows and a few old codgers.

The death of Bob Clarke, and its effect on his grandmother, would ripple like an earth tremor, exacting an ominous toll on the status quo. Bad news never echoed simply the factual truth — it always carried extra meaning.

Joe got out of his car and paused a moment to take in the snow-draped field around him, flat, still, and unmoving, showing no hint of the life it would cradle in the spring.

"I thought I heard you drive up."

He turned at the familiar voice and saw his mother in the open doorway, leaning slightly forward in her wheelchair as if wishing it to fly.

He climbed the three steps up to her and kissed her worn, warm cheek. "Hey, Mom. How's she doing?"

But she knew him better than that. She stroked his face, fixed his eyes with her own, and asked, "You drove all the way up here to ask that?"

"Only in part," he admitted.

"It's about young Bobby?"

He tilted his head slightly to one side. "I think so; I need to find out more."

"I'm glad," she said, and rolled back to let him in.

The home's interior matched its faint odor of faded lavender sachet — neat, a little cluttered, totally embracing.

"She's asleep right now," Joe's mother told him in a quiet voice. "I can wake her if you think it's important."

Joe equivocated. "You've spoken to her, right?"

She understood his meaning, as she had his entire life. This woman had made it her mission to teach her two sons how to truly read, express themselves, and think past the obvious.

"Until she ran out of words," she said.

He nodded and rolled her over to a nearby chair in the living room, onto which he perched so they could continue speaking, their heads close. "Then I think I'll just talk with you."

She took that in before asking him, "So, you have suspicions?"

"I do, but they're vague and circumstantial, and I need some science to give them weight."

"Like an autopsy?" she guessed.

He smiled. "Exactly like an autopsy, and some crime lab stuff, too."

She seemed pleased by his response. "I told her she'd done the right thing. Our idiot state's attorney didn't want one, but Candice told the police she would raise hell if it didn't happen. She hated the idea of it — them cutting him up — but I assured her she was right. It would eliminate all doubt."

"That he was driving drunk, you mean?"

"One way or the other," she answered carefully. "I didn't know him like she did. She swears he didn't drink — at least not beyond a single beer every few months. I'm less sure about any teenager's ability to be so firm in his convictions."

He closed his eyes briefly, receiving her words and careful phrasing like a catechism. She valued the English language as others did fine art, and he reveled to this day in hearing her speak.

"How had he been behaving recently?" he asked.

"Normally, according to her. There were no unusual money problems, no romantic entanglements, no conflicts with his friends. He didn't like working at Taco Bell, but only because he thirsted for better. Candice said that's what baffles her most: There wasn't the slightest indication that something was wrong."

She laid her hand on her son's knee. "What do you think you have?"

"Maybe nothing," he admitted. "There're details here that might connect this to a couple of other cases I've got, but I don't know yet. I just had to come up and look at it myself."

She seemed satisfied with that. "I wish I

could help. But from what I've been told, there's nothing to pursue here, at least not from Candice. She's as baffled as if she'd just been hit by a meteorite."

He studied the floor. "That lack of an explanation is one of the connections with the other two cases."

He shook his head as if emerging from a daze and stood up. "Oh, well, like I said, probably time and a few lab rats will give me more."

His mother hesitated before asking, "Have you heard from Gail?"

He looked down at her, taken off guard by the change of topics.

"Gail? No, not in a long time. She's up to her neck in the governor's race."

"She called me a few days ago," the old woman said, sounding wistful. "She sounded sad."

He pursed his lips and kept quiet. His mother was genuinely fond of Lyn, and very happy for Joe that they'd found each other. But Gail had become like a daughter over the years, a bond the two of them would enjoy forever.

"She was probably just tired," he finally suggested.

"Well, that's no doubt true," she agreed. "But she was wrestling with something in particular."

He sat back down. "Spit it out, Mom."

"She wanted your help, but was too embarrassed to ask."

"Embarrassed?" Joe exclaimed, embarrassment not being one of Gail's common emotions. Also, while they'd parted on highly civilized terms, and maintained a genuine friendship, they'd also not kept in frequent contact, recognizing time's value as a healer.

"What's she after?" he asked. "It can't be that bad."

But his mother shook her head. "She didn't tell me. That's why I asked if she'd called. I guess she's still unsure if she should bother you."

Joe paused, weighing the older woman's combination of concern and awkwardness.

"I'll call her from the road," he promised. "It'll be good to catch up anyway. We haven't talked since she threw her hat in the ring."

He stood back up and walked to the door, his smiling mother coming after him. "Beware what you ask for," she warned him, clearly relieved to be free of her obligation. "That campaign is all-consuming. I guess that's the way it always is, or has to be. But last time we spoke, it was all she could talk about. And the minutiae! 'Reynolds said that, and Ivory said the other, and I can't believe Mattison would pull a stunt like saying Reynolds's last press conference had some elements of merit.' It's amazing any of them stay sane."

Joe listened as he buttoned his coat and pulled on his gloves. These were all familiar names, as they were to most people in this tiny, politically aware state. Governor Jim Reynolds — Gail's true opponent — who'd actually signed the VBI into being a few years back; Jyll Ivory, the Progressive candidate, also running for the top spot; and Peter Mattison, the House Speaker, a Democrat like Gail and one of the losers to her in the primary, but who, being more conservative, older, and probably a closet misogynist, still wouldn't rally around the party flag and at least shut up. They and their peers, opponents, detractors, and rivals seemed to Joe like riders on a merry-go-round — forever circling before the public eye, clamoring for attention and a variety of golden rings, and rarely changing over the years.

He'd give Gail that much. She'd stepped down as a state senator to make this run, but otherwise, she was a relative neophyte. She'd only held office as a Brattleboro selectman before winning her senate seat a couple of years previously, and she worked hard to be known as low-key, effective, pragmatic, and respectful of others. On that basis alone, she was likely to get his vote.

Joe kissed his mother again at the door, thanked her for her help, promised to pass along anything that might give Candice comfort, and exchanged the warmth of the house for the cold of another ice-blue, eye-scorching, sunny day.

He couldn't deny that he was curious about Gail's seeking him out. She was an intelligent woman with whom he'd once thoroughly enjoyed sharing a life. She spoke her mind, believed in causes, and yet had always made time for the two of them.

But there had also been an element of intellectual drive, beating ever more loudly in the background, foretelling — if only in hindsight — how things might change. The fact that a violent and traumatic rape had been the catalyst had thus been misleading in one peculiar way: It had suggested that some of Gail's subsequent choices had been based on emotional turmoil rather than intellectual need. Being a high profile rape victim had historically marked the beginning of her political ascent — she'd refused anonymity and led candlelight awareness parades down Brattleboro's Main Street. But Joe knew that all the necessary elements — Gail's impatience with the status quo, which included him, the frustration with her own achievements, and, finally, her own innate ambition — had been simmering all the while, like the proverbial pot waiting to boil.

The rape had been a nightmare, and had left a permanent scar, but her career path afterward had been built on the energy the rape had helped unleash. Hardly a recommendation, but he hoped from his place on the sidelines that perhaps she'd turned it into that scrap of flotsam that would keep her from yielding to an undertow of sorrow.

The outcome of this election was clearly going to play a huge role in that.

Burdened with thoughts of all this, and with growing suspicions about Bob Clarke's death, Joe climbed back into his car and headed not for home, but toward Interstate 89 and Burlington, following the route young Bob had taken hours earlier in the back of a hearse.

Once under way, he hit the hands-off remote on his cell phone and ordered up Gail's number.

"Hello? Answering for future Vermont Governor Gail Zigman," came a cheery unfamiliar woman's voice.

Gunther burst out laughing.

"Hello?" she repeated, placing a slight edge on its brightness.

"Sorry," Joe managed. "Didn't mean to be rude. This is Joe Gunther, returning Gail's phone call in a kind of roundabout way."

The response became guarded. "Okay. Will you please hold?"

There was an audible click as she disappeared to confer with someone else about this potential crank. Joe, for his part, negotiated the traffic routinely collecting in the right lane for the Woodstock exit, after which the road pretty much permanently opened up for the diagonal route all the way across Vermont's Green Mountains to Lake Champlain on its western edge. It was a road he'd traveled hundreds of times, in all sorts of weather and at all times of day, never tiring of it once. The visual soul of Vermont, as he knew it and loved it, was in evidence all the way, from mountains to valleys, rivers to pastures, cities to lonely farms. With his windows closed and cut off by the growl of his engine, he could still smell and hear what his memories had instilled of baled barn hay and the rush of ice-choked streams. He knew this state as a diagnostician knows the quirks of the human body, and never tired of discovering more.

"Hello? Is that you, Joe?"

This voice, he knew. "Hey, Gail. Am I tearing you away from some rubber chicken dinner?"

"Don't I wish. No, I was on the other phone, trying to raise money. It's what politicians do instead of breathe, pee, or eat."

"Congratulations on winning the primary, by the way. Mom was telling me this has taken over your life."

"It's got to," she admitted, sounding both enthused and weary. "But it makes me yearn for when I ran for selectman — a couple of debates in the school gym, one or two interviews and a few yard signs, and that was that. God — the good old days."

"Rough competition, too," he commented politely, immediately fearing that he might have opened a door to more than he wanted to hear.

Which made her response a relief. "You don't want to know. I have never met a more pigheaded, mean-spirited, small-minded, self-serving bunch of needy egomaniacs."

He was laughing again. "And this is the

company you're fighting hard to keep, right?"

She joined him. "Right. And if you ever quote me — assuming I win — I will issue you an order to kill yourself."

"And issue the ME an order to declare it natural causes," he suggested.

"You got it."

"Still," he said, knowing her well, "you're having a ball."

She sighed. "Yes, more's the pity. And it is the only way I know to get things done in the long run. As the Chinese say, 'Keep your friends close, and your enemies closer.' No more protesting out on the streets for me."

"Jeez," he said. "I hope you're not saying stuff like that in public."

"No, no. I try to keep a cork in it. Don't want to lose whatever momentum I may be gaining."

"Things are looking good?"

"Yes," she admitted, sounding surprised. "This state hangs on to its incumbent governors like grim death, which makes the latest numbers a minor miracle. I just wish my own party members would be as supportive of me as they are critical of him."

Joe sensed he was pushing his luck maintaining control of the conversation, so he took advantage of her pause to jump in. "I bet. Mom was telling me how frustrating it was. She also said you were fussing about asking me something."

Gail's voice became tinged with embarrassment, and as a result, true to form, slightly aggressive. "Dumb idea. One of my people came up with it. You'll think it's obnoxious."

There was the challenge, he thought, coming on top of the earlier hemming and hawing to his mother. "Try me," he urged. "I'll let you know if I do."

"All right," she agreed without hesitation. "Do you know the state trooper who's assigned to drive the governor around?"

"Sure," he said, surprised. "Well, I know a couple of them; he actually has a detail that does that. They work in shifts." This wasn't a big secret, but still unlikely to be common knowledge outside of the state police. However, as Gail well knew, Joe made it a practice to know what many others didn't.

"How 'bout the name Felix Knowles?"

He frowned. "He's one of them."

"What can you tell me about him?"

He paused, wondering not only where this was going, but about its very nature. He wasn't used to fielding such questions from Gail.

"Not much," he conceded. "Why?"

He heard an element of relief, despite her actual wording. "I thought so," she said with a laugh. "I told them it was a waste of time."

"What was?"

"Asking you for the dope on Knowles."

"And you'd want that for . . . ?" he asked leadingly.

She laughed uncomfortably. "Oh, you know politics. It's complete nonsense. In a staff meeting, somebody came up with the suggestion that Knowles might be pissed off at the governor for some reason, and that that might make him a good source for our side. It's just the kind of idiocy that floats up sometimes. Awkward, really."

He watched the road ahead of him slipping beneath his car like the display in a video arcade game. He blinked a couple of times and glanced into the rearview mirror to see a sports car planted on his tail. He signaled and shifted into the slow lane.

"I'd say it was a little beyond awkward," he commented.

Again, that familiar aggression crept into her voice. "It's what you have to do — break off the bad ideas from the good ones. It's just a process."

"But you didn't break it off," he pointed out.

He could almost see her looking around

whatever room she was in, seeking some excuse to cut this short while knowing she had to say something.

"Joe, I'm doing this for the right reasons. You know that. I'm sorry if I stepped on your toes, but you actually called me. Not to fault your mom, but this conversation wasn't supposed to happen. I haven't sold my soul here."

"I know that," he reassured her, if half-heartedly. "It must be tough, having all this crap hitting you from everywhere."

He heard voices in the background, and Gail answer behind a hand cupped over the phone's mouthpiece. When she returned, she was back in forward gear. "I'm so sorry. I have to cut this short. I really wish I didn't have to."

"No problem," he told her, almost rushing her. "Me, too. Take care and good luck."

"It was nice talking to you, Joe. I mean that."

I bet, was his initial reaction, but he caught the genuine softness in her tone, and recognized the atonement implied.

So he matched her as best he could with, "You, too, Gail. Don't let them get to you."

In the silence after they hung up, he considered her dilemma — surrounded by monomaniacal advisors, wannabes, and occasional hacks, eating poorly, sleeping little, posturing constantly, fielding questions daily on everything from health care to her use of dangly earrings. It wasn't surprising that a bad idea might occasionally wend its way to being acted upon.

But it still made him angry. And it frustrated him to know that while she'd been correct in associating herself with the good guys — one of which she was — she'd also yielded to temptation and not acknowledged its moral emptiness.

He shook his head, as if debating with a ghost in the passenger seat. A diplomat, he felt he could be when necessary. A politician? He had his doubts.

CHAPTER TEN

The three of them — Joe, Beverly Hillstrom, and David Hawke, head of the state crime lab — had decided by conference call to hold an emergency meeting in Beverly's office. Physically, she was the farthest off, functioning from the depths of Burlington's Fletcher Allen Health Care hospital complex, next to Lake Champlain and under fifty miles from the Canadian border, but she also had only a single deputy medical examiner to help her out, who happened to be out of town.

And, of course, she was the current custodian of Robert Clarke's body, as well as Doreen Ferenc's and Mary Fish's.

The medical examiner's office was a bright, modern, if diminutive facility, a far cry from the small suite above a dentist's office that Joe had first visited decades ago. It was tucked into a hospital that seemed to have been under construction since Jesus was learning the alphabet — during which time more than one of its executives had been brought before a judge for cooking the books. Sadly, the so-called OCME had also slowly evolved from a sunlit satellite located on the complex's fringes to a totally encapsulated, windowless haven, swallowed whole by the surrounding behemoth.

But haven it was, in large part because of Hillstrom's personal style — an uncanny tempering of almost icy efficiency with a passionate belief in her employees and their shared mission. It was a combination that bred both respect and loyalty from people far beyond her immediate reach.

Joe walked the length of the office's short central hallway, after braving the mother building's maze to get here, and met his two companions in Beverly's picture-perfect, compulsively neat corner sanctum. David Hawke rose from the small conference table and exchanged handshakes. A small, athletic man with steady, watchful eyes, Hawke shared a reputation in his own lab almost on a par with Hillstrom's.

The latter, dressed in pale green scrubs, stayed seated at the table and merely reached up to accept Joe's quick hug, offering, "Would you like some coffee, Joe? It's a long drive."

Joe poured himself a cup from the side table, speaking as he did so. "I really appreciate you both doing this on such short notice. It's not like we don't have enough to do without adding spontaneous field trips."

"From what you said on the phone," Beverly responded, "we may be facing a series of interconnected homicides. That's definitely worth a little collective attention."

Hawke had settled back down before his own mug of coffee and a couple of files. He tapped the top one with his finger. "I think I'm up to speed on Doreen Ferenc," he said. "And I was just given Mary Fish's electrical cord, but what's the story on all the drops of blood? I ran the one you found on Doreen against CODIS and the state data bank. I sent those findings to your office, but other than it being from a male, I got nothing. No hits. The one from Mary is still being processed, but now there's a third heading my way?"

Joe joined them at the table. "Okay, we can start there. Three drops of blood found at three scenes, none of them apparently associated with the victims, all of them appearing carefully placed, and . . ." He stopped dead in midsentence.

"What?" Beverly asked, concerned. "Are you all right?"

Joe rubbed his forehead. "No. I mean, I'm fine. I just suddenly thought of something. All of them were wet; at least they all looked damp. They glistened."

"What're you talking about?" David asked.

"The three drops," Joe explained. "They weren't dry. When we found Doreen, I sat with her for a while, studying the scene, trying to rebuild what happened. The blood on her head was glistening. I remember thinking the same thing on the photo of the one I saw on the truck dashboard; it looked shiny."

"The sample from Mary Fish's foot was still damp," Beverly said softly.

Hawke frowned and pulled his cell phone from his belt. He hit a speed dial and told the person who answered moments later, "Do me a favor, would you, Gina? Have the blood samples in the Ferenc, Fish, and Clarke cases analyzed for anticoagulant. That last one should be coming through the door shortly."

He paused a moment to listen, before saying, "That was fast. Great work. Thanks."

He snapped the phone shut and addressed the two of them. "Just got the results on the Mary Fish drop. Same as the first: male depositor, no hits on any database."

He paused to judge their reactions before

smiling thinly and adding, "It also doesn't match the first one."

Joe stared at him. "It's a different male depositor?"

"Right."

"Great," Joe muttered. "Just what we needed; a little extra wrinkle." He shook his head and then eyed David again. "What's the significance of the anticoagulant?"

Hawke gave a small shrug. "Hard to tell. In a way, it makes sense, if the blood was placed there instead of having come from a wound. You can't just walk around with blood in a Ziploc or a bottle and pour it out at will. It'll dry, just like it does when you cut yourself. When medics collect blood in the field, or techs at a blood bank or the hospital, they use Vacutainers with anticoagulant in them, to keep the specimens fluid."

"And you're thinking that may have happened here," Joe suggested.

David raised his eyebrows. "You're the one who brought it up."

"Theatrics," Beverly murmured.

"Yes." Joe understood her reference. "Like you said on the phone when you called my office the other day. You suggested the rape might have been staged. I hate to tell you this, but you and Willy Kunkle are on the same wavelength. He thinks both the Doreen and Mary scenes were set up to make us reach the wrong conclusion."

"But why?" she challenged him. "When both of them fell apart almost as quickly? Doesn't make much sense."

Instead of answering what he didn't know, Joe switched topics. "Tell us about Bob Clarke. You were able to autopsy him, weren't you?"

"That's why I'm still in scrubs," she answered. "He's definitely a homicide — catastrophic blow to the back of the head." She reached forward and touched Joe high on the nape of his neck, just below the skull. "It was either carefully aimed or very lucky, but it certainly did the trick. Death must have been virtually instantaneous."

"Did it cause bleeding?" Hawke asked.

She shook her head. "Closed injury, in case you were hoping for a source for that blood. And I checked the mouth and nose, too. No open wounds."

"He had to have been struck while he was outside," Joe offered. "You can't deliver a blow like that inside the cab of a truck. And if he died immediately, that would explain why his body looked placed behind the wheel."

Beverly had more to tell. "There was

something else," she continued. "When I examined his stomach contents, there was a significant quantity of Scotch. Knowing you were coming, I ordered a quick blood alcohol reading. He was clean."

"As in clean, clean?" Joe asked.

"As a whistle. No discernible amount of alcohol reached his bloodstream."

"So he downed a bottle of Scotch seconds before being murdered?" Hawke asked.

"Apparently."

Joe leaned back in his chair and ran his fingers through his hair. "Jesus. That's how his grandfather died."

"Murdered?"

"No, no. He was a DUI fatal — the real McCoy. Years ago."

Joe got up and refreshed his cup at the side table, still talking. "Along the same lines, Doreen was raped by her father when she was a kid. He ended up in jail, the family moved, and Doreen never married; never even had a romantic relationship, as far as we can tell."

"What about Mary Fish?" Beverly asked.

"We don't know," Joe confessed. "We haven't interviewed her partner yet, and she has no apparent next of kin. The partner was sedated and in the hospital yesterday. Interesting notion, though, if each of these folks was posed to reflect something traumatic from their past."

He sat back down with a full mug. "Okay, let's step back a bit and see what we're facing; I mean the evidence, not the theories."

"You were talking about the three drops," Hawke reminded him.

"Right," Joe agreed ruefully. "God — getting old. Okay, so now we know we have at least two out of three belonging to separate John Does. Dave, what can you tell from an anonymous drop of blood?"

"Just what I told you," David said, spreading his hands apart. "They're males. That's it."

"What about if one of them's sick with something?"

Hawke was already shaking his head. "Times have changed. We don't have the budget for that kind of digging anymore."

Joe studied him for a few seconds, scowling with frustration.

David pulled a brochure from his pocket and placed it flat on the table, adding, "One of these fellows might be able to help."

It was from the University of Vermont, whose campus was across the street from where they were sitting.

"That's been on my desk for a while," David explained. "It's part of an annual series of seminars UVM's been hosting for years. They have them on engineering, architecture, mathematics, you name it. Scientists and scholars from all over the world come here to kick around ideas. It's low-key, low-profile, and very worthwhile. The Federation of American Societies for Experimental Biology is one of the groups using it, and they're the ones in town this week, as luck would have it. I only thought of it because I knew you'd be asking me for things I couldn't do or couldn't afford."

He leaned forward and flipped the mailer open. "Right there — a talk entitled 'Novel Uses of Synchrotron Light Sources.'"

Beverly couldn't restrain herself. She reached out and twisted the document around so she could read it, since Joe was merely staring at Hawke.

"What does that tell me?" he asked.

"The theme of the session is forensics," Beverly tried explaining. "This is terrific. What an opportunity."

David Hawke took pity. "Joe, these are mostly high-level DNA researchers, cutting-edge people who gave us DNA profiling in the first place. Very smart. And they're having a little brain session all this week a few hundred yards away. It occurred to me that we could do worse than to approach one or two of them and ask for help."

"They would do what you can't?" Joe asked.

"Maybe. Wouldn't hurt to ask. They have a lot more money than I do."

"These are big names," Beverly commented, nodding. She looked up at him. "Joe, it's an academic standard for types like this to pitch in on interesting cases now and then; it keeps them fresh, makes them feel useful, and gives them a glimpse of the real world. It's a little like lawyers working pro bono — it helps them sleep at night. And the tools some of them have at their disposal are incredible. A synchrotron alone is capable of analyzing things down to the atomic level — a huge help in exactly what you're looking for."

Joe retrieved the flyer and glanced over it. He couldn't pretend to understand much, but the words "forensics," "DNA," and "analysis" surfaced periodically.

"We know anyone here?" He waved a hand across the pages.

"I know of Eric Marine," David said. "He's requested a couple of my articles, with favorable comments, which never hurts. I recognize over half the participants of this seminar, of course, and several are even friendly acquaintances, but Marine looks like our best shot for a couple of reasons." He suddenly smiled broadly. "The first being, I'd like to meet the man; the second is that he works out of Brookhaven National Lab on Long Island, which is exactly the kind of place that could help us out."

"Never heard of it," Joe admitted.

"Huge campus," Beverly explained. "Particle colliders, the synchrotron mentioned here, a brand-new nanolab. Physicists at Columbia University pushed to get it built after losing a bunch of their top people to western schools after World War II and the Manhattan Project and other projects. They were afraid that if they didn't have something really nifty to offer locally, the resulting brain drain would leave them a second-rate school. So they took over an army camp and created this incredible facility. They study everything from how the universe was created to what happens to an astronaut's blood after six months in space."

"They're not going to let us in there," Joe said flatly.

"It's not military," Hawke insisted. "It's almost totally open. That was the point from the get-go. People from all over the world, including places that make our government shudder, come there to do research —

thousands of them, every year. There're ten labs just like it across the U.S. It's actually pretty neat — pure science, no national flags hitting anyone across the face. All you need to do is apply. If your experiment is judged to be interesting, it'll be done at no cost to you. The only provision is that you must publish your results. If you want your findings to be kept confidential, then you have to pay full cost. It's what the scientific community envisioned from the start before politicians and wars messed everything up — a global community of scholars brainstorming ideas."

Joe slid the brochure back across the table to him. "Okay, okay. I'm welling up. What're you proposing?"

"Well, I know this is rushing things a little, but this bunch'll only be in town for a few more days, and I would think an approach on our home turf has got to play in our favor. Of course, we also have to analyze the drop of blood from Bob's pickup, but I can speed that up."

David scratched his head, organizing his thoughts. "You're going to have to consider two things first." He held up his hand and lifted one finger. "Number one, we'll have to make the bait tempting enough for Marine and company to find it appealing.

For that, we have to show that we've done our job the best we can, and that our needs are crucial and can't be met without them. This'll be helped by my budget being already in the red."

He raised the second finger. "Number two, keep in mind that, while someone like Marine has all sorts of wild ways to coax information from blood, it's not truly proven stuff. Some of it's even controversial, so no court will allow it to be presented. Still, as with psychological profiling and the use of ESP, it can come in handy in making a case, on a purely investigative level.

"Oh," Hawke added, "and there's another thing I almost forgot: If you opt to do this, we're going to have to manage how we handle the evidence, to maintain case integrity. Some of my testing destroys whatever sample it analyzes. That's why we always try to hold a little back. In choosing who gets first crack at what, we'll have to keep that in mind."

Joe pointed at the brochure. "Okay. Let's say using Brookhaven's a possibility, or any other outsider, for that matter. What can we expect to get, case by case?"

"With Doreen," Beverly volunteered, "it's mostly negatives. No semen and no knife tip broken off in the bone. In fact, it doesn't

148

appear as if the knife even nicked a bone. It did go through her nightgown, though."

Joe hesitated before asking, "Which gives us what? The dimensions of the blade?"

She smiled. "Well, yes, to a certain extent, although the hole usually widens on the way out, as the knife's withdrawn. I actually meant whatever residue might be on the blade, microscopic traces of which could have been wiped onto the fabric of the nightgown."

Joe raised his eyebrows. "Okay. A long shot."

"Admittedly," she conceded.

"With Mary," David picked up, "we've got the footstool, which gave us nothing, the note, which had only Mary's and presumably her roommate's fingerprints on it — we'll collect the roommate's prints after she calms down — and not much else. The most promising item is the electrical cord used to hang her, from which I'm hoping we can collect some sweatprints or touch-DNA, although we'll have to farm that out to another lab — or to Brookhaven, if they're willing and able."

Joe had read about sweatprints and touch-DNA, where a person's fingerprints might be too smeared to lift, but the skin cells and oils and residues within the print were still available for testing. "That's looking good?" he asked.

Hawke gave him an equivocal, "It's looking possible. The cord was new; its surface is smooth and nonabsorbent; the killer may not have been wearing gloves. Who knows? There, even without Brookhaven, I'd be willing to take a shot, budget be damned."

"Don't we also have the ink analysis route with the suicide note?" Joe asked.

"Sure," David conceded. "But without a standard, it won't do us much good. It's like a fingerprint without an AFIS match or a blood drop with no hit in the data bank."

Joe shook his head. "Hold it. Isn't that precisely what we're talking about? We already have blood with no hits. That's not stopping us from trying to see what else we can get out of it."

David held up both hands in surrender. "Granted. We'll put the ink on the table, too."

"What do you think you have with the third case?" Hillstrom asked Joe, hoping to be helpful in light of his frustrated expression.

"Well," he said, "given what you discovered in the poor guy's stomach, I have a bottle that might have somebody else's fingerprints on it. I also have the truck."

"It wasn't Clarke's?" David asked, surprised.

"No, no. It was Bobby's, all right. But it occurred to me driving up here that if he didn't go off the road himself — and that's looking likely with the head injury Beverly found — then the truck had to have been pushed, possibly by another vehicle."

"Leaving a mark on the bumper," Beverly suggested.

"Could be."

"Well," David stated. "That, we could check out pretty easily."

"What about clothing?" Joe asked him. "Does touch-DNA work there? We're assuming the killer pulled down Doreen's underwear and lifted Bob into his truck. He couldn't have done either without touching them and leaving DNA — assuming he wasn't wearing gloves."

"Big assumption," Beverly couldn't resist saying. "This is clearly a careful man."

Hawke was also looking skeptical, if for different reasons. "I don't know. The underwear's as big a reach as finding residue from the knife on the nightgown. And with Bob, even if the bad guy didn't have latex gloves, he probably was wearing something. It was in the middle of the night in the late fall, for crying out loud — frigging freezing. Still,

151

the underwear, the nightgown, the ink analysis, and even the bumper might all be good for Eric Marine's curiosity. Actually, come to think of it, if we did gather enough evidence through cutting-edge science, maybe we could get it into court, after all, and establish legal precedent. That is how it happens sometimes; DNA didn't have an easy time at first."

Joe reached out and patted his arm. "Slow down, Einstein. There could be a Nobel in this for you, too, but I doubt it. For all we know, Eric Marine's never heard of you, had some student read your articles, and has a policy against helping outsiders."

Hawke pulled a face. "Damn, Gunther, you sure can rain on a parade."

"Just being cautious," Joe said. "Right now, we have a whole lot of nothing, much less anything to bring to a jury. I'll have the sheriff's department transport the pickup truck to you in a closed carrier, so you can give it your full attention without putting a team out in the field. I'll also interview Mary Fish's partner for any relevant background information. How much longer will Eric Marine be in town?"

Hawke didn't bother consulting the brochure. "Three days, assuming he doesn't skip out early."

"I'll talk to him," Beverly volunteered, making both men stare at her. She smiled in response. "I've heard about him, too, and read his papers. Plus, I don't think it will hurt if a colleague of the opposite gender makes the appeal. Maybe I can meet him for lunch or something."

Joe was laughing by now. "All for the cause, Beverly, all for the cause. You are too much."

"And that little secret had better accompany you both to your graves," she said severely.

David Hawke saluted her and stood up. "Aye, aye. Can I go now? I've played hooky long enough."

"Go," Joe told him, "and many thanks. This has been truly above and beyond."

Hawke gathered his files and moved to the door. "Not really. As Dr. Hillstrom said, if all three of these are connected, we've got something more than worthy of our collective attention." He paused and added, "I'll run using Brookhaven by the state's attorney, just to make sure we're on safe ground with all this."

Beverly waited until the door had closed behind him before asking her old friend, "And what more can I do for you?"

"It's going to sound a little weird," he

warned her.

"Go ahead."

"I'd like to see Mary and Bob. I'm going to do my best to tell their stories and maybe let them rest in peace. I just wanted to meet them, if only this once."

Beverly smiled and patted his hand, rising from the table. "I don't think that's the least bit weird, Joe."

She led him back down the hallway and out into the lab, the last door of which opened onto the autopsy room, an arena he'd visited often over the years, usually with Hillstrom officiating.

She crossed over to the wall cooler and pulled open two of its drawers, revealing the pale, slightly yellow-tinged bodies of a young man and an elderly woman. The woman's face was dark and discolored and her tongue protruded slightly from between her lips. Both bodies had the familiar Y-shaped cut decorating their torsos.

"Tell me what you know," Beverly requested.

Joe studied the faces for a moment, barely registering the signs of death that would have derailed most observers. He had seen hundreds of corpses in his career, and before that in combat as a young man. He had learned to read life's sign language in what was left behind.

"Mary I know the least," he began. "Hard-working, dependable, devoted to the woman she lived with and the people she worked for, even though her boss is clearly an idiot. From what I could tell, she had a quiet, comfortable life, and filled her time away from the office with classical music, show tunes, and a huge collection of DVDs of classic Hollywood movies. It looked like she and Elise, her other half, loved cooking, staying home, and each other. Of course, Elise and I have yet to meet, and you know what they say about first impressions."

Beverly chuckled slightly. "That they're usually correct?"

He conceded the point. "Not what I was thinking, but for Elise's sake, I hope so. Maybe those memories will eventually overshadow the effects of that fake suicide note."

He shifted over to the young man. "Bob Clarke's grandmother, Candice, is best friends with my mom, so him I know more about. Terrible upbringing until his father was locked up as a habitual offender, then the proverbial gift from God. He reacted to Candice's offer to take him in like a starving man hits a meal, and repaid the favor with respect and hard work and abstinence

— at least as far as any of us knew. At the time of the transition, I know my mom was pretty nervous. Candice is no spring chicken, and not in the best of health; Mom thought the effort might do her in. But of course, it was just the opposite — both of them bloomed in the other's presence."

He stood there for a moment, looking down at both bodies, and then finally stepped back. "Thanks, Beverly. That helped add a little perspective."

She placed her cool hand on the nape of his neck and smiled. "I know the feeling. Good luck finding who did this."

CHAPTER ELEVEN

Springfield's hospital sat above the town, less overlooking it than standing slightly aloof, like a doting nanny standing off to one side, ready to care for her accident-prone charges. It was gray and damp when Joe pulled into the parking lot, and he paused a moment before entering the facility to appreciate a climate so many other Vermonters his age had come to thoroughly dislike.

He didn't deny that the late fall/early winter cusp, especially, could be challenging, and that some years its unrelenting grayness could seem biblical in duration. But he was born of this part of the earth, and while he'd traveled far in his time, the nostalgia he'd felt when away was only reinforced when he was back in its embrace. Familiarity in his case led only to comfort and a sense of belonging. As with all love affairs of the type, the occasional crankiness was easily forgiven.

And so he walked slowly across the parking lot, feeling the mist against his face, very much aware of the two people he'd left in Hillstrom's cooler, fellow New Englanders who'd been robbed of any more such experiences.

Elise Howard had been placed on the hospital's top floor, in a quiet room facing a steep embankment covered with evergreens, across the feeder road to the upper parking lot.

Joe stood quietly in the open doorway, studying the thin, frail woman in bed as she gazed out the window, as unmoving as if she'd joined Mary Fish at the morgue.

He tapped softly on the wall beside him and watched her slowly turn her head away from the view, as if letting go of the one rope that was keeping her moored.

"Yes?" she said in a whisper.

He advanced into the room and took a seat between the window and the bed, so that she could look over his shoulder if she chose, instead of having to watch him.

He squeezed her hand, less in a shake than in a simple touching of sorrowful humans, and uttered his all-too-practiced standard introduction.

"Hi, Ms. Howard. My name is Joe. I'm a

police officer. I am so sorry to be meeting you under these circumstances."

"So am I," she said, which pleased him as a response. It implied that the numbness accompanying her misery hadn't dulled her ability to react with precision and truthfulness.

"I hope my being here isn't too much of an intrusion," he continued.

"No," she sighed. "I knew someone would come eventually. I imagined it would be a funeral director or someone like that."

"That can be arranged," he offered. "For the moment, we all just wanted to let you be, at least until the initial shock had passed."

She nodded. "Thank you."

He assumed the need to pursue a funeral director had passed. "I would like to chat with you a little about Mary, though. Would that be all right?"

"Yes."

"And I know this sounds a little stupid, but I want to show my respect by asking how you'd prefer to be addressed. As Ms. Howard? Elise?"

She had returned to the window, but this brought her focus back squarely to his face. "How long have you been a police officer? I'm sorry . . . I forgot your name."

"Joe. And a long time."

She allowed for a thin smile. "It shows. You're very good. Elise will be fine."

"Thank you," he said, and leaned forward to prop his elbows on his knees, placing his face near hers, but slightly below it, so she wouldn't feel cornered.

"How long were you and Mary a couple?"

"Thirty-two years," she answered without pause, the number no doubt having been floating in her head for several days. "And before you even ask it, they were the happiest years of my life."

"What do you think of how Mary died?"

Her eyes narrowed. "What do I *think* of it? What an absurd question . . ."

He held up his hand to stop her. "Not how you *feel* about it, Elise. What do you literally think happened?"

She teared up and blinked several times, fighting to keep her composure. "We were doing fine," she finally said, barely audible.

"No disagreements?"

She tilted her head slightly. "No. I'd been complaining about wanting some time just for us. At first, she'd been a little impatient — she was the one who brought in the money, you see. But after a while, her enthusiasm grew, until she was talking about it more than I ever did. We laughed about that. It wasn't a bone of contention."

Gunther remained silent, letting her continue the conversation to his advantage.

She finally took a deep breath and asked him, "Could she have been murdered?"

"That's what I'm trying to determine," he admitted.

Her mouth fell open, her shoulders went slack, and she became so pale, Joe thought she might pass out.

What she said, however, surprised him. "I thought so."

He watched her a few seconds, concerned, but she remained staring at him, alive and conscious.

"Why do you say that?" he asked.

Her answer was disappointing. "I couldn't think of any other explanation."

He pursed his lips thoughtfully before proceeding. "Elise, I have to be honest with you. Most people are killed by someone they know and for reasons that make sense — or at least they're explainable. Random stranger killings are very rare, especially around here."

"All right," she said, as if he were detailing a theorem.

"If everything was going well between you two, then what else might've gone sour for Mary?" he pressed her. "Schools can be hotbeds of jealousy and disappointment. Mary was in a powerful position, being Raddlecup's number two. Did she ever discuss what happened at work with you?"

"All the time," Elise said. "And it was Raddlecup that caused most of her problems. The rest of them usually went to her to avoid him, and she was wonderful with them."

"How did that make the relationship between Raddlecup and Mary?"

"It was fine," she told him. "He loved her; she saved his bacon every week and made it crystal clear that she never wanted to replace him."

Joe paused a moment before asking, "The way she died was very personal. It wasn't like someone fired a gun into the air and the bullet just happened to strike her. Does the staging of a fake suicide tell you anything?"

Again, she paled, and Joe feared he might have overestimated her reserves, but she took a deep breath and said quietly, "No."

"There's never been a death like that — a hanging — in either one of your families?"

"No."

She was looking down by now, apparently focusing on the edge of the bed. Only by doing the same did Joe notice her tears silently dripping onto the sheet. He reached for her hand and squeezed it gently.

She looked up, her weathered cheeks glistening, and gave him a wan, apologetic smile. "I'm sorry. She was the love of a lifetime."

He nodded sympathetically. "I lost my wife to cancer decades ago," he admitted. "I never wanted to marry again."

"Then you know the feeling."

"There may be another angle to this we haven't discussed," he said after a moment. "Could it be that someone wanted to hurt you by doing this?"

She straightened and pulled her hand away, if only to wipe her cheeks. She looked startled by the suggestion. "Me? Why?"

"I don't know," he answered.

She frowned. "This has become such a terrible world."

"Did you think of something?" he asked hopefully.

She closed her eyes briefly, seemingly exhausted. "I can't think of anything else."

She lay back and rested her head against the pillow. Joe rose and squeezed her shoulder. "I'm so terribly sorry, Elise. Thanks for speaking with me."

She merely nodded and gave him a tired smile.

He saw himself out.

Bill Allard was Joe's boss, making him and the commissioner of public safety the only two people between Joe and the governor. The VBI was a quirky entity, having resulted from a typically political cocktail of hysteria, heedless speed, and a pinch of spite. One motivator behind Gail's advisor's thinking the governor's trooper/chauffeur might want to dish dirt on the boss was that many in the state police had interpreted VBI's birth as a direct slap in the face.

That very sensitivity was one of Allard's concerns when he entered Joe's office in Brattleboro the next day.

"The Colonel's curious about the Mary Fish case," Bill announced after he'd settled into Joe's guest chair, a fresh cup of coffee in hand.

"Ain't we all," Joe quipped. "What's Neal want to know?"

Neal Kirkland was the colonel in charge of the state police, an old school warrior not well disposed to his troopers taking a backseat to anybody.

"The way he heard it, we might've hip-checked his boy off the stage."

"Dave Nelson?" Joe asked, genuinely surprised. "He seemed pretty grateful at the time, and I think we're on solid ground claiming it's a homicide."

Bill hastened to finish the sip he'd begun. "No, no. Not Nelson. It's whoever he reported to, or maybe whoever that guy reported to. You know the routine. By the time it reached Kirkland, we'd ripped them off, kicked sand on Nelson's shoes, and called him a sissy."

Joe sighed. "I went through channels. If they wanted to stop us, they had the opportunity. You came all the way down here to tell me this?"

Allard grimaced. "My sister's getting a divorce. She lives in Greenfield, so I thought I'd drop by and hear her out. You and I both know how this works, Joe — the supervisor gives his stamp of approval to you, and then bitches to his boss that he didn't have a choice and took a bullet to keep the peace. It's bullshit, but Neal talked to me, which means I had to talk to you, and that's that."

He took another swallow before adding, as Joe suspected he would, "Except for now, we have what's looking like a serial killer. That's right, isn't it?"

"Yes," Joe admitted reluctantly. "I was hoping I wouldn't have to use that phrase, though."

"Don't you have three murders, all by the

same perp?"

Joe sat back and scratched his temple, feeling his own frustration rising. "Maybe. What we've got is two homicides and one death that stinks to high heaven. You've read everything I sent you so far, right?"

"Yeah," Allard conceded. "All the way to last night's update. You mentioned bringing in a consultant for the high-end forensic stuff. Dave Hawke can't handle that?"

Ah, Joe thought, the crux of the visit. "Nope — too expensive and too technical. Plus, if this Eric Marine he mentioned takes the bait, most of the expense will probably go away, absorbed by the pursuit of some greater scientific good."

Bill stared at him balefully.

"Okay," Joe admitted, "we've got pretty much squat right now. A few drops of blood, some evidence that may or may not have a little DNA on it, and a growing bunch of interviews leading nowhere fast. We need a break, Bill, and it would be nice to get it before somebody else ends up dead and the newsboys connect the dots."

"Ah," Allard said, as if struck by an old lingering memory.

"They been pounding on your door, too?" Joe asked.

"Too? Who's been after you?"

"Just Katz," Joe conceded. "The Burlington TV crew was at the Doreen scene, and they've made a few calls that Lester and Sam handled. But Stanley's the only one to have gotten through to me. It's all been about the one case, so far, but it won't be long before something leaks out, which would make it really nice to have something to say."

"And what about that one pure, straightforward murder?" Allard asked. "I mean the old-fashioned stuff — interviews, surveillance, document checks, alibis, and the rest? Anything at all?"

"That's what I meant by the interviews going nowhere fast," Joe told him. "We like Chuck McNaughton for something dirty, in part because we think he's a creep, but he's got a solid alibi. Lester's theory is that he could've hired a hit, which is possible, but we don't have a motive. He and Doreen don't appear to have had a thing going; it doesn't look like she was blackmailing him or about to squeal to the cops; for that matter, we've got nothing saying he was cooking the books or doing anything she could've squealed about. His biggest transgression so far would be interesting only to his wife's divorce lawyer, assuming she had one.

"Plus," he added, almost as an afterthought, "if he did hire a hit man to whack Doreen, then it's looking like he used him to kill Mary Fish and Bob Clarke, too. Why do that? To throw us off? Seems a stretch."

"And Doreen's mother's death right after is still looking like a straight suicide?"

"Yeah, although I will admit it brings up a small detail I can't get out of my head."

"What's that?"

"I didn't put it in any report to you," Joe admitted. "But I was struck by how two of these cases seemed to hark back to the dead person's past history — Doreen's rape by her father and Bob's grandfather dying drunk at the wheel of a car."

" 'Specially since Doreen wasn't raped this time, and nor was Bob drunk," Bill filled in.

"But that's my point. I think Margaret Agostini may have killed herself not just because her daughter was murdered, but because she'd been told that Dory had been raped, too. But it's just a hunch — there's nothing to go with it."

Allard rose, placed his partially empty mug on the counter alongside the coffee-maker, and headed to where he'd hung his coat by the door.

"I'm sorry, Joe. I should know better than to meddle. You've clearly got this as surrounded as possible right now. I'll get out of your hair so my sister can give me a snoot full of real drama."

"Not a problem," Joe assured him. "I'll let you know what we find out."

Bill settled his coat on his shoulders and gave him a wistful smile. "I should've taken retirement when they offered it, right?"

But Joe shook his head. "Not from where I'm sitting."

Willy pulled the car close enough to the snowbank to allow him to get out and keep the car out of any traffic. "Goddamned road crews. In New York at least they know how to keep the streets clear."

Sam stared at him. "In *New York?* What the hell're you doing running New York up the flagpole? You're the one who keeps saying what a dump that place is, including the snow removal. You *hate* New York. Plus, it's warming up; half the snow's gone already."

Willy scowled at her. "Whatever." He waved his hand at the remaining mounds of the stuff. "Ya gotta admit. This shit sucks."

Sammie merely shook her head. Willy hadn't lived in New York in over twenty years, where he'd briefly been a cop. Moving to Vermont had amounted to a partial salvation, in fact, even though it hadn't softened his attitude any.

They were parked in the minute village of Westminster West, really a small cluster of buildings lining the curve of a road between Putney and Saxtons River. Known for its artists and left-leaning politics — regardless of whether either one truly represented the majority — West West, as it was colloquially known, was nevertheless as quaint as rural New England had to offer. It boasted the no-muss, no-fuss, archetypal gathering of church, library, and clapboarded Greek Revival homes that so caught the eye of those busloads of summer tourists. It also helped deflect the reality that trailer parks had as much to say about genuine New England as any place like this.

"That the address?" Willy asked, pointing to a small house tethered to the road via a narrow, crooked path through the snow, as wide as a hand shovel's blade, and now slathered with a layer of soft, slippery mud. The lights behind the ground floor's windows cast a series of pleasant yellow rectangles upon the white patchy blanket covering the yard.

"Michele Starr," Sammie confirmed. A shadow passed before one of the windows. "Looks like somebody's home."

They got out quietly, easing their doors

shut out of long habit, and looked around the neighborhood. The village was tucked in for the night, the street empty and still, the smell of chimney smoke on the breeze, and the sense of the night air having enclosed the community like a star-packed celestial lid.

"Goddamned cold," Willy barely murmured, unimpressed, using his one good hand to gather his collar more tightly around his throat.

They traveled the shoveled lane in single file, arbitrarily choosing the sucking mud over any mysteries beneath the recently rain-drenched snow to either side. A no-win set of options that Willy growled about the entire distance, his grumbling unnaturally loud in the surrounding silence. At the door, they listened carefully for a few moments, again out of habit, but heard little beyond what sounded like a muted radio program.

Willy pressed the doorbell.

A moment later a small, slim, older woman stood before them, a tentative smile on her face. "Yes?"

Sam looked over the woman's shoulder, enjoying the fresh smell of recent cooking that hit her face. An old, slow-moving cat crossed the hallway in the distance without a glance in their direction.

171

"Are you Michele Starr?" Willy asked.

"Yes, that's me."

They both displayed their credentials. "I'm William Kunkle and this is Samantha Martens, of the Vermont Bureau of Investigation," he intoned. "We'd like to ask you a few questions, if that's all right."

"My goodness," she said, without opening the door any wider. "What about?"

Sam recognized the gentle paranoia of someone whose age put her in the 1960s as an adult in her twenties. "It's okay, Ms. Starr. We're not after you for anything. We think you once knew Doreen Ferenc, and we wanted to know a little more about that."

Michele Starr remained looking receptive, although the mention of Doreen's name clearly made an impact, but the door remained where it was, despite the cold rushing in, and her next questions were hardly inviting.

"Why? And how did you find me?"

Willy had reached his limit — rarely a huge leap. "Lady," he said, "you're not in trouble and we're freezing our asses off. Doreen's been murdered and we need help. We found you 'cause that's what we do. It's that simple. You gonna let us in or not?"

The expression changed to shock, as if Willy had channeled Michele's mother in

172

reminding her to tend to her manners. The door swung back at last and their small host ushered them in.

"I am so sorry. We're told so often to be careful nowadays, and this horrible thing about Doreen . . ."

They both filed in and stood slightly hunched in the hallway, letting the heat work its way inside their clothing.

"It's okay," Sam said. "Totally understandable."

After that, the social niceties fell into place by rote. Coats were hung up, hot drinks were offered and the radio turned off, the cat was introduced to little effect, and they all ended up seated around a woodstove with glass doors, enjoying the source of the home's warmth.

"Feeling better?" Starr asked Willy pointedly as he took a sip from his cup of coffee.

"Lots," Sam answered quickly, not trusting him to be civil yet. "Thanks so much for understanding. It's sometimes a quirky job and we catch people by surprise without meaning to. I am sorry."

The woman was working hard to maintain appearances. "It's nice to have unexpected company now and then, especially when it turns out I don't have to worry."

"Don't have any skeletons in the closet?"

Willy asked.

"The price of a boring life," she told him.

Sam was looking around the living room, noticing an unusual number of framed black-and-white photographs, not unlike what they'd seen at Doreen's house.

"You read about Doreen in the papers?" she asked.

Michele nodded mournfully, her voice indicating a crack in her politesse. "Yes. Poor girl. I actually knew her once, a long time ago."

"At Ethan Allen Academy?"

Her eyebrows rose. "You *have* been checking up on me. Yes, during one of the summer sessions they used to host. I taught photography at the school and it was a good way for me to bridge the summer break. I don't have any family, didn't have a summer home, and I needed the money. It worked for everyone. Dory was one of my students."

"Did you also know Mary Fish?" Willy asked.

There, Starr's response was spontaneous and happier. She smiled broadly and her eyes softened. "Oh, yes. Mary was like the Queen of the Nile there — all things to all people. One of the nicest, most loving women I've ever known."

174

"And a boy named Chuck McNaughton?" Sammie added. "He was a student there."

There the older woman frowned. "Of mine?"

"We know he attended the school."

She shook her head. "The art department was sort of cut off from the general population. English teachers got to meet everyone, but art was an elective. I didn't know a lot of the kids who attended all four years."

Willy pursed his lips. Lester's discovery earlier in the day that Dory and Chuck had both been at Mary Fish's school for a brief moment had seemed like just the break they were craving.

"Funny you should mention English," Sam now said. "Because McNaughton was at the school taking remedial English, the same summer that you and Doreen were there."

Starr's only response was to look at them wonderingly, which made Willy think that she was either truly clueless or among the best liars he'd ever known. But his gut told him the latter was wishful thinking.

Still, there was something about her that he couldn't ignore — something guarded that they hadn't squarely hit.

He tried a different approach, using her earlier distrust and sadness. "Michele," he asked, "let me tell you how we do this. We spend days looking into people's lives, layer by layer, figuring out what they were doing when and who with. It's only after we're finished that we finally conduct the interview. You're a smart woman. You can figure out why we do it that way."

"I didn't know the McNaughton boy," she insisted. "I swear. I have no reason to lie about that."

Sammie saw her own opportunity to maneuver. "Mary is dead, too, Michele. She was found hanging by the neck a few days ago."

Michele sat back in her chair as if pushed by a large hand, her face drained and her mouth open. "What? Mary? Oh, my God."

She ducked her head, covered her face, and began sobbing.

Sammie rolled her eyes in frustration, but Willy followed up quickly. "Michele," he pressed, handing her the napkin she'd given him with his coffee. "Talk to us. What's going on?"

She raised her face to answer. "I was in love with Dory, but she wasn't interested. Mary was the only reason I didn't lose my mind and my job, both."

"Dory was gay?" Sammie blurted.

"No," Michele wailed. "That was the

176

problem. I didn't know what she was, but I loved her anyhow. She was only in her mid-twenties; she didn't seem to have anyone in her life. In those days, everything was perception and guesswork; it's not like now, when you can just ask. It was subtler, more of a courtship, and I thought I was making a connection. But when I took the next step, she slammed the door in my face. I completely fell apart."

"And that's when Mary showed up," Willy suggested.

"She knew about me," Michele admitted. "All of us tended to know about each other; there were signs only we recognized. But she was older and committed to Elise, and she was incredibly discreet in any case, because of her position. Still, she sought me out, and gave me comfort, and by doing that, she saved my life."

She wiped at her face ineffectively, still sobbing. "I can't believe she's dead. And she hanged herself? Why?"

"We don't know," Willy said blandly.

"What happened after Dory turned you down?" Sam asked.

Michele took a deep breath and straightened in her seat. "Nothing. She left. Most of the summer had gone by anyhow. I never heard from her again, or even about her until I read the papers." She paused and shook her head. "And now poor Mary. What's Elise going to do? Mary was her life."

Both detectives ignored that question.

"In your conversations with Doreen," Sammie asked after a pause, "when you were getting to know each other, did she ever mention that her boss had a son at the school?"

"McNaughton was her boss's son?"

That clearly answered the question.

The conversation wound down from there. Sam and Willy took a couple of more half-hearted stabs at the subject, but what had seemed so full of potential hours ago now seemed to have dissolved into simply another example of Vermont's uniquely sparse population commingling as to defy all likelihood. It was no cliché that up here, far from the urban mob, almost everyone did in fact know everyone else.

Except for where it might have helped the case.

CHAPTER TWELVE

Eric Marine was a white-haired, bespectacled man with a face whose every feature mirrored the motion of his mouth. When he smiled, everything lifted with happiness, and when he frowned, it all sagged with disappointment. The man's innate expressiveness, and his habit of reacting to everything said to him, led to an ever-shifting facial landscape that Joe, for one, couldn't stop watching.

Fortunately, Marine was looking only at Joe's companion. "David Hawke," he was saying, shaking the latter's hand. "How wonderful. Such excellent papers — informative, original, even challenging sometimes." He suddenly took in Joe. "You are very fortunate. Dr. Hawke and his team were among the early ones to grasp the significance of DNA work — extraordinary, given the small size of your state." His other hand suddenly shot up to his forehead as he blurted, "No offense."

"None taken," Joe said.

They were standing in the lobby of Burlington's Hilton Hotel, just across Battery Street from a sweeping view of Lake Champlain, whose iron-gray surface was flecked with whitecaps. Far in the distance, crowned by a solid plane of cold, bruised sky, the razor-sharp outline of New York's Adirondack Mountains stretched out like an arrested tidal wave of snow-frosted rock — as dark and disturbingly ominous as the smaller, more benign Green Mountains to the east were rounded, gentler, and more inviting.

"Dr. Hillstrom was telling me that you two gentlemen were interested in the forensic capabilities of BNL," Marine said brightly, not pausing to add, "Of course, as you might have gathered from my talk at this conference, this is an area of some interest to me. I have been thinking for quite a while what a shame it is that our life sciences and especially our NSLS and CFN technologies have been so rarely considered as potential resources." He laughed and held up a finger for emphasis. "Not that I don't recognize the standard barrier, which is money, as always."

He walked away suddenly, forcing them

to follow him to a small cluster of comfortable armchairs, grouped out of the way near a gigantic window facing the view. Joe noticed that David was smiling broadly, clearly in his element. For his part, Joe had only deciphered that BNL stood for Brookhaven National Laboratory. This was going to be a challenging conversation.

Marine happily plopped into one of the chairs and sighed. "You people live in the most beautiful part of the country. The lab is located in a very pretty setting, too. Don't get me wrong. Five thousand acres of fields and forest." He laughed again abruptly. "And lots and lots of wild turkeys, not all of them employees."

Joe and David joined in politely, making Marine wave dismissively. "I know, I know. Bad joke. No need for flattery. My wife already tells me what a bore I can be. Still, it is so nice to get out and see another part of the world."

He changed gears and slapped his hands on the arms of his easy chair. "Okay, enough of that. You gentlemen have a problem, and I am wasting your time."

He stared at them both expectantly.

Joe was the first to jump in. "Dr. Marine, we have . . ."

"Eric," the scientist interrupted.

Joe smiled. "Right. Thanks, and please call us Joe and David. Eric, we have three homicides, two of them not known as such by anyone but us so far . . ."

"Why?" Marine interrupted again.

Joe thought fast to figure out what he meant. "Because one was disguised by the killer as a suicide, and the other as a car crash involving alcohol."

He paused. Marine nodded, smiling widely. "And all three were conducted by the same person? How intriguing."

"The evidence suggests it," Joe agreed cautiously. "But that's one big reason we're knocking on your door. As you know, whenever we're lucky enough to get a picture of a bad guy, or a fingerprint or a DNA sample, we always have to cross our fingers that somebody or some database will give us a match. So far, even though we have a pretty decent collection of samples, we've gotten no matches."

Hawke cleared his throat to contribute, but Marine stalled him with a raised index finger. "Hold on, David. I'd like to hear Joe's wording first. It's often useful to build from the layman's view upward."

Joe laughed awkwardly. "Well, you'll get what you're paying for. Okay, as of this morning, after David delivered his latest from the third killing, we have a collection of three carefully placed blood deposits, two male, one female, all laced with anticoagulant . . ."

"Ah," Marine exclaimed. "Beverly told me about these, but the findings hadn't come in for the third. So it's looking like a calling card, too."

"Right," Joe agreed, relieved that Hillstrom had done some groundwork. "We don't know how or why, but more than anything, they connect all three cases, like three different paintings all bearing the same signature. And we also have these."

He reached into his pocket and extracted a stapled sheaf of paper, which he handed to the Brookhaven biologist. It was a documented listing he and David had prepared earlier of everything from Doreen's sliced nightgown and bloodstained underwear, through Mary's electric cord and supposed suicide note, to Bob's truck bumper and empty Scotch bottle, along with the three mysterious blood drops and all of Hillstrom's autopsy findings.

Marine took his time with the pages, nodding occasionally and muttering things neither of his companions could overhear. Eventually, he placed the pack on his knee and addressed David Hawke.

"And you can do what with all this?"

"The standard entry analyses," Hawke replied. "Trace, DNA, and biological sampling for starters. We can also farm out things like the touch-DNA we hope may be adhering to the electrical wire used in the hanging. But I know our limitations, and I'm pretty sure that what we have so far is what we'll end up with in the long run. I was crossing my fingers that with your resources, you could save us a lot of time and money and give all or some of this the best shot possible, instead of our nibbling away at it until we have nothing left to test."

"This is a hugely important case to us, Eric," Joe picked up. "In the rest of the country, a stranger killing three apparently unrelated people is third-page news. In Vermont, if word got out, it would spread like a wildfire and the politicians would go nuts. Roughly speaking, we get ten to twelve homicides a year here, total. We really need to give this everything we can."

Marine pressed his lips together briefly before responding. "I will see what I can do. Speaking for myself, I can run those three unknown blood samples through several tests not available to David, and I won't have your constraints. Just to confirm, you are following a purely investigative route, is that correct?"

Both men nodded in unison.

"That's perfect. Some cutting-edge research into genetic predictors of externally visible characteristics may come in handy here. Traits like ethnic origin and hair and eye color are starting to surface with a higher and higher degree of predictability. This is a subject of interest I've been exploring and promoting for years."

"With all that in mind," David cautioned, "we will have to follow some basic rules of evidence. Someone from Joe's office will accompany or at least account for the whereabouts of whatever you take at all times, and my office will supply you with known control samples to be subjected to the same tests you administer to the actual ones. That way, down the line, nobody can claim that any results mysteriously appeared just because of your process."

"Understood," Marine agreed, adding, "Which brings up another route I'm hoping to follow. We have a synchrotron light source at BNL, capable of extraordinary things, and with the additional advantage that it doesn't alter or destroy samples. So, once we're done, and you find reason to either preserve the evidence or use it for more tests, it'll be available. The same's not true for the drops of blood, though. You do understand that?"

"Yes," Hawke told him, "but it doesn't matter. The three samples are large enough that you'll have plenty to test and have some left over. We can live with that."

"I hate to sound stupid here," Joe volunteered, "which was bound to happen sooner than later, but what is a synchrotron?"

Marine laughed. "Good question. Not stupid at all. Let me explain it this way: If you're about to read something small, and the failing daylight isn't quite enough, you turn on a lamp and put on your reading glasses. Not only does the page brighten up, but the words seem to jump out at you."

"Okay," Joe encouraged him.

"Well, the synchrotron is a pinpoint light source," Marine continued. "But of a brightness to rival the sun's, and we use it to produce X-rays, ultraviolet light, and infrared rays to study things at their atomic level in all sorts of different ways. It's the ultimate reading lamp for objects down to a billionth of a meter small. As a result, it can allow us to see all the various components that constitute a sample. That's where the reading light metaphor falls apart, naturally, since now we're talking about characteristics unique to a specific sample, which is more like a fingerprint, no?"

He looked at Joe happily, content that his explanation had been like the light itself. But David knew to add a bit more.

"Remember Beverly's idea that something might have come off the knife and been deposited along the edges of the cut in Doreen's nightgown?" he asked. "That's way beyond what I can do here at the lab, but the synchrotron would be like a flashlight in a dark cave, as Eric was saying. It could give us trace evidence at the atomic level, if there is any, which might help us identify what environment that knife had been exposed to earlier. Plus," he added, "if he runs the electrical cord through the light source before he runs any DNA tests, the fact that the synchrotron leaves everything intact means we virtually get a free sweat-print test thrown in."

Marine picked up on Hawke's educational tone. "Sweatprints are a perfect application of the light source, since they represent the minerals and other compounds that adhere microscopically to a person's skin, and are often left behind when something is touched. That's in addition to any DNA that might be there, too — what we were calling touch-DNA — even in the absence of an actual fingerprint."

"And you have access to this light source?" Joe asked.

Marine gave him a wink. "That's the beauty of how we do things down there. It's more like a college than a lab. That can mean jealousies and rivalries and cliques, of course. We've earned seven Nobels, after all; the stakes are high. But by the same token, there is the kind of collegiality, collaboration, and friendship that overrides all that, and allows for much work that often stays off the radar. Of course, it depends on the device — there's not much leeway using the ion collider, for example; people are on that to discover the source of the universe. Best not to mess with them. But the light source has some sixty-eight beams to work from, and more researchers using it than anything else on campus. People slip in quick projects all the time with a wink and a nod. Besides, one of our missions is improved national security. This kind of fits that bill, not to mention that forensic applications are begging to be better explored with the synchrotron — it's a journal article in the making, easy. I can make this work all sorts of ways. Don't give it a thought."

In the ensuing moment of silence, Joe and David glanced at each other.

"Sounds good to me," Joe said.

David nodded and addressed Eric. "You got a deal, assuming the SA approves. I'll wrap everything up, including my control samples, and sign them over to Joe or whoever he designates, and we'll see you in a few days. Is that timing okay?"

Marine was all smiles. "From what I understand, gentlemen, we have a murderer to catch. Of course it's okay."

"A synchoron?" Willy spat out. "Sounds perfect for something stupid."

"Synchrotron," Sam corrected him. "And you're just pissed because a machine might do something better than we can."

Willy tilted his seat back and put his feet up on his desk. "I still think it's a common link, like with McNaughton. Maybe we missed with Michele Starr, because she didn't know if Doreen and Chuck knew each other at the academy. But that doesn't mean they didn't."

"What're you thinking about?" Joe asked from his favorite spot on the windowsill.

"It's always sex or money," Willy answered him. "No matter how you slice it. And for all we know, it's both here, since McNaughton is no pauper and definitely no saint. I think Doreen knew something and I think that's why she died. Maybe she and Mary

Fish and young Chuck were all in the same place at the same time years ago by pure coincidence, but I'm not a big fan of coincidence — something happened back then."

"What about Bob Clarke?" Lester asked.

"I don't know," Willy conceded. "Could be he's there to throw us off. You know, the classic scam: Toss a bomb onto a bus because you're really pissed at a single passenger. The cops can never figure it out — was it a terrorist? Were any of the victims connected? Blah, blah, blah. Bob's a smoke screen."

The silence in the room stood in for the general skepticism.

"Lester," Joe asked, "you've been digging into Doreen's background. What do you think?"

"So far," Spinney answered cautiously, "I think we have a woman with a nightmare childhood who cut her losses, made some life choices, and focused on living in a comfortable, sex-free, financially rewarding rut. She reminds me of a shell-shocked soldier, happy to spend the rest of the war with her head down in a trench."

"Yeah," said Willy, "except how she ended up is exactly how she started — raped. That tells me her killer knew her better than you do."

"What else did the killer know?" Joe asked generally.

"How Bob Clarke's grandfather died," Sammie suggested.

"That's interesting," Joe said, thinking back. "Because it's not clear that he knew much about Mary Fish. Elise told me that no one in Mary's family had ever hanged themselves; it seemed like both of them came from pretty normal upbringings."

"Except that they were gay," Willy pointed out, "and Dory was asexual. What was Bob's orientation?"

Joe shook his head. "Good question. I don't know. That's part of what we need to find out."

He slipped off his perch and stood before them. "Look, it's just a matter of time before the story breaks on these three cases and we're swamped with reporters and politicians cashing in. I have no clue if this synchrotron or Eric Marine's high-end DNA work is going to produce anything usable, but Willy's right in a way. We can't abandon what we know how to do. Lester, are you pretty happy that you've dug deep enough into Doreen?"

Lester looked uncomfortable. "I don't

know where else to look, boss, but that doesn't mean I didn't miss something."

"Fair enough. Still, you're at a point where you can be interrupted. I want you with me when I escort Hawke's samples down to Long Island. I have no idea how Brookhaven is laid out or how we'll maintain custody of this stuff, so more's the merrier, at least to begin. Sam and Willy? Bob Clarke's the name of the game, first and foremost. He's the latest case; we need to bring him up to snuff. One advantage we have is that whoever is killing these folks likes to show off. We never finished that line of thought, by the way, the one about what the killer knows."

"He can get hold of blood," Willy volunteered.

"And it's blood with anticoagulant," Sam added.

"What else?"

"That implies a hospital or clinic or something involving medicine," said Lester, whose wife was a nurse. "Any fool can get hold of a syringe and suck somebody's vein, but only in a medical setting do you have vacuum tubes with anticoagulant. That's how they store it before the lab gets it."

"Maybe a blood bank?" Willy suggested.

"Maybe," Joe agreed. "Find the person

who knows all three victims, knows the histories of two out of three of them at least, and who works at or has access to a medical facility, which might also have a blood bank."

"And who lives in the southeast corner of the state," Sam added. "That's where the murders all happened."

"Okay," Joe agreed. "Fine. I know we're making presumptions, but we have to start somewhere. And by the way, while Lester and I are in the Land of the Geeks, for however long that takes, don't be shy about pulling in extra manpower from the other units. We are not alone, and we shouldn't act like it when there's so much at stake."

"Do we get to pick who we play with?" Willy pointedly asked.

Sammie groaned from her corner of the room.

Joe laughed. "You get to suggest. I get to pick."

"No fun, Dad," Willy complained.

Joe grimaced. "Don't even go there."

"Long Island?" Lyn said, her eyebrows arched. "That's where they have all the mansions."

"You're thinking of Rhode Island," Joe told her.

"The hell I am. The North Shore? The Gold Coast? Playground of the Vanderbilts? Orson Welles used one of those palaces in *Citizen Kane.*"

Joe leaned back to study her more closely. They were in bed, comfortably entangled, with the TV on mute on the dresser across the room.

"How do you know that?" he asked her.

She pressed the back of her hand theatrically across her forehead. "I am but a cipher. He clearly cares not. Perhaps I shall return to Tara."

He poked her in the armpit, making her quickly ball up in self-defense.

"I was a movie nut growing up," she admitted from under the sheet.

He ducked under the covers to see her face, now curtained with a hank of long hair. "I had no idea," he said. "You never said. We should rent some."

"Oh, yeah — I was just too busy setting up the business until now," she said. "So where is this place?"

"I looked it up. It's actually pretty neat. It was an army base in both world wars, converted to a lab in the forties. It's kind of a science camp on steroids — thousands of lab rats, billions of dollars worth of equipment. It's got its own zip code, it's so big —

in Upton, New York. People visit it from everywhere to study all sorts of things: how to make a better mammogram, what space dust is made of, what the AIDS virus looks like."

She swept the hair away from her eyes. "And you're going there why?"

"We're hoping they can run some tests our crime lab can't," he said simply.

"How long's that going to take?"

"Honestly? I don't know. The scientist helping us seemed to think pretty fast, but I'm bringing Lester with me just in case something goes wrong or I have to leave early."

She slid up closer to him and laid her hand on his bare chest. "You're talking days."

He kissed her. "No doubt. I wish I could bring you with me."

She smiled. "Is this where I tell you I'll do something unspeakable so you won't forget me?"

"Sure," he said hopefully.

She held the smile a few seconds and then killed it. "Well, forget about it."

He tried to read her expression. "Really?"

She slid her hand lower and laughed. "Naah."

CHAPTER THIRTEEN

Willy paused on the third-floor landing of the building's wooden fire escape, watching and listening for any movement besides his own. He was on South Main Street, in Brattleboro. It was both late and frigid enough for even the night's oddest denizens to be falling asleep. And he was about to break and enter.

He was poised outside Susan Allgood's dark and quiet apartment, paying little attention to the cold biting into his exposed skin. There were a few lights on behind a window here or there, a couple of other-worldly glows from television sets, but no shadows moving, and no sounds aside from the distant rumble of an unseen vehicle, or the occasional clang that punctuates every urban setting like a fitful heartbeat.

He knew where Sue was, or had been fifteen minutes earlier, when he'd monitored her inebriation at the local bar. She'd been alone then, and he doubted she would have picked anyone up in the meantime.

Plus, he knew that she valued her relationship with Chuck McNaughton enough not to mess it up with a one-night stand. And while she may have been a little buzzed right now, she wasn't drunk. Willy was confident of all this. He'd been watching her for several days, studying her as a zoologist might a collectible specimen.

He reached under his parka and extracted the switchblade he always kept clipped to his waistband. It had a long, thin, nasty-looking blade that he honed regularly on a strop at home. He rationalized carrying it — and a backup gun and another knife and a set of brass knuckles his boss knew nothing about — on the basis that a one-armed man had to compensate to stay even with the pack. But long before he'd lost the use of his arm to a bullet, back during his days with the Brattleboro PD, he'd carried the same hardware — along with the paranoia demanding it.

He worked the blade up under the window's sash and made contact with the lock. Typically, it wasn't even set, allowing him next to pry open the lower frame and open the window enough to where he could swing his leg inside.

He'd been here once before — legitimately — when he'd first met Sue to ask about Chuck McNaughton. That conversation had actually begun in the same bar and continued here, where he'd finally let himself out after she'd fallen asleep on the couch in a drunken stupor.

He might have sympathized, given his own alcoholic history, but compassion was not an overused tool in Willy's box of instincts, and he'd merely left feeling contemptuous of her, McNaughton, and even of Chuck's wife, who Sue was convinced knew all about them, but ignored it for the comforts of his healthy income.

Breathing in the warmth of the dingy apartment, Willy quietly closed the window, opened his coat, and settled into an armchair facing the front door.

No one knew he was here, including Sam. The two of them were supposed to be digging into young Bobby Clarke, figuring out how he tied into the other two bodies in this nonsensical mess, all while Saint Joe went bugging a bunch of nerds with a few blobs of blood. Ridiculous. McNaughton was the bad boy who'd employed Doreen, attended the school where Mary worked, was cheating on his wife, and was supposedly embezzling from his own company.

Typical Gunther to get all mental and complicated about a straightforward murder.

But rocket surgery this wasn't. Or whatever. McNaughton was dirty, and Willy was going to prove it.

It didn't take long. The scratch of a key at the lock and a fumbled-with doorknob alerted him to her arrival; the quiet implied that she hadn't gotten lucky at collecting a last-minute companion.

She entered slowly, dragging her feet, and closed the door behind her without turning on the light. From the glow through the window behind him, Willy saw her cross to the kitchenette counter, dump her purse and gloves, and slip her coat off her shoulders, letting it collapse in a pile on the floor. She then perched on one of the stools by the counter and struggled to remove her high, patent-leather boots, sighing deeply as she did so.

"Don't keep going," he cautioned her as she dropped the last boot and seemed about ready to lift her tight-fitting sweater up over her head.

She screamed, straightened with a jerk, and tilted backward off the stool, barely catching herself on the counter's edge.

"Who the fuck's there?" she demanded,

199

fear thick in her throat.

Willy turned on the dim lamp by his side, revealing himself.

She shielded her eyes.

"Hi," he said. "Remember me?"

The scowl answered first. "You fucking asshole. You almost gave me a heart attack. You can't be in here. That's not legal."

He smiled. "And yet, here I am."

She shook her head. "No, seriously. This isn't right. It's a crime. I could call the cops. The real ones."

"Cool," he said. "We could compare my crime to yours; see who they find more interesting."

Her response was telling. "What do you know about me?"

But he made a disapproving face. "That's not how this works, Sue." He pointed to a phone mounted on the wall near her. "There it is, if you want to call."

She straightened and smoothed the front of her sweater, hoping to regain some composure. "Why're you here, anyway? I told you what I know last time."

"You told me about Oklahoma. That's not why I came back."

She reached out for her purse, extracted a pack of cigarettes and a lighter, and lit up, pausing to inhale deeply. "So?"

"So, I like you," he lied. "I like your spirit. You're a survivor, like me. Not too proud, but not a sucker, either. You know how to take care of number one."

She grimaced and waved a hand around the dingy apartment. "Yeah, a real success story. I have a nose for a bullshitter, too."

"That explain your attraction to Chuck?"

"Fuck you."

"I'm not your type," he countered pleasantly. "I am here to help you out, though."

"I don't need help from you."

His eyes widened. "Oh, I doubt the state's attorney would agree."

Her expression darkened, the cigarette all but forgotten. "What the hell's that mean?"

"You brought it up," he told her innocently. "When you told me about Chuck dipping into the company well. You know about guilt by association, right?"

She looked as if she'd been hit by an electrical bolt. "*That is bullshit.* I don't have anything to do with that. *That's* what you meant by me being guilty of something? That's *his* fucking deal."

"It's not what I meant," Willy said blandly, in fact not knowing precisely what she was talking about. "But you have direct knowledge of an ongoing criminal act, plus, you benefit from it."

"What?"

"Accessory to grand theft," he intoned on the fly. "They could throw the book at you, 'specially since the best you'll be able to swing'll be a public defender."

She shook her head vehemently. "No fucking way. I don't get enough out of this deal for that."

"What can you give me, then?" he asked. "Like I said, you're low-hanging fruit right now — a lot easier to grab than he is. Only you can change that."

She stabbed her unfinished cigarette out directly on the counter. "This is not fair."

"It is what it is," he said, introducing a new angle for her to consider. "You gonna go back on the Oklahoma alibi?"

"I would in a heartbeat," she promised. "But there were others there, too. It was a goddamn convention, for Christ's sake. There were hundreds of people."

"What about him and the business, then? What you told me before?"

"What about it?"

His voice hardened slightly. "Don't get cute, or *I'll* use the damn phone and this conversation'll stop. You do not want that to happen, trust me."

"Shit," she muttered, and fumbled around for a second cigarette.

After lighting up and exhaling, she asked, "All right. What do you want to know?"

"What's he doing crooked?"

"Well," she sneered, "he's cheating on his wife, for one."

He dismissed that impatiently. "Old news, kiddo. You implied he was dipping into the till."

She scowled at him again, clearly feeling boxed in. "I don't know the details," she said quietly.

He slid forward in his chair, as if preparing to leave. "So you jerked me around," he said flatly. "That's cool. I gotta tell you, though, we already know he's dirty, and we know you benefit, so we're back where we started: It'll take us longer, but we'll toss him in the can, and we'll toss you in, too, for obstructing justice and being a pain in the ass."

"You can't do that," she shouted at him.

He stood up. "Watch me."

She stubbed out the second cigarette, slid off her stool, and blocked his exit. "Wait. Sit down. He's got a scam going."

Willy stayed standing. "What kind?"

"He steals stuff. He runs a trucking company, duh. Things get lost, insurance kicks in, and he sells what ends up in his garage."

"That sounds pretty piddly."

She rolled her eyes. "I didn't mean his real garage, stupid. We're not talking a flat screen now and then. He's got a system."

"And you know this because you cook his books?"

She looked disgusted. "I know this because I'm his fast fuck. He talks on the phone — doesn't even know I'm in the room. I'm like invisible."

Willy smiled. Not anymore, he thought. "You know who he talks to on that phone?"

She hesitated, studying his expression, and finally smiled back, at last back on familiar ground. "Yeah," she said. "I do."

CHAPTER FOURTEEN

The trip to Long Island, and along much of its length, was a numbing succession of highways and interstates — traffic-clotted, featureless, and flat, punctuated for the most part by either commercial structures dedicated to servicing travelers, or blighted residential buildings made grimy by the spewing of so many nearby vehicles.

By the time Joe and Lester reached the Brookhaven lab signs and entered its long, curving, tree-lined access road, their eyes took time adjusting to what seemed like an estate or a huge park, until the guardhouse came into view.

There again, as with everything associated with Brookhaven so far, it seemed more like a formality. The guards were armed and watchful, but the glance at credentials was cursory, the names of the two Vermonters on the guest list being the real lock opener.

Thereafter, however, the world around

them took an unexpected historical slant.

Lester acknowledged it first. "Damn, this is like a used parts warehouse for old movies — for whole buildings."

Joe understood what he meant. Most of the surrounding architecture reflected the history he'd mentioned to Lyn — BNL, barring face lifts and a few modern additions, was an old army camp. And looked it.

"I like it," he said.

Spinney stared at him. "You fond of the Los Alamos look?"

Joe laughed. "It ain't pretty, but it's practical and useful. Why throw out perfectly good buildings just because they don't have 'designer architect' stamped all over them? Drives me nuts to pass by colleges with huge tuitions and see that most of the money's been wasted on ugly, billion-dollar buildings. It offends my Yankee spirit."

Lester watched the buildings slip by. "Well, you should be in hog heaven."

Eric Marine had directed them by e-mail to one of a row of what might have been military admin buildings decades earlier — low, long, and plain. The word "biological" appeared somewhere on the small plaque marking the entrance.

"You want me to stay with the loot or come with you?" Lester asked as Joe swung

206

out by the curb.

Joe held up the keys. "We'll button her up. I'm not worried at this point. We better both meet the cast of characters."

They'd come down in a rented SUV in order to hold all the bundles Hawke had given them, some of them bulky, others secured in protective packaging.

The building's interior was a perfect match to its shell, built to withstand being washed down with a fire hose, although not looking as if it had been thoroughly cleaned in decades. But it was clutter only, as Joe saw it, which again appealed to his vision of an environment filled with people more interested in learning than in sitting on Color-Me-Beautiful office furniture.

Joe knocked on the properly numbered door, heard a grunt, and twisted the knob, revealing two men, heads together and bent over like gardeners admiring a plant, peering at a computer screen.

The grunt had not been in response to Joe's knock, which clearly had gone unheard.

"Dr. Marine?" Joe asked quietly.

The white-haired biologist looked up, his eyes wide.

He blinked a couple of times, transparently shifting gears, and then issued a wide smile. "Ah, my police officers. How wonderful. Wayne. These are the people I told you about."

The other man turned away from the screen and took them in. Bald with a close-cropped fringe, he was trim and athletic, with a sportsman's aggressive zeal in his eyes. He crossed the small room and extended his hand. "Wayne Shepard. Glad to meet you."

Joe responded with his own formalities, introducing himself and Lester, while Eric filled in with, "Wayne's the one I thought might help us the most with your various problems. He's my contact at the light source — the one I go to when I need access — and he's said he'd be happy to help with this, too."

"I really appreciate it," Joe told him.

"Not a problem," Shepard responded in a clipped voice. "Happy to help out law enforcement whenever I can. The more the light source can be used for people like you, the better the rest of the world will understand its benefits. Funding comes with popularity; simple as that. Look what happened with the early CT scanners — every hospital I know lined up for one, even if they were only three blocks apart and could have shared with no problem. Dumbest thing I ever saw, especially since, in no time flat, advances in technology antiquated most of the first generation machines. You want to see the device?"

"The light source?" Joe asked. "Yes, I'd be delighted."

They all four piled into the rented SUV, Wayne Shepard acting as tour guide from the front passenger seat. No remnants of snow here. Only brown grass extended between the buildings, adding to the drabness of the passing scenery of chain-link fences, metal buildings, a dominating and ominously cheerful, candy-striped smokestack, and an even more suggestive dometopped building that hinted of long-discontinued nuclear experimentation.

But to Joe, the impression of pragmatic functionality held true. Drabness didn't go to depressing, and several of the newer buildings were even quite upbeat, with expanses of window glass and soothing, if modest, architecture. As Shepard described building after building, and how several had once been used for one reason, and then either remodeled or discarded later on, there grew in Joe a sense that this vast, hyperactive place was a shrine for the pursuit of knowledge on a passionate level. It was as if the clichéd image of the absent-minded professor with chalk-dusted trousers, a four-day beard, and a disregard for self-image had been superimposed over an entire region. Appearances counted for little in contrast with results — it was in many ways a place where minds were mastering matter.

Shepard ordered them to stop in front of a white, sleek, two-story building whose modernity struck a discordant note with all around it. With its tinted windows and bland, rounded appearance, it reminded Joe of Gort, the robot in the 1950s sci-fi movie *The Day the Earth Stood Still.* Gort had also been capable of throwing a mean beam of light.

"This is it," Shepard announced, climbing out of the vehicle. "The National Synchrotron Light Source, or NSLS, came online in the early eighties; already old hat."

"All anyone can talk about here," added Marine, joining them on the sidewalk, "is how the next generation, the so-called NSLS-II, will produce X-rays ten thousand times brighter than this one's." He pointed to a huge field across the way. "It'll go in there, where the old railway tracks used to deliver recruits during World War I."

"That was less than a hundred years ago," Shepard commented, heading toward the building's entrance. "When a simple flash-light was considered fancy technology, and didn't work half the time."

Eric patted Joe on the shoulder as they entered the lobby. "Not to worry. This one works."

Joe caught Spinney's eye, wondering if he, too, was beginning to feel trapped on the edge of a parallel universe, where everything looked familiar, but where less and less made sense.

And that was moments before their hosts led them to an observation window over-looking the equivalent of a vast factory floor — cluttered, harshly lighted, and to any lay person's eye utterly chaotic.

Now even the familiar slipped from Joe's frame of reference. Below them, under a cavernous ceiling lined with air conduits, sound-absorbent batting, and multi-ton, load-bearing I-beams, was what appeared to be a gigantic jumble of machines, work-stations, electrical cabling, and shiny steel tubing, much of the latter wrapped in crinkled aluminum foil to look like some strung-up alien fridge food.

It was a tightly packed mechanical maze, eight feet in height, but it appeared free of any recognizable form or function, and inac-cessible to even the smallest human being.

"That's the NSLS," Wayne Shepard said with pride. "Over two thousand researchers use it every year, coming from all over the world. It runs like this twenty-four hours a day."

Joe kept his eyes glued to the acreage before him, watching for even the slightest movement among all the gleaming steel. Finally, like a ladybug scurrying through grass, a single person in a red shirt moved hurriedly in the distance, half obscured by the crisscross of cables, wires, and piping.

Lester seemed to be reading his mind. "There's one," he murmured, in a tone half suggesting he might now pull out a bird book and record a sighting.

"Would you like a quick tour?" Marine suggested.

They all four descended a staircase to a massive electronically controlled door, which Shepard unlocked with a wave from his pass card. As he pulled on the handle, a fog of mechanical noise swept over them, explaining the quilted batting Joe had seen hanging from the ceiling. It was not the kind of noise requiring ear protection, but it was vibrational and ubiquitous — a dull steady thrumming that spoke of extraordinary energy being continually expended. Joe didn't want to know what kind of electricity bills were called for to rival the sun's brightness.

He felt a hand on his elbow and turned to see Eric Marine proffering a folded slip of paper.

"I thought this might help explain things a bit. It's a haiku I wrote to explain all this."

Joe studied him for a moment, suddenly seeing an aspect of the man he hadn't glimpsed before.

He took the paper and opened it up. "A haiku?"

The scientist smiled up at him guilelessly. "Read it. It may not be as goofy as you think."

Joe did as he was told, and read:

Synchrotron Radiation
A sun factory
One eight six K electrons
delta momenta

"Ah," he commented politely.

Marine was openly laughing by now. "Translation?" he asked.

"Please."

"In a nutshell," Marine explained, "synchrotron radiation is, I think, actually brighter than the sun's. I used the word 'factory' because light is manufactured at a synchrotron. One eight six K is the speed of light in a vacuum, one hundred eighty-six thousand miles per second, which is about the speed here. Delta is the math symbol that signifies 'change in' and momenta is the Latin plural of momentum. Meaning, all told, that synchrotron radiation is only produced where there is a change in momentum of the electrons. In this case, movement in a straight line will not produce synchrotron radiation, but movement in a circle will."

Wayne was becoming impatient with his more artistic partner's antics. "Magnets speed up the electrons around and around in a tube," he said loudly and quickly, "until they get fast enough to throw synchrotron radiation down a number of straight tangents to hit whatever targets we've put there to be analyzed. People have compared all this to a car speeding around a circular track. The headlamps give off light, and the tubes tangential to the track carry that light to the targets. That's it. Let's take a look."

And with that, he turned his back and began the tour.

That took place in a moving huddle, so that they could all hear what Shepard and Marine had to say. It was a more detailed version of what Joe had heard in the hotel lobby in Burlington, and therefore even less comprehensible. But he did end up with the basic understanding — correct or not — of several dozen workstations using X-rays, ultraviolet, or infrared light to peer into the tiniest inner workings of things physical, chemical, and/or organic, from land, sea, and outer space. Marine's earlier metaphor of the ultimate reading light being applied to the world's smallest newsprint seemed remarkably apt, at least to Joe's mind.

They did meet other people, of course, if not many, including some working within the entrails of all the tubing, wiring, and supporting architecture. It made for a tight fit, to be sure, but not quite as impenetrable as Joe had thought from above. And there were scattered mementoes of a quaintly human flavor sprinkled about — laptop-equipped desks decorated with family photos, calendar art, personal trinkets, and political cartoons. They evoked a slightly warped, sci-fi equivalent of prehistoric cave drawings — faint scratchings of Homo sapiens in a technological universe.

The most curious thing for Joe, however, was the paradoxical nature of the whole thing — a vast building dedicated to producing a beam of light, which, in the end, remained nowhere to be seen. Indeed, this famous light was so concentrated, and so rigorously controlled, that in the long run, it wasn't like a flashlight in the dark at all, but rather a space-age contraption so high tech and valuable that nary a drop of its prized product was allowed to leak into the surrounding space. It may have been a form of man-made sunshine, but it wasn't to be wasted.

Back outside in the quiet of the lobby, Lester gave voice to one of Joe's growing concerns, "I guess I can see how you can take a grain of space dust and figure out what it's made of," he said. "But how're you going to study our stuff? We brought a sawed-off part of a truck bumper."

Wayne laughed at his wonderment. "Not to worry. We get strange materials all the time. We just adapt the stations accordingly. We've analyzed plastics to be used in artificial knees, human bones to study arthritis. We even once took a close-up look at the sludge from New York harbor to see what pollutants were in it."

"We can take a piece of metal or wood," Eric added, "that's been hit by a bullet, and find out not only that it *was* a bullet, but potentially what kind and from what box on its owner's shelf, assuming we have access to that."

"If you study an object closely enough," Shepard added, "you can usually discover its unique qualities — just like matching a print to a finger."

"The difference," Marine picked up, "is that a fingerprint is hardwired biology. What we're talking about is the ability to finger-print a sample's environment." He pointed at Spinney's head. "Today, you woke up, presumably washed your hair, and set out to come here. All during that trip, your hair was exposed to a series of changing environments, each of which probably deposited samplars, however tiny. All of those, as well as the nature of the hair shaft itself, could conceivably be identified and charted from infrared spectroscopy."

Joe had already grasped as much. What was nagging him now was more practical.

"How fast can it be done?" he asked.

"Depends," Shepard admitted. "And of course, we're dividing to conquer here, with both Eric and me working simultaneously. Still, none of this should take more than a couple of days to process, even if we have to crunch the data for a bit longer afterward. But by then, you'll be back home catching crooks, right?"

Everyone laughed politely, but certainly the two cops had no idea what they'd be doing in the interim, especially given their baffling surroundings.

They returned to Eric's office, made a couple of phone calls to gain access to the lab's high security vault, and then laboriously transferred the samples from the Vermont truck to there, documenting the move carefully. Joe made clear that nothing was to be removed from the vault without either him or Lester being notified, so that samples could be escorted to whatever testing environment was called for. The two scientists smiled condescendingly a couple of times during this lecture, but Joe could tell that they were mostly posturing. It was clear they understood the need to maintain a chain of evidence, to the point where Joe was left wondering if his reason for being here had less to do with security, and more with curiosity, impatience, and anticipation.

By the time this was wrapped up, and the two cops brought to the dorm room they would share for the next few days, night had arrived and the entire campus had begun glowing from within, with hundreds of windows, skylights, and streetlamps replacing the daylight, giving the lab an appropriately industrial appearance.

"Some place, huh?" Lester commented as they later made their way toward an on-campus restaurant/bar that Eric had recommended before heading off for his own home and family. "It's like the place everyone in high school said I should go to."

"You were a science guy?" Joe asked him, enjoying how warm the air was in comparison to Vermont, if not the relative dullness of the naturally flat surroundings.

"Not really. It was my physique. I always looked like a stork. People just assumed I was smart. Probably helped me be better in school than I might've been."

Joe trudged on for a few seconds before reacting. "Let's hope the same thing works for our evidence — that it winds up better than we think it is."

CHAPTER FIFTEEN

The moon was full, bright, and opalescent, its milky shimmer coating the snow-covered countryside like a glowing layer of cream. It reflected off the earth's white surface enough to light up the somber sides of the otherwise dark wooden buildings scattered alongside the narrow stream creasing the bottom of the gully. Overhead, there wasn't a cloud in the sky.

The entire scene was eerily still and as beautiful as a Romantic painting, its canvas stretched out as far as one could see.

"Shit," Willy growled to himself, swinging out of the car.

He was alone, of course, having not told anyone of his plan, including Sam. Not that she wasn't capable of a little guerrilla action herself. But that was the problem; Willy could never tell which way she might choose — independent or company line. And lately, especially with his obsession to nail Chuck

McNaughton, he suspected she'd blow the whistle on him.

That, Willy could live without. He knew he was right. No matter if Chuck hadn't killed Doreen Ferenc or Mary Fish with his own hands, the man was definitely dirty. And wasn't it VBI's mission to catch bad guys, even while distracted by an unadvertised triple homicide?

Of course it was.

Willy supervised the scene from where he'd parked in a pull-off beyond the compound's dirt driveway. It was an abandoned lumber mill, not far from Guilford, maybe five miles south of Brattleboro. Dating back over a hundred years, it was a hodgepodge of metal-roofed wooden shacks, several quite large, scattered across the acreage like carelessly tossed dice. There were a few of these operations around the county, in various states of disrepair, some even functioning in their original role, timber harvesting and lumbering being viable if threadbare occupations in a rural state like Vermont.

But this mill had fallen silent long ago, and looked it. It had sat here ever since, below the road, barely visible behind a screen of scraggly evergreens, seemingly lost to time. Even the local vandals had lost interest in making it look worse than it already did.

Which made it perfect for its current use.

Willy worked his way across country, downhill, through the trees, now grateful for the moonlight that kept him free from the underbrush.

Not that there was a huge risk of getting tangled up. Willy had been trained as a sniper by the military, albeit many years ago. His area of expertise — indeed his literal killing ground — had been the jungle. His instincts remained strong, despite his lack of practice and his ironic disability, and even with the moon's help, he still moved with the unnerving silence of a shadow slipping along a wall.

He had come here tailing a clueless Robert Prozzo — Bobby, as Sue Allgood had called him, and the man she'd identified as McNaughton's partner in crime.

Bob Prozzo was no stranger to Kunkle, as was often the case with the area's bottom-tier dwellers. Willy had even used him a couple of times as an informant, although with marginal results. Bobby was a thief, a burglar, a drunk, and more — a man self-abandoned to need and instinct. He had no inner level balancing right from wrong; he merely acted on immediate desire. It might just as well have been a physical disorder at this stage in his life, and Willy treated it as such.

But without empathy. Willy had found himself faced with significant moral choices in the past, and had selected poorly. It had been a costly and painful journey, and could have resulted in a compassionate rebirth. But it had not. As a result, Willy wasn't going to cut anyone any slack who even remotely reminded him of himself. His was the zeal of the reformed, demanding a brutal, unsparing honesty.

Sue had told him that, as far as she was privy, McNaughton was using Prozzo as his front man to rip off the company. Not to an obvious extent — he didn't want his insurance claims for lost shipments to attract attention — but even the occasional light load, paid for once in a settlement and again on the black market, could buy a lot of toys.

Plus, Willy imagined, it didn't hurt that every time he did it, Chuck was poking his father's ghost in the eye. Therein probably lay the true appeal.

Willy reached the relative shadow of the nearest building and paused to listen carefully.

He had first picked up Prozzo as the latter was leaving his house, and had tailed him on a roundabout journey that had ended at the trucking company. This in itself had hardly been startling; Willy's background check on the man had found him to be employed by McNaughton, giving him legal access to the property.

But things had blurred thereafter. Willy had followed his quarry inside, and watched him cull half a truckload of high-end products from off the loading floor and an assortment of other places. It soon became clear that the strategy was to skim generally and generously, no doubt supported by an inventory control system purposefully in need of overhaul.

A couple of hours later, in what had originally been an empty ten-wheeler, Prozzo at last headed back out onto the road, aiming south.

And this is where he'd ended up. With Willy hanging far behind, his headlights out, Bob Prozzo took the abandoned-looking lumbermill's driveway, and electronically opened not just the entrance gate, but the largest building's double doors, impressing even Willy. To have an entire property off the radar in which to store stolen goods was classy enough. To have it surreptitiously wired with garage openers and God knew what security — to guarantee that a large truck could be on the open road one moment, and gone the next — that was raising the bar.

It also made Willy wonder about covert surveillance.

He looked up, studying the eaves and the outer corners with the small monocular he always carried in his pocket. Sure enough, he eventually located a small camera, discreetly tucked under the roof's overhang.

"Gotcha," he told himself, and began considering how to approach the old barn's entrance.

He didn't have to worry. The sweep of a pair of headlights touched the treetops at the periphery before taking a plunge as the vehicle headed down the driveway, also opening the gate remotely.

Willy seized his opportunity. Knowing that as the building doors opened, all eyes would be focused there and not on any television monitors, he waited until the mechanical rumbling began before simply stepping out into the open and running for where the new arrival was headed — the ramp to the same large shed Prozzo had used.

He arrived at the corner just as a black SUV thudded across the rough threshold of the building, disappearing into its embrace. Prozzo, and whoever else might be with him, had killed the lights to prevent attracting attention.

They'd also granted Willy a final advantage, allowing him to tuck in behind the car, bent double and moving fast, so that he was inside and hidden behind a small stack of boxes as the double doors swung back shut and the overhead lights reignited.

Willy watched as, in the abrupt glare, Chuck McNaughton emerged from the vehicle and stretched lazily.

"You get it all?" he asked.

Willy shifted his view to see Bob Prozzo approach the back of his own truck and throw open its rear door with a loud clatter.

"Lock, stock, and plasma TV," Prozzo bragged. "You got the buyers lined up?"

McNaughton waved that away dismissively. "You handle your end, Bobby; I'll handle mine. Just like always."

It was a custom-made cowboy moment, designed for Willy to step out, deliver a punch line, and make the arrest. But for once, he'd prepared beforehand. So, he merely took out his cell phone, took several pictures of the scene, and settled back to wait for an opportunity to leave as quietly as he'd arrived. This time — given how much crap he'd catch anyhow — he was going to play it by the numbers, more or less.

The frustration of not being able to pin even one of three murders on his top-of-the-line suspect would at least be mollified by escorting him to jail for embezzlement and grand theft, assuming his legal strategy worked out.

Besides, Willy further comforted himself, none of this meant McNaughton hadn't killed anyone; it just meant it wasn't the only crime he'd committed.

Willy was nothing if not a dog with a bone.

Straight from a full day back at the office, Joe entered Lyn's apartment on Oak Street, shouted out a greeting, got a mumbled reply from the bathroom, and headed for the armchair facing the woodstove in the living room.

The apartment was on the top floor of a Victorian showcase, all excess and carved hardwood and historically accurate, over-the-top paint colors, and Lyn had honored the effort by decorating her digs appropriately. It was warm, Old World, and very comfortable. Her bar's success had transformed a financial risk into a sound move, and he came here now as much for the refuge she'd created as to see her in its embrace — it had become a double balm for when things were running rough.

As they were now.

"Boy, you look done in."

He glanced at her standing in the doorway, dressed in a pair of flannel pajamas she knew he loved to remove.

He smiled tiredly in appreciation. "Not dead yet."

She laughed, taking his meaning. "That'll keep. First things first. How 'bout something hot to drink?"

"Deal."

She faded back to the kitchen, still talking as she fixed him a cup of cocoa. "Bad day at the office?"

"I read somewhere," he told her, "that George Bernard Shaw once said that being attacked by critics was like being nibbled to death by ducks. I know what he meant, assuming he ever said it."

"I read the paper this morning," she conceded.

He stared at the glass-doored stove before him. He could see a pair of logs burning with mesmerizing intensity. Stanley Katz at the *Brattleboro Reformer* had finally discovered his bloodthirsty roots and issued an editorial demanding an explanation for the "cloak of secrecy" that the VBI had dropped over its recent investigation, which clearly invoked "the darkly disturbing images of secret police organizations so reviled in third world autocracies."

"I know he has to sell papers," Joe conceded. "I just wish he didn't have to be such a jackass about it. I can't wait for when he's told we actually have three murders."

"You two go back, don't you?" she asked, still making industrious sounds from the kitchen.

"No, you're right. Nothing new there."

"So, what else?"

He rubbed his eyes. What else, indeed? "I still haven't heard from Lester on Long Island. The lab guys there are taking their time, which I hope'll mean good news. Willy couldn't stand just doing his job, of course, so he rounded up one of our primary suspects on a grand theft charge, which now means the guy's lawyered up and unapproachable for anything else. I got a call from someone in New York or someplace, claiming to be from Fox News, wanting to know if I'm the cop who used to sleep with the woman now running for governor."

Lyn rounded the corner carrying a tray with mugs, cookies, and the artificial sweeteners and fake creamers that Joe so loved.

"Are you kidding me?" she asked.

"The race is down to the wire. Not much time left, and it's no sure thing for either

229

side. People are looking for ammo." He thought back to the last conversation he'd had with Gail, about her own camp's efforts in that area.

Lyn set the tray on the low table between his chair and her own. He sat forward to doctor his drink the way he liked.

"How do you feel about all that?"

He looked up, struck by her muted tone. "What?"

"Gail. Her race. If she wins, she'll end up being your boss, won't she?"

He smiled at the repetition of that theme. "No more than any other governor. Bill's my real boss, then the public safety commissioner. You could even argue the entire legislature comes next, since they could kill VBI with a single vote."

That clearly hadn't addressed her concern. She was still studying the contents of her cup, not making eye contact. "A lot has come out in the press."

He took a stab at filling in the blank. "About the rape? It's a big deal in some people's minds."

Now she looked up. "Not yours?"

He tilted his head, considering his answer, not sure where this was going. "It changed her life, Lyn. I'm sure it changed us both."

"And broke you up?"

"As a couple?" He hesitated. "Probably. The rape made her more anxious. What I did for a living finally got to her. People rationalize memories, especially as time goes by. Maybe she'd tell you something else was to blame, but that's what I remember."

He stopped playing with his cocoa and reached out to touch her forearm. "Why the questions?"

She broke eye contact, now staring into the fire, as he'd been doing earlier. She sighed. "Just feeling insecure, I guess. Things are going well between us. It makes me nervous."

He could understand that. Life had not been easy for her, despite her present success. One bright light was her daughter, a journalist in Boston, but even she was a product of a divorced couple, and no one knew what had happened to Lyn's ex.

With a track record like that, happiness had to be considered warily.

"Gail and I have moved on, Lyn," he told her. "It's a rare friendship now, but it'll never go back to what it was. Even back then none of our friends could figure out how we lasted as long as we did."

"But you did."

Forgetting the cocoa, Joe slid off his chair and crouched by her side, holding her hands. "So will we."

She leaned forward and placed her face against his neck. He could feel the dampness of her tears.

"God, I hope so," she muttered into his collar.

CHAPTER SIXTEEN

"Come on in," Eric Marine gestured to Joe and Les, ushering them into a conference room down the hall from Eric's office. "We've set up a miniature classroom in here."

Joe allowed Lester to enter first, noticing how tired he seemed. The younger man had conceded upon Joe's return to the BNL campus that babysitting a pile of evidence had not only been more boring than he'd imagined, but had involved incredibly weird hours. Apparently, both Marine and Shepard had fit in this project whenever the opportunities arose, including a couple of times in the middle of the night. Joe was both pleased and impressed by their enthusiasm.

The room was essentially two offices stuck together, but it had several chairs around a table and a pull-down screen against one wall. A projector hooked to a laptop sat in the middle of the table.

"Have a seat, gentlemen," Wayne Shepard greeted them, looking up from the computer screen. "I think you'll be happy with what we've dug up."

Joe smiled his appreciation. "We're up for some good news. Les also told me how you burned the midnight oil on this. We really appreciate that."

Shepard shrugged. "No big deal. We do that a lot. Sometimes, access to a light beam is catch-as-catch-can."

"Besides," Marine said with a laugh, settling into one of the seats, "it's fun to surprise the younger guys once in a while. They think we're such hopeless old coots."

Shepard crossed to the windows and dropped the blinds before sitting down at the keyboard.

"Okay," he began. "Knowing that neither one of you speaks our form of scientific triple Chinese, Eric and I discussed how to explain all this without sounding condescending."

"Thanks for that," Lester said softly.

Shepard punched a key on the computer to introduce the first slide. "So, here we go. We started with a good assortment of test items. As listed here, you gave us three blood deposits and either swabs from or pieces of a pair of women's underwear, a nightgown, a suicide note, an electric cord, an empty bottle of Scotch, a pair of men's pants, and a section of truck bumper. All from three different crime scenes."

The others in the room remained quiet, watching the screen.

Shepard continued. "The first thing Eric and I decided to do was to break our findings into two separate reports, one for you, which is what you're about to see, and another for David Hawke, which will be couched in terms he will appreciate with his background and knowledge."

Joe smiled. "Very delicately put. Thank you."

Eric laughed. "Well, it wasn't just for you. We know you have others in your chain-of-command who will want to know what happened here."

Joe could instantly think of several. "True enough."

"Finally," Eric added, "you should know that we've been in touch with David throughout our research. In some cases, while he's obviously capable of extracting DNA and is much better at handling evidence than we are, we have a lot more data available to us. Without getting complicated, that just means that we've been exchanging e-mails about DNA patterns and whatnot that have been very helpful to both parties."

Shepard somewhat impatiently moved to another slide. "First, the bad news: There were a couple of things that simply gave us nothing of note." He punched through two slides as he spoke. "The young man's clothing — Bobby Clarke's. There was mention in the paperwork that perhaps the killer had placed the body behind the wheel of the truck, thereby depositing some trace evidence on Bobby's pants and coat. I had no luck at all there, I think because whoever attacked him wore gloves. It's getting cold up north, no?"

Joe nodded mournfully, remembering David making the same observation days earlier. "Yes — especially at night."

Shepard appeared unfazed. "The second dead end, so to speak, was Mary Fish's purported suicide note. You already know that it matched neither her personal printer nor the one in her office; all we could tell was that it came from someone else's."

"That having been said," Eric amended, "we did capture its fingerprint, scientifically speaking. If you ever do come across the printer you think produced this document, we should be able to match the two."

Shepard's face lit up at the suggestion.

"Yes, of course," he said. "And that's true for much of what we're laying out for you. A good deal of this amounts to snapshots taken of members of a crowd — it will be up to you to connect the picture to the right human being."

"Understood." Joe nodded.

"What about the Scotch bottle found on the floor of Bobby's truck?" Lester asked. "Isn't that a dud? Our guys at the crime lab said it had been wiped clean."

Eric beamed. "Yes, but with what?"

Shepard interrupted. "That'll come later." He pointed at the laptop. "I don't want to get out of order."

Eric Marine couldn't stop himself. "He used a dirty rag," he whispered loudly and in a rush, at the same time waving on his colleague and urging, "Okay, okay. Carry on."

Shepard moved to the next image. "Let's keep with the victims and address the drops of blood later. Chronologically, that means Doreen Ferenc to begin with." The slide showed the fragment of Doreen's nightgown surrounding the knife gash.

"Having just said what I did about staying in order, I'm going to make an exception with her underwear and address it later in a different context. As for the nightgown, though, I think Eric told you of the likelihood of particles on the knife blade ending up on the edges of the fabric's entrance hole."

Another image showed a huge magnification, although of what, Joe had no idea.

"And indeed," Shepard continued, "that was the case. I found gunpowder, engine oil, wood dust — primarily oak — and traces of HC_2H, in a formulation suggesting oxyacetylene use, since acetylene as a gas would disappear all on its own."

"Gunpowder?" Lester echoed, just as Joe muttered, "Acetylene?"

"Let me," Eric dove in, although his colleague had made no effort to speak first. "This part is really for your ears only, since, as scientists, we should restrict ourselves to fact. But I love Vermont, and visit it every chance I get, and I think I've gotten a small feel for the place in the process."

He rested his elbows on the table, emphasizing his keenness. "What Wayne just mentioned strikes me as perfectly reasonable. Joe, do you carry a knife?"

"Sure."

Eric shifted his attention momentarily. "Lester?"

Les pulled out a pocketknife and displayed it.

"My point precisely," Eric resumed. "And both of you presumably use your knives for all sorts of purposes — cleaning your fingernails, opening mail, gutting fish, for all I know. Right?"

Both men nodded, getting the idea.

"Well — and this is pure theory, as I said — here I think you have the knife of a man who maybe loads his own ammunition, is familiar with or works on cars and wood processing equipment, and is within proximity to or handles an acetylene torch, all of which could easily involve the use of a knife blade in time of need. A real Vermonter, in other words."

Lester was scratching his head. "That's good to hear."

"When you load ammunition," Eric persisted, "you sometimes separate individual flakes of gunpowder to achieve an exact measurement, no?"

Les's expression cleared. "So you use a knife blade. I got it."

Joe had removed a pad from his breast pocket and was jotting notes to himself.

"There's a little more," Shepard told them. "Again, it's mostly supposition, and unlike Eric, I don't know Vermont at all. But acetylene is actually more rarely used than people think. Oxyacetylene welding was very popular back when, but arc-based welding has almost totally replaced it."

"Still used for metal cutting, though," Joe finished for him.

Shepard smiled. "Correct. I was thinking that very point might help you home in on a target more accurately."

"Point taken," Joe thanked him, adding to his notes. "Although we probably have more people clinging to the old ways than you do down here."

Shepard nodded. "True." He turned to his computer and advanced the slide show another image.

"This," he described unnecessarily, "is the electric cord used to hang Mary Fish. It is also — to echo Eric's thunder — a nice supporting piece of evidence to the theory he just laid out."

Again, a picture followed, taken on a micro scale too extreme to recognize.

"Here's where things get interesting to me," he said. "It turns out that the cord was beyond simply being new; it was virtually unused, meaning that its surface was factory-pristine."

"I read in a report that Mary's companion said the old one had worn out," Joe explained. "They might've bought its replacement but never used it."

"Well, that was good for us," Shepard said. "Not that we couldn't have worked with an older sample. It just would've upped the challenge."

"So you got a print?" Les asked incredulously.

"Not exactly," Shepard explained. "We extracted a little DNA from a microscopic smear — Eric was telling you that we contacted Dr. Hawke and exchanged some data — but we also lifted some minute environmental evidence left behind by the skin oils — evidence that supports what Eric was saying. All this is where the synchrotron and DNA analysis work hand in glove, with the first securing a sweatprint's physical deposits, and the latter zeroing in on its genetic code material."

Another close-up picture. "Engine oil matching that left by the knife," he said. "And again the acetylene signature — both substances that are prone to resisting a quick scrub, unlike gunpowder or sawdust."

Shepard sat back. "I have to warn you about something, by the way. Remember how you were told that while the synchrotron process leaves a sample untouched, and that the same couldn't be said for DNA analysis? Well, there was too little of this touch-DNA to save a leftover sample. I was told that all of this was for investigative purposes only, though."

Joe was already trying to put him at ease. "No, no. That's fine. Totally understood. Not a problem."

"All right." Shepard nodded and moved to the next slide, this one vaguely familiar to the cops, if not in fact intelligible. "This is actually not your standard DNA profile," he explained. "We had to resort to something a little fancier called Copy Number Variation to compare what little DNA was on the underwear to whoever handled that electric cord last — there simply wasn't enough material to do otherwise — much less a standard DNA profile. And yes," he added quickly, "we did run it against Mary Fish's and Elise Howard's genetic code to rule them out; it's definitely someone else, a male."

"You found DNA on the underwear?"

"Next up," Shepard said, smiling. The next slide showed that article of clothing. "At first blush, we were ready to categorize this alongside the suicide note. The comments David left for us indicated the working theory of the false rape, and that the underpants had been pulled down solely for staging. In the old days, that would've been it, and little time would've been wasted running tests."

He turned toward them like a happy snake-oil salesman, his eyebrows high and his expression bright. "But no longer. Infrared spectromicroscopy lets us see things we never thought possible. Following the theory of the case, I worked out in my mind how the victim was attacked, laid out, and then positioned, and calculated that only a finite area of the underwear would have been available for the killer to pull down around her ankles."

As he was speaking, he was showing various aspects of the garment, once again ending up with what looked like a microscope slide. "The key turned out to be the same mineral and chemical signatures that we lifted from the electric cord. Once we found them, we were able to extract more touch-DNA." He hit his keyboard dramatically with his finger. "And voilà. A profile perfectly matching the Copy Number Variation sample from the Mary Fish scene. Proof that the same man was at least at the scene of both murders. Agreed?"

Joe was momentarily caught off guard, suddenly realizing that Shepard was actually looking for an answer.

"Absolutely," he blurted. "Incredible work."

"Sadly," Eric added now, "I wasn't able to extract anything beyond gender from either sample. They're just too small. Still, with any luck, you'll be able to run this through your state data bank at least and secure a hit."

"Fingers crossed," Lester said softly, his inflection betraying his doubt.

"All right," Shepard resumed, advancing his show with another image. "Down to the last victim, young Bob Clarke. Here, the paydirt was with the supposedly wiped bottle and the truck bumper." He cut a slightly disapproving glance at his colleague. "Eric already mentioned how, when the bottle was wiped clean, the cloth or rag used exchanged its trace evidence for the finger-prints that it erased. The report I read said that no rag was found at the scene, is that right?"

"Correct," Joe told him.

"Then we assume, with some small risk of error, that the killer used his own. This assumption is borne out by what we did find on the bottle's surface."

"Don't tell me," Lester commented. "Oil and acetylene."

"Among other things, yes," Shepard agreed, his earlier glee still somewhat dampened by Marine having stolen his

244

surprise. The reaction reminded Joe of how childish humans could be, regardless of their educational achievements, and maybe — sometimes — because of them.

"Other things?" Joe prompted.

Shepard's eyes widened slightly. "Ah, yes. Well, not surprisingly, a rag kicking around on the floor of a vehicle or even a glove box, if that's where he kept it, will pick up a lot of microscopic debris. Still" — the prior shine in his eye made a grudging re-appearance — "I was able to locate the sawdust. No gunpowder, though."

Joe smiled broadly, in part to encourage him. "I can live with that. Oak, again?"

"Not only that," Shepard conceded, gaining momentum, "but mixed in with the oil were minute metallic flakes, symptomatic of the used engine oil found in every car. My guess is that whoever this is used the rag to either wipe his dipstick or to clean around the pan lug when he last changed his oil. The beauty with that is the same as with DNA — once you locate your suspect's vehicle, we should be able to connect the old engine oil on the bottle to the oil in that car's engine."

"Cool," Lester murmured.

"Which brings us" — Shepard moved to another slide — "to Bobby's truck. Here, you must pass along my kudos to David Hawke and his staff, who really did an extraordinary job with all of this material, to be honest. But the truck bumper was tricky and especially well done."

The picture was of the bumper fragment Joe and Lester had brought with them. Shepard pulled a pen-sized laser pointer from his breast pocket and began moving its hot red dot across the image.

"What we noticed on this otherwise unremarkable surface, employing a variety of light sources, was that it had recently been disturbed, I think we can now safely say by the application of a second bumper used to push Bobby's truck off the road."

Lester was scrutinizing the picture and clearly seeing nothing at all. "You've got to be kidding."

"Actually, no," Shepard answered him. "The photograph doesn't do the evidence justice, to be sure, so it's not quite as amazing as you might think. In fact, there are a couple of small aberrations visible to the trained naked eye, but I emphasize the word 'trained,' which is where David comes in. As you *can* see, this was not a new bumper, and it had clearly seen better days. He was able to distinguish old injuries from new, which gave us this . . ."

A new slide appeared.

"Which is what?" Lester asked of the chart before them.

"A readout of the deposits on the surface of the bumper," Shepard informed them. "Again, similarly to most of the samples we've been discussing, the assemblage of artifacts constitutes a unique fingerprint of the offending bumper — everything from transposed dirt, soap from a recent car wash, more oil, our friend the acetylene, and sundry other items of little interest either because they're so common, or because we can't link them to anything."

"Acetylene traces were on the bumper?" Joe asked.

Shepard looked at him appraisingly. "Yes. I was struck by the same thing. What do you make of it?"

"That the user of the torch and the car were in proximity," Joe said, "implying that the acetylene isn't being used in a commercial environment, but a home one, like a garage."

Marine smiled. "That's what we were thinking."

"What do we do with that?" Les asked.

"Nothing yet," Joe said. "But I still like it."

"I ought to add something about the oil

in this instance," Shepard then pointed out. "It's not engine oil."

"Oh?"

"It's much lighter, more refined. I really had to dig around to find an explanation."

"Did you find one?" Joe asked him.

"Not really."

Joe smiled. "You said you hadn't been to Vermont. We use light oil to undercoat our cars, to stave off rust from road salt."

Shepard laughed. "That's it. I even found some salt residue."

"It's been snowing up there."

Shepard nodded. "How wonderful. All right, then. There you have it."

He again sat back in his chair, this time indicating that his role had reached an end. Joe read the body language and expressed his thanks. "Dr. Shepard, this has been incredible." He cast a look at Eric Marine before continuing. "I know we're not through — we still have the three drops of blood — but this alone has already given us a huge advantage. The guys back home will hate me when I hand them all this extra homework, but it's exactly what we were hoping for. Many, many thanks."

He looked at Marine again as Shepard went to studying his knuckles self-effacingly, but with a pleased expression. "Dr. Marine?"

Eric happily pulled the laptop toward him. "The blood. Let's hope this will be a kind of cherry on top of Wayne's ice cream sundae."

He fiddled with the program briefly and brought up his own set of pictures, all of them charts and graphs that both cops recognized, at least in theory, from past exposure to DNA explanations, often rendered in court to equally bewildered juries.

"As you know," Marine began, "we were given three samples, one from each murder scene. We didn't know the order in which they were originally collected by your suspect, so we kept to the same sequencing order we applied to Wayne's list, *i.e.,* Doreen's was Number One, Mary's, Number Two, and Bobby's, Number Three. For reasons that I'll soon explain, this turns out to have been a fortuitous choice."

Like Shepard before him, he played the keyboard as he spoke, but since the image contents meant even less to the two laymen, they didn't pay the slide show much attention. Marine didn't appear to mind.

"Again, as you knew before coming here, none of the DNA extracted from these three samples matched the victims they accompanied, the other two people killed, or each other. They were pure stranger deposits. My objective approach, therefore, was to work from the basis that at least two out of the three did not belong to the killer, unless, of course, there are actually three killers involved, all of whom left blood samples as a form of signature."

"Oh, Jesus," Spinney said, half to himself. "I never even thought of that."

"It's unlikely," Eric agreed. "But possible. On the other hand, it doesn't really alter my findings, and to be honest, I'm speaking more of how I was thinking before Wayne found what he did, which seems to connect all three cases to one perpetrator. Not only that," he added, "but as you'll also soon find out, I'm now pretty doubtful that any of the samples belongs to our guy."

He lit up the screen with something the two Vermonters could understand — a list.

He introduced it by explaining, "I thought about wowing you with some of the magic we do here, and which your crime lab can only dream about. But then I realized you'd have little clue about what I was describing. That's the reason for the separate report just for David Hawke.

"So" — he pointed at the screen — "I kept it simple. Drop Number One. He's a male with brown eyes, chances are he's black and — with consultation with one of my colleagues working on the NASA radiation effects team here on campus — I figure he's being treated for an aggressive form of cancer."

Joe let out a laugh. "You don't have his cell-phone number?"

Marine looked pleased. "It is fun, I will admit." He then held up a cautionary finger. "But let me say, before Wayne does, that it all comes with a caveat. The methods I used are cutting-edge stuff, some of it controversial, and none of it, as far as I know, admissible in court — except for the gender reading, of course."

"But they aren't wild guesses, either," Shepard put in supportively, as if softening the implication that he might be more rigid than was reasonable.

"No, no," Eric followed. "Absolutely not. I wouldn't have put this forth otherwise. There is a growing body of increasingly reliable research centering on what we call EVAs, or Externally Visible Characteristics. These are traits like skin, hair, and eye color, and maybe obesity, height, and whatnot; speaking of which, gender is actually an EVA. Anyhow, the goal is to come up with some Star Trek–style device where

251

we'll eventually be able to put a drop in one end, and get a picture of the blood's owner out the other. That's all science fiction right now, of course, but we are making baby step inroads."

"With ethnicity, for example," Joe suggested.

"Right," he said brightly. "It turns out some of these EVAs are easier to nail down than others, gender being one of them. Even so, as with gender, none of it is flawless. Still, it seems that red hair and blue and brown iris color are getting much more predictable."

"And black skin color?" Lester suggested.

"Right," Eric agreed slowly. "To a slightly lesser degree, but I thought it looked good enough to suggest."

"Any idea on the type of cancer?" Joe asked.

The DNA man ducked his head a moment, choosing his words. "This gets trickier. Medicinal radiation is designed to minimize damage to DNA, for good reason. Also, localized radiation is going to affect the body's general blood supply less than radiation that's being applied to let's say leukemia or bone cancer. Now, of course, we can't actually know the realities involved here, but my sources — who have a huge

knowledge of irradiated blood samples —
are leaning toward something long term and
generalized."

"Like leukemia?" Joe reiterated, to be sure
he understood.

"Correct," Eric reassured him, before following with, "but that could be completely
wrong."

Joe shrugged. "I'll take it anyhow, given
what we've got. Is that it for Drop Number
One?"

Marine hit a keyboard button. "It is. This
is Number Two. She's a female with blue
eyes, but that's about it, except for the two
small details that I promised to explain."

Joe smiled at the obvious come-on.
"Which are?" he played along.

"Let me proceed with one at a time, or
none of it will make sense," Eric said. "To
begin with, the DNA is degraded."

"What's that mean?" Les asked. "The guy
left the sample lying around?"

"That's a distinct possibility," the scientist
agreed. "But I was intrigued by an additional hypothesis: that the blood was
extracted from someone dead."

"What?" Joe blurted out.

Eric held up a hand while striking another
key, explaining, "This is Drop Number
Three, which is not only what made me

return to Number Two to consider my hypothesis, but which also explains the second unusual feature I mentioned about Number Two. Let me start by saying that Number Three is significantly degraded, far more so than Number Two. That coincidence made me consider the possible parallels between either collection techniques or — shall we say — the raw material used."

Mimicking his colleague earlier, Wayne Shepard chuckled and muttered, "You'll love this."

His partner continued. "Here's the kicker that lends it credibility: Number Three is contaminated with just a smidgeon of leftover Number Two DNA."

Marine beamed at them both as if he'd just delivered the goose to Tiny Tim's family.

Lester merely stared back at him. Joe had to concede, "I'm sorry, Eric. I'm afraid I just don't get it."

"Think funeral home," Wayne suggested.

"The blood came from there?" Joe asked, his mouth open.

"Not definitively, but it fits," Eric said enthusiastically, his face cheerful. "It strikes me as more reasonable that this person stole blood from two corpses, in the privacy of a funeral home, than that he was using a technique so sloppy that he consistently ruined his samples. I mean, how would such a worker stay employed? And the contamination is the smoking gun: He extracted Number Two's blood first, using a clean syringe, and then followed by immediately drawing Number Three's sample, with the same syringe, thereby tainting Three with a bit of Two's DNA. That not only links the two samples, but it puts them in a logical sequence."

"But do funeral homes use anticoagulant?" Lester asked. "And where did he put Two's blood to make room in the syringe for Three?"

All three of them looked at him.

"Good point," Joe said, impressed.

"Maybe it's not a funeral home," Wayne suggested. "A hospital morgue would have blood tubes nearby. Your bad guy could be filling his pockets as he walks down the hallway — a little here, a little there. Still, scientifically, there are anomalies, perhaps indicating that we're completely wrong."

Joe scratched his forehead. The transition from evidential dead end to suggestion overload was fogging his brain. "No. I like it. It's not that it doesn't make sense. It just takes getting used to. Okay, okay. Let's leave that where it is for the moment. What more did you get on Number Three?"

But Eric had to admit defeat. "That was it. A male. Nothing else stood out. Sorry."

"Except that both Two and Three could be dead," Lester pitched in.

Eric couldn't allow that, as hopeful as it sounded. "Or that their blood was carelessly collected. Degraded blood is just that, no more or less. It doesn't necessarily speak of its host."

There was a telling silence before Lester said hopefully, "We still have the fact that all the blood was stored in tubes with anti-coagulant."

"And the likelihood," Shepard added, "that both Two's and Three's blood was collected at the same time in the same place, regardless of whether that was a funeral home or a hospital morgue or someplace else entirely."

"Which tells me," Les contributed, "that both bodies were sharing a rack. That means records that can be checked for a blond, blue-eyed female who was stored alongside a male."

Joe nodded and stood up, smiling broadly and releasing the two scientists from any more speculation. "We've got a ton better than that, even, all because of you two and your willingness to help. There's more on our plates now than I know what to do with until we sort it out at home."

He leaned over and shook their hands warmly, adding, "But that's what we're supposed to know how to do."

Eric Marine looked saddened that they were parting ways. "You'll tell us what happens?"

Joe laughed. "Not only that; I may be bugging you for more details as we go. In fact, count on it."

Wayne Shepard stood also. "We will. It's been a real pleasure putting science to such use."

CHAPTER SEVENTEEN

Joe sat on the edge of the conference table and took in the scattered debris of coffee cups, doughnut boxes, discarded stirrers, and crumpled napkins. There had been fifteen people circling the table moments earlier, from various departments and agencies, convened from as far away as Burlington's VBI office — the largest in the state — for a top priority, highly confidential law enforcement meeting to explain the Brookhaven findings and coordinate a massive, and discreet, task force response.

And now they'd left on their various assignments, trickling out of the Brattleboro corporate headquarters' parking lot of Vermont Yankee in unmarked cars so as not to attract attention. VY, as it was commonly known, often made its conference rooms available for quiet assemblages — yet another public service that the state's sole nuclear energy provider probably offered to atone for sins no such plant believed existed.

It had been a risk for Joe to expand the numbers of those cops in-the-know, but he didn't have much choice. He needed the manpower. Besides, word was going to get out soon enough that they were pursuing a triple murder serial killer, after which the Stan Katzes of the world would turn the entire investigation into a free-for-all.

"You don't look happy."

Sammie Martens was standing in the distant doorway, watching him.

He gave her a half smile. "Just meditating."

"You got a lot of good stuff at Brookhaven." She stepped inside and resumed the seat she'd had at the meeting.

"Yeah," he agreed. "Something'll come of it. Sooner the better, though."

"You good with inviting VSP to play?"

He crossed to the white board and began erasing his talking points. He'd started from the beginning, with Doreen, and taken them all for the entire journey. It had lasted two hours, including questions, and he'd covered a lot of wall space.

"They're a good outfit," he said, slightly irritated. "The divide-and-conquer days are over, or ought to be. We may bitch about each other, even with good cause, but we more than most have to set an example. Where's Willy, speaking of which?"

She let out a short laugh. "He thinks he's in the woodshed."

Joe stopped to look at her. "You're kidding. A) I didn't think he cared, and B) he should know me better. I'm just glad he thought ahead to get a judge involved and make busting McNaughton legal. It would've been nice if he or the SA had told us that he had a search warrant all along."

She raised her eyebrows. "You're not pissed he went after McNaughton?"

Joe spoke as he resumed wiping with long, cursive strokes. "Chuck McNaughton's a weasel. I never thought he did in Doreen, much less the other two, but I'm happy he's staring at jail time for something. If Willy was trying to get my goat, he'll have to do better than that."

"You think the real guy is done killing?" Sam asked, changing the subject.

He paused again, his eraser poised over a list he'd been adding to throughout the meeting. "Hard to say. I mean, look at this." He tapped the board. In his neat block handwriting was the stack of assignments his much expanded team was currently pursuing:

Oil undercoating shops — customers
Funeral homes — employees & records
Hospitals — employees & morgue records
Rescue squads — employees
Lumber stores — customers for oak, especially
Acetylene suppliers — customers
Known welders
Doctors' offices — for black men with cancer
Gun shops and reloader suppliers — for gunpowder
Newspaper obits for recently deceased blond females

"Somewhere in here," he told her, "is a guy with a serious grudge. Logic says he'll surface in several areas at once — like a woodworking welder who works at a funeral home and volunteers at a hospital. But we thought we'd find a common thread when we put our three murder victims under a microscope, too."

"And got nothing," Sam added quietly.

"Exactly," Joe agreed, and continued erasing. "So, we have no rationale to pin on him. I haven't a clue why he's done this — or why he's still doing it, maybe. And I sure as hell don't know if he'll keep going. The cliché is that these guys don't stop, but I think that's a dangerous assumption here."

"Why?" she asked.

"It misses that he might have a goal. It's not like he has an appetite for kids, or brunettes, or people who love Chihuahuas. This all looks totally random to us, as if he walked down the street and shot a few people in the head on a whim. But he's an arrogant son of a bitch, too, and I'm betting he has a huge chip on his shoulder."

"Because of the blood drops?" she asked.

"Yeah. Why do that, unless you need to stand out somehow?"

"He wants to be caught?" Sam suggested.

Joe scowled. "Maybe, but that's too easy and it doesn't tell us anything. I think it's more that he needs to look good — to himself, and maybe to someone else, too."

"He's showing off."

"He's looking for respect," Joe corrected, adding, "I'm just not sure who his audience is. But if I'm right, and he achieves whatever stature he's after, he'll more than likely stop."

He finished erasing the list. "Not that I'd mind that," he admitted. "God knows, we don't need people to keep killing in order to catch them."

He stopped again to fix her with a quizzical look.

"What?" she asked.

"I was just reminded of something. A thousand years ago, when I was a rookie, I handled a small break-in at the high school. Someone stole some supplies — no big deal — but I was asked what I was going to do about it, and I answered, 'Nothing.' They were ticked off, of course. Thought I was being lazy. But I asked them, 'Why do you do something like this? Because you're in need of some pads and chalk and a few pens? You do it to brag about it later. You have to tell your buddies.' "

Sammie was smiling. "And your buddies will trade it with us when we bust them for something else down the line."

"Right."

She nodded, but couldn't resist asking, "Okay, Obi-Wan, did you nail your man?"

He laughed. "Nope. Guess we never busted the right buddy."

Gini Coursen looked up into her son's face. "Move it a little higher."

Ike Miller reached behind her and pulled the pillow closer to her shoulder blades, catching a whiff of her body odor in the process. He stepped back, his expression neutral. His mother didn't actually suffer from any ailments that her own terrible habits hadn't brought on, but that didn't mean that by this point she could barely function.

"Where's the remote?" she asked.

He located it in a fold of the comforter spread across the bed and dropped it on her lap. Across the dark and dingy bedroom, an enormous plasma TV set filled the room with a kaleidoscope of projected colors as a rapid succession of young women advertising shampoo swirled their hair like the skirts of contra dancers spinning across the dance floor.

Gini Coursen began flipping channels, looking for anything with either canned laughter or contestants screaming with their hands above their heads — her two favorites.

Ike watched her profile as she hunted, his emotions torn.

"You want something to drink?" he asked.

She didn't turn her head. "Why?"

"No reason. Just thought you might."

"What I want is the newspaper."

His gaze dropped to the floor. "There's nothing in it."

She stopped mangling the remote long enough to stare at him. "Why not? I thought you had this figured out."

"I do, Ma," he murmured, both angry and embarrassed.

She shook her head and went back to patrolling the channels. "Doesn't look like it. This big plan of yours. Ben would've been less talk and more action."

"That's what put him in jail," Ike blurted out, instantly regretful.

Gini looked at him, openmouthed. "What did you say?"

He held both hands out to his sides, palms open. "It's true, Ma. I mean, I loved him, too, but he did . . ."

She hit his thigh with the back of her hand. "Don't you go there, you shit-bird."

He stepped back, his face red with fury, "Shit-bird? After what I did for you? You really think Benny would've given a flying fuck?"

Now it was her turn to rue her words. She reached out to him. "Ike — honey. You're right, you're right. I didn't mean it that way. It just came out."

"Well, stop it," he cautioned, but his voice had lost its edge.

"I just miss him sometimes," she said, her sincerity jarring with the commercial music in the background.

"I know, Ma. I do, too," Ike conceded.

She was finally able to take hold of his hand. He found hers too soft, warm, and damp for comfort, but he didn't let it go.

"Do you?" she asked.

That sparked his ire again, and he took advantage of it to break off contact. "Jesus . . ."

"I'm sorry, I'm sorry," she quickly wailed. "It's just . . . Sometimes, you act so hard."

Ike moved toward the doorway, hating this sort of emotional tar pit. He liked things more orderly.

He looked around at his mother's domain — cluttered, dirty, smelling of mold and human being. What she called her nest, and he tried not to think about. "You all set for now?"

"Tea?" she asked, with the little-girl smile he hated.

"Right." He turned on his heel and left, walking rapidly, only stopping once he'd reached the kitchen.

That wasn't much cleaner — he was no neat-freak himself — but nothing smelled, and she virtually never came in there, preferring her bed and not willing to use the walker. That somehow helped it seem brighter.

Instead of pouring her tea, he sat at the kitchen table by the window. He was at the far end of the house. The hallway, his bedroom, and the bathroom they shared lay in between her nest and here. He actually

266

wasn't sure what this house was called — a prefab, a converted trailer. It didn't have wheels, but it was long and narrow and didn't have a cellar. It was a dump, too, and on a plot of land that looked more like a car graveyard than a homesite, there were so many wrecks scattered around.

It was also buried in the woods, off a dirt road few people traveled, shrouded by a tangle of uncared for trees and an odd and sudden outcropping of huge granite boulders that he presumed had been left behind by a glacier long before.

They didn't own any of it, including the car corpses. They were renters, beholden to a landlord Ike had met only once and who'd never shown any interest in them, their welfare, the integrity of the property, or even — to a large extent — the rent, which he seemed happy to get whenever it appeared.

Which is exactly the way Ike liked it — from the cars to the mud to the leaky roof and poorly insulated walls, to the sagging wooden garage across the way where he kept his office, which is what he called a plank desk against the far wall of a dirt-floored shack equipped with an enormous and no doubt dangerous woodstove. His computer was there, though, and his collection of printouts and news clips. That's where he did his thinking.

Crazy old lady. He dug a cigarette from the pack in his breast pocket and lit up, enjoying the smoke being pulled down deep into his lungs. Why couldn't she just let go of Benny? Son of a bitch had never done squat for either one of them.

He drew in again on the cigarette, looking out at the leftover snow still frosting some of the car innards, where the sun couldn't reach. But there was no getting away from Benny.

There was only putting him in the shade. He was stealing Ike's limelight. Like always.

Ike's eyes settled on the morning paper lying before him, where he'd dropped it in disgust earlier. Stupid cops. You try to make things interesting, and all they do is drop the ball. No wonder there was so much crime in the world.

Ike Miller reached for the disposable cell phone on the table, looked up a number in the phone book, and dialed.

"*Brattleboro Reformer.* How may I direct your call?"

"I want to talk to the editor."

"He's not in at the moment. Would you like to speak with someone in the newsroom?"

Ike hesitated. "Is he any good?"

The woman at the other end paused. "I'm sorry?"

"Sure. Put him on."

There was a moment's silence, followed by, "Newsroom. Patrick."

"I got a story for you."

"Who is this?"

"You don't need to know. I'm about to make your day."

"Oh?"

"Yeah. You people have a serial killer running around you don't even know about."

CHAPTER EIGHTEEN

"Joe, that's not how this works. I do not spill my guts and then have you say, 'No comment.' The very fact that you're still on the line means I got something here, so don't bullshit a bullshitter."

Joe stood at the corner of High Street and Main, Brattleboro's commercial heart, and found himself thinking about the Dunkin' Donuts that used to stand there for what seemed like years eternal, before being replaced by a community park and a Thai restaurant.

He really had a hankering for a doughnut, bean burritos notwithstanding.

"You there? Hello?"

"I'm here, Stanley. I'm considering your offer. I'm also still recovering from the shit you dumped on us about depriving the public of what they've got a right to know. Isn't that a little worn-out, even for you?"

"I didn't make you an offer," the editor

protested, completely ignoring that last comment. "I called on you to confirm or deny. That's it."

It was a good restaurant. Joe would concede that. He and Lyn ate there often. And the whole corner looked better than when it had been the remnants of a long-forgotten, 1930s garage.

Maybe he missed the working-class tackiness of the scene more than the doughnut shop itself. He'd lived in Brattleboro for so many years, and knew so many of its down-and-out from his decades on the police department, that he'd come to see all that as its reality, more than the chamber-of-commerce gleam of new restaurants and spiffy community parks.

"Spare me, Stanley," he told his phone. "You're going to run a front-page screamer based on one anonymous wacko telling you Jack the Ripper is back? I don't think so."

"Something's up, Joe," Stan Katz insisted. "I can hear it in your voice. A good cop you are; an actor you're not. I can still write a frontpage piece making you and your fancy outfit look like cow manure. There's an election on the horizon, Joe, in case your old girlfriend hasn't told you, and VBI is a political creation. You hearing what I'm saying?"

"I hear you talking, Stan. I don't hear much substance."

But he knew Katz was right. All the sparring aside, they would have to meet.

And Katz knew it, too, which is why he didn't respond.

Joe sighed and crossed the street, leaving the Dunkin' Donuts memorial park behind. "I'll see you in a few minutes, Stanley."

The *Reformer* had once been shoved into a few rooms on Main Street, not far from the Latchis Hotel and Theatre, a 1930s art deco landmark, and right in the middle of the town's bustle.

Now, it was relegated to a single-story, flat-roofed, mostly windowless brick slab, wedged between a cemetery and the interstate, and so removed from the community's center that — if anyone even knew where the building was — they'd have to drive to get there.

It had been a sound financial move, no doubt, but — perhaps as with the passing of the doughnut shop — one Joe had forever rued.

Not that he was particularly sentimental about the newspaper. Like most cops, he saw the press more as a business dependent on sensationalism than as a bastion of free speech and liberty. On the other hand, he had to concede that the *Reformer* was hardly a mud slinger, and that Vermont's media in general had a gentility about it that almost smacked of the 1950s.

For that, he wouldn't complain, which was in large part why he pulled into the *Reformer* parking lot a half hour after receiving Stan Katz's call, and ten minutes after phoning Bill Allard, whom he'd felt honor-bound to warn.

Allard, no surprise, had not been happy.

The building's interior was no more inspiring than its outside — essentially an out-of-the box, open-floor layout with a few walls for offices, conference rooms, and probably an outmoded darkroom, the move from downtown having predated the Internet and digital photography by several years.

That being the case, Joe saw Stan immediately upon entering, seated at a computer somewhere in the middle distance, pounding on a keyboard as if it were on fire. Joe gave his old nemesis that much — upon being promoted to editor, he had eschewed a corner office to stay with his reporters.

Of course, that also meant they had to go shopping for a place to talk privately, and finally ended up in an office belonging to someone with an unhealthy addiction to cat-related paraphernalia.

"Celia won't mind," Katz said upon entering. "She's out sick."

Joe looked around, frowning. "I can see why."

Katz shoved a chair his way and settled opposite him.

"So, what've you got?" he asked.

Joe laughed. "Right — this where I tell you everything we have on Jimmy Hoffa because we're friends and I trust you?"

Stanley smiled and shrugged. "You look tired. I thought I'd try." He paused to collect his thoughts a moment before resuming. "Okay," he then said, "let's do this by the numbers. One of my reporters got a phone call earlier from a man who didn't identify himself, but who said that the police were working on three deaths that were in fact homicides committed by the same person. Those deaths were Doreen Ferenc, whom we know, and two more named Mary Fish and Robert Clarke. Do you care to comment?"

"Not yet," Joe answered. "Can I ask a few questions?"

Embodying the very attitude Joe had just been considering regarding the Vermont media's soft touch, Katz replied, "Shoot."

"Did you trace this guy's number?"

"It was a private call, and Pat — the

reporter who took it — said it sounded like a cell. Probably a drop phone. Was he lying?"

"What did he sound like?"

"Young. Was he lying?"

"Were there any background noises?"

Katz sighed. "No. You're killing me."

"Was the call recorded?"

"No."

"Okay," Joe allowed at last. "What do you know about Fish and Clarke?"

Katz nodded. "Fish we heard was a suicide; Clarke I know nothing about. The AP wire had something about a car crash up north, so I'm guessing that was him. Were they murdered?"

Joe studied him in silence for a moment. The two of them first met back when Joe was a lieutenant detective and Katz a fired-up cops-and-courts reporter — both far more ambitious, Type A, and antagonistic than now.

"Ground rules first," Joe said.

Katz sighed. "Oh, for Christ's sake. Aren't we beyond that crap?"

"You wish," Joe told him. "You know goddamn well what we're talking about here. You print your kind of headline and we'll not only have a panic, but you'll have done exactly what this nutcase wanted you to do.

You actually want to be that easily manipulated?"

"So they are murders and he is the serial killer."

Joe leaned forward to make better eye contact. "Focus, Stanley. You're not going to get shit unless you deal with me."

Katz laughed. "Why? Because you'll call the *Rutland Herald* out of spite?"

"No," Joe spoke slowly. "Because he will unless you and I come to an agreement."

Katz furrowed his brow. "Lay it out for me."

"We're both screwed here. This guy is going to let the cat out of the bag. If you don't produce a story, he'll go elsewhere; if you produce a story with my help, then maybe we buy some time with my personal guarantee that I'll let you interview me for an exclusive after it's all said and done."

"All said and done?" Katz asked incredulously. "Like when the guy's in jail two years from now, after trials, appeals, and every other goddamn delay? Such an offer."

"If I don't cooperate, you got nothing," Joe stated.

Katz rubbed his forehead. "All right, all right. Let's push that aside. What're you putting on the table?"

"I give you that all three murders are connected to a single killer, but I hold back a few details that're key to the investigation and will make the prosecution that much easier. You and I have done that before."

Katz acknowledged the point with a slight tilt of the head.

"In addition," Joe continued, "you print that we've got a good handle on the bad guy's identity and that the killings were absolutely targeted and not even remotely random. Nobody's at risk in the general public."

Katz was scowling. "Is that true? Any of it?"

"Would I lie to you?"

"You always have."

Joe sat back and looked at him silently.

"That's it?" Katz demanded.

"It makes your story official," Joe said. "You can write about the guy calling it in, and you can quote me responding to it. It gives you the scoop, maybe satisfies the wacko, and doesn't cause a stampede."

"Because in fact," Katz suggested, "you have no idea who this is and the killings were totally random."

"Wrong on both counts," Joe said with a straight face. "And if you go there, I'll make sure you look like a total idiot before it's done — right up there with the *National En-quirer.*"

Stanley swiveled his borrowed chair around and looked beyond a row of porcelain cats on the windowsill to the silent traffic on the distant interstate outside. Joe let him ponder.

"All right," the editor finally said, not bothering to look back. "Let's give it a try."

Sammie killed her car engine and let her hands drop into her lap. She'd been more tired on other cases, more stressed, and more doubtful of success. This time, they had troops to spare, a clear-cut perp to pursue — even if they didn't know his name — and a strategy linked to the Brookhaven findings that made sense. But she still felt exhausted.

It hadn't been fun, visiting funeral homes and rescue squads and hospital administrators, sometimes doubling back to get warrants for a simple list of employees or customers. But she'd been there before. Mind-numbing research and digging were often part of the job. It beat working at a desk, and it sometimes led to unexpected successes. She'd solved more than one case by stumbling across a key missing piece while examining something unrelated.

278

Still. She was bushed.

She swung out of the car and approached the barn labeled "Thurber's Undercoating." At least this time, she wouldn't be dealing with a blank-faced bureaucrat. Schuyler "Sky" Thurber and she went back a few years.

She entered the barn through a small side door, into a large warm cavern, pungent with the sweet, cloying smell of the fine, light oil used to protect car underbodies from road salt and sand. In a far corner, corralled off for safety with a steel grate, stood an enormous woodstove, flanked on both sides by attending rows of piled wood.

"Sky?" she shouted, not seeing anyone around. In the middle of the huge space was a large, semitransparent, plastic campaign tent, big enough to seat fifty people. But in its midst, poised on a lift, was a Subaru station wagon.

"In here," came a baritone voice. "Who's that?"

"Sam Martens," she answered, approaching the tent. "I didn't see you in there."

She gingerly peeled back a flap and glanced inside. The odor associated with the whole place was thicker in here, explained by the walls of the tent being slick with a thin film of oil.

"Careful," the slightly muffled voice said. "You'll trash your clothes."

She saw a pair of legs approaching from the far side of the elevated car, encased below the knees in green rubber boots. A man stepped around the corner, his head covered with a filthy ball cap and his face blocked by a respirator. As he neared, he gestured to her to step back, and then followed her outside to the barn's main room.

There, he peeled off a long pair of rubber gloves and removed the respirator with a single, long-practiced sweep of his hand, revealing a broad Scandinavian face sporting a perfect row of large, white teeth.

Sky Thurber leaned far over and kissed Sam on the cheek. "How's the girl?" he asked brightly. "You look like you could use a little beach time."

She laughed and squeezed his hand, the only part of him she dared to touch. "You look like you just got back from some."

He laughed in turn. "I did. Margaret and I went on a cruise. Can you believe that? Just like the ads — fancy meals, swimming pool, gambling. I didn't see any of those pretty girls. They musta been on a different boat. But it was great. We're thinking of doing it next year, too."

He led the way to a small cluster of chairs

located near the woodstove. In the background, a small squad of parked vehicles was visible, no doubt waiting their turn in the tent.

Sky pointed to one of the chairs. "Sit anywhere you want. That one's mine, though — only one that'll guarantee your butt'll never get rusty."

He burst out laughing as they both settled down. She'd known and loved this man and his family ever since she'd helped them out fifteen years earlier on an embezzlement case. For some reason, they'd all just clicked, and had stayed friends forever. Sammie Martens had no family, and the Thurbers, among few others, had been quietly enlisted.

There would be no need for a warrant here.

Sky stuck his big feet out before him and clasped his hands across his stomach. "So," he said, "what piece of detective work brings you here?"

"That obvious?" she asked.

He gave her a gentle smile. "Samantha, when you come here to cry, you look like a lost puppy; when you come here to help me work and get distracted, you dress like I do; when you come here to see Margaret and whatever kid may be hanging around, you bring gifts. Now, you look like a cop. If you were a man, you'd be wearing a tie."

She was laughing. "I wish I were a better undercoater, Sky, 'cause then we could switch jobs, although if we did, my bosses would get a great detective, and you'd lose all your customers."

He wagged a finger at her. "Don't sell yourself short. You're better than you think, and trust me" — he waved his hand around — "this doesn't take a genius. Plus, I'd be a terrible cop. I like people too much."

She nodded her agreement. "You're probably right there. It helps to be a little hard-nosed."

He was studying her as she spoke, and now asked, "You sure you're okay? I saw the paper this morning, about the three murders. You're right in the middle of that, aren't you?"

She nodded.

"Thought so," he continued. "I told Margaret the same thing. 'Poor Sammie,' I said, 'knee-deep in evil again, I bet.' "

"Well," Sam conceded, "you were right."

"Is that what brings you here?"

"It is," she admitted. "We're collecting lists of people who either benefit from certain services, like this one, or who have certain specific occupations. Afterward, we'll compare all the lists to see what names overlap."

His eyebrows rose. "And you want people who get their cars oiled? That's a lot of folks, if you're getting to all my competitors, too."

"We're trying to," she said. "That's where the math kicks in. When we get enough lists, the names appearing across the board are likely to be few and far between."

He shook his head in wonderment. "That's amazing, how you do that." He suddenly grasped both chair arms in his large hands and pushed himself to a standing position. "Well," he said, "let's not dilly-dally. I got a list on the computer. We were about to print it out for our company Christmas card."

He led the way back across the barn floor to a small cluttered office in the far corner. A school desk was the largest thing in it, the shelves were sagging with trade magazines and catalogs dating back years, there were pictures of family and friends — including one featuring Sam and Willy, who was frowning, of course. Sky carefully settled behind the computer, cleared its keyboard of unopened mail, and turned it on.

"What other lists are you looking at?" he

asked. "If that doesn't break any rules to ask."

"No, no," she said. "It'll sound a little weird, but it's welders and hospital employees and funeral-home workers and ammo reloaders and woodworkers, among others. Kind of a hodgepodge. That's just some of them."

He was nodding as he scrutinized the screen, waiting for the computer to fully awaken.

"Like a hunter who has a home shop with a table saw and a welding rig, and who volunteers nights as a hospital aide."

Again, she laughed at his clear-sightedness. "Exactly. You are *good,* Sky. That's amazing."

He shook his head and started typing. "Nah. I'm just describing damn near everybody I know. Hell, I'm most of those myself, except for the medical stuff. I don't like blood, so I volunteer as a firefighter. You know that."

"I do," she allowed.

He foraged around amid the displaced mail until he found a pair of reading glasses that he daintily perched on his nose. "There. That's better."

He glanced up at her quickly. "What about

a psychological profile? You have anything there?"

She shook her head. "He's killed three people, as you know from the paper. But, to be honest, people killing people isn't that abnormal. I'm not sure a profile would tell us much."

He frowned, as much at the screen as at her comment. "I've heard that," he said, "but I don't really want to believe it."

He suddenly pushed himself away from the desk and shoved the glasses up into his hair to better study her. "You're looking for someone who does all these things, or comes into contact with them, but you're also looking for someone who's not right in the head." He held up his finger. "Maybe anybody can kill once, 'specially in the right circumstances, but three times?"

She wasn't sure what to say, and merely muttered, "I guess."

Sky lurched forward and started stabbing the keyboard again. "Tell you what: You don't tell anyone what it means, and I'll put some asterisks by the people I think might be crazy enough to be who you're after."

She opened her mouth to speak, but he cut her off with a raised hand. "I know, I know. You've got other undercoaters you're talking to and a dozen lists to read and then you'll find out that your villain didn't even own a car. None of that matters. I just want to do this, okay? I know it's probably libelous or some damn thing, so all I'm saying here is that the names I'll check are a little weird. It's just my two cents worth, okay?"

The printer began chattering, somewhere behind a stack of bills, and in five minutes Sam found herself back outside in the driveway, seated behind the wheel, and scrutinizing Sky's customers.

Nothing leaped out. She recognized a few names because of past DUIs or other old cases she'd handled while on the PD. Scanning the addresses didn't do much for her, either.

What stuck in her mind, though, wasn't the actual list. It was the fact that Sky had thought of marking certain names in the first place.

CHAPTER NINETEEN

In general, interactions with forensic labs are done electronically or by mail. So many boxes of weapons, buccal swabs of DNA, cast impressions of tire treads, photographs, reports, and other paperwork are put in the mail that the U.S. Postal Service is considered a reliable and acceptable link in any chain of custody. Indeed, the efficiency of this mundane but reliable system was often preferred over hand deliveries.

Joe, however, tended toward old school. He felt that handing over an item face-to-face, or at least following up in like fashion after the article had arrived, was not only good manners, but proof of the object's importance in the overall scheme of the sender.

Of course, he understood being hectored by matters of routine. But there were exceptions, and he believed this was one of them.

The Brookhaven findings — along with

the gains he was hoping might come from them — were of a unique nature to Joe. Born of a process he'd never guessed existed, they were aimed at catching a criminal he wanted to stop more than he had any other in a very long time.

Whoever this man was, standing invisible behind the dead bodies of three innocent people, taunting the police with his ominous blood drops, he was certainly not the average crook, bent on conventional malice. This one ran deeper, more cruel and calculating, and in search of a goal they could only hope he'd reached, assuming that meant no further killings. Joe didn't want to even consider the fallout of finding another victim. That was one more reason for driving to the crime lab in person — to escape his desk phone and the pile of news-hyped messages from people demanding to know what social plague had gripped bucolic Vermont.

The state's forensic lab was for the moment on the top floor of one of a cluster of ancient, inefficient, dour red brick buildings now blandly called the State Office Building Complex, but known in 1891 — the time of its creation — as the Vermont State Hospital for the Insane. At its peak housing some fourteen hundred patients, the actual hospital portion of the campus now barely functioned, and was annually threatened with extinction. But it was far from isolated; all around its shrunken core, inhabiting the many nooks and crannies it had once called its own, was a gathering of state agencies cut loose from nearby Montpelier. As bureaucracy had grown, the world becoming more complicated, demanding, and politically compromised, the state's leaders had latched on to the erstwhile insane asylum's fall from popularity and gradually filled its emptying buildings with entities as diverse as Natural Resources, Corrections, Children and Families, Environmental Conservation, and — more relevant to Joe — the Department of Public Safety. It was this latter building that housed not just the state police headquarters and the crime lab, but also the central office of Joe's own Vermont Bureau of Investigation — even if that did only amount to just enough room for Bill Allard and a secretary.

Joe prowled the forever-packed parking lot for a hole, lucking out at last at the far end, and walked toward the old, hulking edifice, noticing how much the snow had yielded to the warmer temperatures of a normal October. At least the lab would eventually be free of its confines, he reflected

— almost ten million dollars had been secured at long last to build David Hawke and his team new quarters, allowing what was a highly regarded, nationally certified operation an environment more befitting its true quality.

Once inside and past the buzzer-controlled entryway, Joe eschewed the small elevator, climbed the two flights to the top floor, forever impressed by the austere architecture, and then wandered down a short hallway to Bill's miniature domain. He hadn't called ahead — not to Bill — but he also wasn't averse to Allard joining the conversation he was anticipating with Hawke.

As so often happened when he dropped by, he found Bill scrutinizing his computer screen as if it were covered with hieroglyphics.

"Hey," he said from the door.

Allard didn't even glance in his direction. Only his eyebrows rose in greeting.

"I'm reading about you right now."

Joe stepped into the small office. "The *Reformer?* Yeah — that was a shoe dropping I didn't expect. That the bad guy would blow our cover."

Bill shook his head. "The *Reformer* was nothing. This is the *Boston Globe*. They're loving that we've turned into Newark."

Joe sat down. "Newark? They say that?"

"Not in so many words, but Newark is mentioned as the epitome of armpits, and Vermont's in the same paragraph. Subtle, it is not."

The phone rang. Allard picked it up, listened briefly, and told his secretary, "Like all the others — I'm currently out of the office."

He hung up and looked at Joe for the first time. "Since eight A.M.," he said. "Nonstop. The press, the politicians, the brass from downstairs. The governor called; I could hear him sweating on the phone. 'Remember,' he says, 'I created you with my pen.' Can you believe that?"

Joe smiled. "Sure I can. Why's he give a damn?"

Allard broke away from the screen and sat back, locking his hands behind his head. "You really don't know?"

"What? It's not like *he's* whacking these people."

"In an election year," Bill explained, "they give a damn about everything, and you know what? They're right. Your old girlfriend chooses to make hay out of this, Reynolds will end up with egg on his face, guaranteed."

Joe scowled, trying to follow the logic.

"It's the same as when New York gets hit with a snowstorm," Bill went on. "The people yell at the snowplow people; they yell at their bosses; the bosses yell back and get the union riled up. The union screams about how the mayor shortchanged their hours, benefits, and operating budget. The mayor says his hands are tied because of shenanigans in Albany; and the next thing he knows, the New York State governor loses the election because of something he couldn't have controlled in the first place."

He pointed at Joe. "Our governor is wondering if you're not a snowstorm."

"Me?" Joe asked.

"You're the one being quoted." He pointed at the screen. "And that's all it takes."

Joe absorbed that for a moment. "Okay," he said. "Did he actually say anything I care about?"

"No, but his attitude was more panicky than I thought it would be. He's starting to really sweat this one."

"And an incumbent, no less," Joe mused.

"Well," Bill admitted, "I won't be voting for her, but your old . . ."

"Gail," Joe interrupted. "I'm getting tired of the girlfriend handle."

Allard chuckled. "Right. Fair enough. Gail. Anyhow, she's gaining yards. The rape victim angle is probably key, not to sound heartless, but even without it, I think she stood a good chance. Reynolds's been there a long time, and people have gotten to attach him to most of their problems — like the guys downstairs and the creation of VBI."

Joe laughed at the irony of that. "You telling me cops'll be voting for Gail because Reynolds created us?"

Bill shook his head like a sage confronting a dense student. "Come, Grasshopper, did I not tell you about snowstorms?"

Joe checked his watch and rose to his feet. "Jesus. I'll leave it to you to ponder that crap. I'm actually here to see David. You want to join us? I want to kick around what he's learned from the Brookhaven stuff."

The phone rang again as Bill stood also. "And leave all this?"

He preceded Joe out the door, ignoring the phone.

The crime lab was down the hall, behind locked doors, but David Hawke's even smaller office was just a few yards away from Bill's, toward the stairwell, and with a single window overlooking an airshaft. Joe could only imagine how much Hawke was fantasizing about his proposed new digs, purportedly less than a full construction year away.

If you believed what you heard.

Hawke gave them his standard affable smile as they crossed his threshold, and rose to shake hands. "Two of you? Should I be nervous?"

"Hardly," Allard reassured him. "I'm just running away from my phone."

Hawke gestured toward the door and ushered them both back out. "Then let me aid and abet. I think it'll be better if we talk in the lab. I can do a little show-and-tell, and we can all escape the phones."

He led the way to the lab's reinforced door and entered both his password on the lock and their names on the visitors' sheet, speaking as he did so. "I was really pleased with what they did down there, Joe. I'm guessing you're pretty happy, too, given all the new avenues this opened up, but on a scientific level — and even just an inter-agency one — this whole deal seemed to me like a home run."

"No, no," Joe joined in. "Me, too. They were great, and I thank you so much for suggesting them in the first place."

Past the security door, they walked down a hallway much like what they'd just left —

dark, old, built for abuse, and additionally cluttered with odd pieces of equipment that looked destined for the dump. As they went, they caught glimpses to both sides of lab technicians hard at work, dressed in white coats and — because of the setting — looking more like World War II researchers than the inhabitants of an up-to-date forensic lab.

Hawke finally led them into a room near the end, with a table in its middle and an assortment of counters, bookshelves, charts, and at least one projection screen lining the walls. From past exposure, Joe knew this to be their one conference room.

"Take a load off," Hawke invited them, waving at the chairs circling the table, whose surface was littered with paperwork, some of which Joe recognized from Brookhaven.

"You want anything to drink?" he asked as they settled down. Both men shook their heads.

David nodded and addressed Joe. "I'm glad you called, to be honest. This whole thing has been so unusual, and is beginning to attract so much attention, that even I was wondering if we shouldn't compare notes."

"You having problems with what was done?" Joe asked, suspicious of Hawke's tone.

But he set them both at ease. "No, no. God, no. The science was top-notch — the kind of stuff I never thought I'd get my hands on, not before I retired, anyhow. I mean, synchrotrons? Copy Number Variations? Sweatprints and touch-DNA? For a guy like me, financed by the state, to get a whiff of some of this is right up there with getting a ride in the space shuttle. Maybe it's only a trip up and back, but, oh, boy," he said, laughing. "What a ride, huh?"

Bill and Joe remained silent, their expressions polite.

Still smiling, David confessed, "Okay, I know. Enough nerdiness. Why don't you start, Joe? You called me, after all. Then I'll tell you what's on my mind."

"You just touched on the biggest thing, David," Joe said. "The press is going crazy and the politicians are ganging up. I just wanted your feedback about what you had me carry down to Long Island. I got the nerdy part," he added quickly, raising his eyebrows. "But I meant the forensics. The publicity'll only get worse, but if we get lucky and pull this crook in, my gut tells me it'll be like a woodchuck version of O. J. Simpson. I'm curious how you feel about that kind of scrutiny, given the route we took with the evidence."

All the glee had faded from Hawke's expression. He looked at Joe carefully. "I did tell you that you can't bring much of this into court. You remember that?"

"Of course," Joe soothed him. "It was along investigative lines I was talking. I've got several dozen people out there right now chasing down gunpowder suppliers, oil undercoaters, acetylene distributors, lumber mills, funeral homes, and Christ knows what else, all based on atom-sized evidence collected by a bunch of wannabe Nobel laureates. You're the one who deals with us day in and day out; you know the scientific standards around which we base our cases. This is the first time I've seen you since Marine and Shepard pulled their rabbits out of the hat."

David was nodding. "Okay. I got it. In short form, I like it. More importantly, I'll defend it if it comes under attack. Fingerprints took forever to meet the legal standard; DNA was a lot faster. It's reasonable to expect that forensic science will be making inroads on a regular basis and that its validity will be increasingly recognized in court. So, the cows are out of the barn; I have no problem lecturing whatever reporter or politician wants to ask me about any of this." He waved his hand over the strewn paperwork before him.

"That's good to hear," Bill murmured.

"True," Joe agreed, "although I didn't have much doubt. You prepared us for that going in. What about the three blood drops, though? At Brookhaven, they wobbled between saying some of the blood came from dead people, or maybe was just left around in the sun too long. I did mention that I had people checking funeral homes and morgues. You think I'm wasting my time?"

Now David began looking vaguely uncomfortable. "Oh, yeah, the degradation and contamination. I looked into those."

Both cops were struck by his tone of voice.

"And?" Joe prompted.

Hawke shrugged awkwardly. "Well, in retrospect, it's a little embarrassing, but after all the data came in, I, too, was struck by those findings, so I did some checking. They seemed so obviously fundamental. Turns out we noticed both artifacts, too, back when we constructed the initial profiles."

"What's that mean?" Bill asked.

"The reason Marine and Shepard were equivocal," David explained, still sounding unhappy, "was because they ended up with the samples. They didn't collect them."

"Why does that matter?" Joe asked.

David tilted his head slightly. "It goes to the degradation. You now know that blood degrades in the body or outside of it and that it's pretty hard to tell which happens where, but there are indicators that help you figure it out — or at least take an educated guess."

"Okay," Joe urged, wondering where this was going.

"Take a drop of blood deposited on a pillow versus one found on a tabletop," Hawke suggested.

Joe began to have an inkling. "Or a forehead," he said.

Hawke nodded. "Or a forehead. The pillow sample soaks in, is sheltered from air and sun to a limited degree, and takes time to dry."

"And degrades in the meantime," Bill contributed, also on board.

"Right," Hawke agreed. "The sample on the flatter, nonabsorbent surface, though, dries pretty quickly and stops degrading almost immediately."

"Especially if that surface is a dashboard, in the cold, in the middle of the night," Joe finished. He looked at Hawke inquiringly. "So, what you're saying," he added, "is that we're on the right track. All three drops were deposited where they would dry quickly, and therefore two of them must've been degraded beforehand, like inside dead people. And to wrap it up even tighter, we have one sample slightly contaminated by one of the others, painting a picture of two bodies lying side by side. What'm I missing?"

"Nothing," Hawke conceded. "It's just that we already knew all that as soon as we received the samples from you, way back when."

There was a stunned silence in the room.

Hawke continued. "Our protocol is to produce a DNA profile and the gender of the donor. That's what you ask for and that's what we give you, along with running the profile through the computers for any hits. The lab technician here who processed all three blood drops noticed at the time not only that one was slightly degraded, but that the other one was even more so. Not only that, he picked up on some DNA white noise in the background of the more degraded sample, although he didn't bother pursuing it. He was following procedure, which is to run the samples a few times more if the results are unsatisfactory to begin with."

"As when they're degraded or dirty?" Bill asked.

"Exactly. The higher end alleles, or genes, if you will, are the ones to go first with degradation, leaving the smaller, molecular alleles. In fact, when the samples are too poor, we can't even enter them into CODIS — the national data bank. We have to settle for just our in-state inventory. That's what happened with the one found on the dashboard. CODIS demands a minimum of ten alleles out of the standard thirteen; we accept a lower threshold, largely because of our much smaller population base."

Joe was studying his friend quizzically, feeling somewhat at sea. "I get it, David, but he was following the rules. Thanks for being embarrassed, and I guess you'll be issuing an interoffice memo for future work, but we figured it out in the end, right?"

"Only because of Brookhaven," Hawke said mournfully.

Joe chose to move on, impatient with this kind of morbid navel-gazing.

"There's something I didn't ask when I was in Long Island," he therefore brought up. "Couldn't they have done a profile of the DNA on the electrical cord? They found genetic material."

"They did get DNA," David agreed, "but

not the kind we enter into our data banks. That's where they can do things I can only dream about. What they found was that the same man left his DNA at both Doreen's and Mary's scenes — on the underwear and the cord, respectively. But they didn't get enough to actually enter it into any system."

"The thirteen alleles you were talking about?" Bill asked.

"Exactly."

Joe was rubbing his temple, trying to extract a memory. "David, I get it that we've got the wrong kind of DNA there. But what about the three blood drops? They're huge and relatively healthy. I know you ran them through the national system and our own and got nothing, but isn't there another way of analyzing them? I thought I read something . . ."

Hawke's face cleared a little as he laughed. "Wow — don't I wish. No, those're all criminal profile databases. We don't know who belongs to those three drops — they're just people, as far as we know."

"He's talking about familial profiles," Bill suggested.

Joe snapped his fingers. "That's what I was looking for. Familial DNA, where one family member shares some of the same profile as another."

Hawke was shaking his head. "God, you guys read too much, or watch too much TV."

"But it's true," Joe protested.

Hawke held up both hands. "It is, it is. You're right."

Joe was on the edge of his seat. "So, hear me out. We have the killer's DNA but can't do anything with it; we have three other DNAs that may not be on record, but we sure as hell know that they were collected and deposited at crime scenes by the killer. Is it an absolute certainty that some relative of even one of them isn't a crook on file?"

Bill and David exchanged glances.

"No," Bill said cautiously.

Joe sat back. "Then let's run all three samples at least through the Vermont database and see if we get lucky. Can't hurt, can it?"

Bill was mulling it over without comment, but Hawke merely shrugged. "We've never done it before. I'll have to run it by the lawyers for permission, but I don't see where it would be a problem."

"It's just knocking on doors," Joe stated. "Like we're already doing."

CHAPTER TWENTY

The Back Stop had always struck Lester as a better name for a bar than a gun store, not that the name sounded all that great for either. Nevertheless, it was Windham County's biggest supplier of weapons, ammunition, and — most importantly to Les — reloading equipment. And in a state unique for its lack of gun laws, that was a statement of substance.

It wasn't located in Brattleboro, the county's anchor town, but west of there, on Route 9, more toward Wilmington and the magnet of the ski resorts sprinkled along the backbone of the Green Mountains, from Massachusetts to Canada, 175 miles to the north. The owners of the Back Stop weren't idiots or woodchucks — they fully appreciated the allure of Vermont romanticism, the appeal of the gun to the American male, and the convenience of being near a cluster of vacation-ready condos. The Back Stop had figured out that while the rest of the family might find joy in visiting outlet stores, spas, ski slopes, or golf courses, the males would eventually find a way to rationalize a trip to a gun emporium.

And Lester had to admit, they'd done a hell of a job. He wasn't a gun fancier himself. He carried one from obligation, qualified with it twice a year, as required, cleaned it perhaps just as often, and otherwise worked hard to forget he even had it. But he conceded that the carefully orchestrated aura of the Back Stop revived the same faint childhood cowboy stirrings in his chest that they clearly did with more gusto in the people he saw trolling the aisles of new and used long guns, occupying an entire wing of the building. The place was dark, woodsy, handsomely dinged and bruised, and smelled of leather, wood, and oil.

Sadly, though, he also knew that the owners weren't locals who'd figured out how to separate well-heeled flatlanders from their cash. They were two Realtors from Stamford, Connecticut, who'd identified an extra wrinkle in the exploitation of Vermont.

Still, he was a realist, and recognized a couple of faces working behind the glass counters. Whoever had set all this up was aiding the local economy, and in a small, rural state of this size, that was only a good thing.

He approached one of the men he knew, who'd once owned a small hardware store before the economy had overwhelmed him.

"Hey, Ed," he said quietly, extending a hand in greeting.

Ed Silverstein cocked his head and smiled. "Detective. It's a real pleasure. How've you been?"

"I'm not complaining. Keeping busy."

"I guess," Ed commented. "They got you working on that triple murder? That sounded terrible."

Les gestured dismissively. "Among other things. It reads worse than it really is. You know newspapers."

Silverstein chuckled. "Oh, yeah. The family okay?"

"They're fine. My son's almost as tall as me now."

The older man laughed outright. "Oh, my God, Lester. No offense, but in your case, that's a scary thing. Does he have to bend over for more oxygen?"

Lester shook his head. "Very good, Ed. I never heard that one before."

Ed looked slightly apologetic. "I'm sorry. I couldn't resist. What can I do you for —

other than more insults from me?"

"No — no problem. I'm too old to be thin-skinned anymore. I need a little research question answered."

Silverstein nodded, his face now serious. "Give me a try."

"I'm wondering about folks who come in here who do their own reloading."

Ed's eyebrows shot up. "I've got just the man for you — he's our specialist. Come with me."

They both walked down the length of the counter, one on each side, until a gap allowed Silverstein to usher Les inside the barrier, and from there to a door leading to an employees-only back room.

They wandered through a storeroom and a shipping area before reaching the store's highly advertised gun repair and customizing section — a large, well-lighted room totally lacking any Vermonty kitsch, lined with workstations and anchored in its middle with several large, felt-covered tables, all covered with guns in various stages of disassembly.

"Jeezum," Les murmured, admiring the contrast with the sales room. "Command Central."

Silverstein glanced over his shoulder as he walked. "This is our version of a casino banking room — where we make all the money. The repairs are reasonable enough. That can be a competitive market. But the custom work? Watch out, credit card!"

He led them to the far end and through one last door labeled "No lighters, matches, or flammables beyond this point. No metals capable of causing a spark."

"Comforting," Spinney commented.

"It is to the guy who works here," Ed agreed.

On the other side of the heavy door, which closed automatically with an airtight sigh behind them, was a room not unlike the one they'd just left, but smaller, laced overhead with heavy-duty fire extinction water piping, and occupied by a single man wearing a soiled lab coat, a face mask, and rubber gloves.

Ed slapped Lester on the back and opened the door again. "I'll leave you two alone — gotta get back to the counter." He pointed to the masked man and made hurried introductions as he turned away. "Les, this is our own Ammo-Mike. Good seeing you again, Les."

Lester muttered something to the closed door before facing his new host, not bothering to offer a hand in greeting. "How're you doin'? Sorry to barge in like this."

The mask stayed in place. "No problem. Who are you?"

Lester smiled. "Right. I guess Ed needs a crash course on manners." He reached into his pocket and pulled out his credentials. "Lester Spinney, VBI."

That caused the face mask to be pulled down to Mike's neck, revealing surprise mixed with a hint of concern — a combination Lester was used to.

"VBI?"

"Nothing serious, and nothing to do with you," Les assured him. "We're just running an investigation that may or may not have something to do with reloaded ammunition. I knew the Back Stop caters to that kind of customer, and Ed brought me to you."

Mike pointed to one of the stools parked by the central table. On shelves all around them were rows of large cans and assorted other containers. Some of them he could tell held powder, brass, or bullets; the rest were a mystery. The heavy worktable itself was a parking zone for arcane equipment, some of it quite large, and all presumably used in the craft of self-loading. Lester, with his lack of knowledge, had no clue about most of it.

"Have a seat."

Lester sat, still wearing his coat. The room

was also quite cool.

The Back Stop technician sat opposite him. "I don't know what I can tell you," he said. "A lot of people load their own ammo. Thousands of them, probably."

"Is it a complicated thing to do?" Les asked. "I've never had anything to do with it."

Mike pulled a long face. "It can be. It's not just black powder shooting that's involved, like people think. More shooters load modern loads than they do muzzle loaders. It's the cost of ammo. Through the roof. If you shoot a lot, it makes sense to buy the equipment and load your own. You could retire the upfront cost in a year or two, depending, and then not only start saving, but start finding out all the ways you can fool with the stuff."

Les furrowed his brow. "How do you mean?"

"Part of the fun," Mike explained, "is combining different bullet weights and styles with different powder loads. You can go crazy with that. And every time you cook up something new, you have to try it out at the range. There, you got interests like rapid firing, distance, accuracy, trajectory, kick, take-down power, and all the rest. And that just sends you back to invent some more recipes. I know people — rich or retired or maybe they just don't have a life — who spend all their time doing this. It's a little crazy."

"But you do it."

Mike laughed. "I'm paid to. I mean, it's interesting, but I'm no nutcase. I used to like it more before I got this job." He waved his gloved hand around to encompass the room.

"So," Lester challenged him, "if it's for do-it-yourselfers, what're you doing here?"

Mike smiled ruefully. "I'm the rich man's loader. Guys from the flatlands call ahead and have me fill a special order for a weekend blowout. Maybe they brag to each other about having custom ammo, or lie that they're doing it themselves. I don't know. It costs them way more than if they just bought it up front from Ed, but to each his own, I guess. I don't try to figure out rich people."

Lester thought back over to the elusive portrait they had so far of their quarry. A rich weekender from Connecticut was not on the A-list.

"How 'bout locals?" he asked. "You get a lot of them?"

"Sure, but I'm not gonna be doin' their loads. They just buy the raw materials from us." He hesitated. "Well, some of them do; the rest'll shop on the Internet, like everybody else."

"But you keep track of the names, I guess," Lester suggested. "So you can send them flyers and junk mail?"

"Sure," Mike agreed. "I mean, I guess so. I don't do that myself."

"But you have lists. Surely."

Mike tilted his head slightly, wondering what the question was. "What's the case, if it involves gunpowder? Sounds unusual."

Lester rose from the stool, nodding. "It is. Wish I could tell you more. Would Ed be the guy to give me your customers?"

"Not really. He's just a counter man. Bill Shiffer does the marketing. Ed'll show you how to find him. You like working for VBI?"

Les paused, halfway to the exit. "Yeah, I do. Good outfit."

"You get all the big cases, right?"

"Yup." Lester resumed his departure, sensing what was coming next — the questions, the I-wanted-to-be-a-cop confessions. He placed his hand on the doorknob.

"You doing those murders that're in the paper?"

"Some of us are," Lester said vaguely. He pulled the door open. "Thanks for your help, Mike."

"Ike," the other man said.

Les stopped. "What?"

The reloader was still seated at the central table. "Ike," he repeated. "Ed slurred his words when he called me Ammo-Ike. That's my nickname here. He made it sound like Ammo-Mike. Happens sometimes. Too many 'M's."

"Ike," Les echoed.

"That's it. Ike Miller. Good luck with Shiffer."

"Thanks," Lester said again, and eased himself out the door.

After his departure, Ike stared at the closed door, as if trying to read its surface.

"I know goddamn well you're working that case," he said under his breath.

He then switched his gaze to the rows of cans, boxes, and bags, and muttered, "But what the hell's gunpowder got to do with it?"

He stood up and walked around the room, thinking hard. He continued talking to himself, "Ike, you may have to start watching your back."

He reached out and removed a .50 bullet, shiny gold and heavy, from a bag at eye level, and hefted it in the palm of one hand, voicing another thought. "Or maybe you should throw a little smoke in their eyes."

■ ■ ■ ■

Joe got out of his car and checked for traffic in both directions. He had just parked on Elliot Street, in Brattleboro, opposite one of the town's taller structures — a seven-story apartment complex reserved mostly for the elderly on limited income. It wasn't much to look at — square in all dimensions — but clad in red brick, like so much else in New England, and a well-known local artifact. As modern as it appeared, it still had been built decades ago, and by now had become part of the social fabric.

He crossed the street. The earlier snow had by now virtually disappeared, aside from a few well-shaded corners where plow trucks had created dirty thaw-proof deposits.

He was here to meet Elise Howard, Mary Fish's companion, who had called to say that she had something to tell him. He'd been surprised by the address change, and had said as much when she'd phoned. Apparently Raddlecup, the school headmaster, had wasted no time in asking her to leave school property, further enhancing the impression he'd left with Joe upon their first meeting. Elise lived on the third floor, on the side of the building overlooking the street. When she opened the door, he'd expected piled boxes and strewn-about packing material. Instead, it was neat, spare, and warm, looking as if she'd been there for years. There were even pictures on the walls, including a significantly sized portrait of Mary, smiling broadly at the camera.

"My Lord," he said, stepping inside. "You move in fast."

"I hate a mess," she admitted. "It used to drive Mary crazy. Back at school, half that little house was filled with her junk — stuff neither one of us really wanted. I just took advantage of the move to throw most of it out. Would you like some tea?"

Joe entered the small living room and took in the simple surroundings, admiring how she'd done such an effective job with so little. "No, I'm all set, thanks. This is really nice."

She sat on the sofa and gestured to an armchair across the coffee table from her. "Please, have a seat."

Leaving his coat on, he settled down and studied her closely. "How're you doing, Elise? Really."

She sighed. "My heart is broken. I feel numb and powerless and spend most of my time wondering why I bother continuing."

He nodded, knowing the sensation well.

"That's partly why I called," she added, surprising him.

"Why's that?" he asked.

"When we spoke in the hospital," she explained, "you asked me two questions I didn't answer truthfully. You asked if there had ever been a hanging in either Mary's or my family, and you asked if what happened to her might have been partly directed at me."

"I remember," he said.

She had been keeping her focus on the small table between them, but now she raised her eyes.

"My mother hanged herself," she told him. "I was a child at the time, and I always thought I was to blame — something my father was happy to let me believe."

"I'm sorry," he murmured.

Her voice was clear, but he noticed that her hands were tightly clenched in her lap. "He was not a nice man, to me or to her, but I was able to get away from him before it got too bad. Maybe my mother killing herself gave me the courage to leave. I'll never know. But I always thought that I had the answer as to why she did it the way she did."

"By hanging?" he asked.

"No. Well, maybe. But I mean the time and place. She made sure that I would be the one to find her, not my father. People said it was monstrous and unbalanced and proved how far over the edge she'd gone, but I knew it was a message to me: Get out now or you'll be next."

Their eyes interlocked, Joe merely nodded.

"That's why I didn't tell you about my mother when you first asked," Elise continued. "I had to be sure in my mind that Mary hadn't done the same thing."

"But I told you she'd been murdered," he protested, his voice very quiet.

"The police tell people all sorts of things," she countered gently.

He was slightly taken aback, less because of the truth of her comment than because of her being the one uttering it. In his mind, he'd always seen her as the more sheltered of the two women. But sheltered obviously didn't mean ignorant, and given what she'd just said, she clearly wasn't that.

"Why did you call me now?" he asked.

"Because of the second thing I avoided," she confessed, her voice beginning to tremble and her eyes to glisten. "I found Mary just as I'd found my mother. At that moment, when I walked into that room, I asked myself what the message was. It lasted only a second, maybe less, before all the rest came caving in — the panic, trying to lift her, being overtaken by grief, now all this numbness. But when you asked me if someone had been trying to get to me by doing that to her . . ."

Her voice trailed off.

"Who do you think it was?" he asked, his body tense with anticipation.

But she disappointed him. Tears now flowing freely down her pale cheeks, she exclaimed, "I don't know, but don't you see? It had to have been somebody who knew me, knew my history, knew that my mother had used herself to guide me away from my father."

"Is that something you've always kept a secret?" Joe asked hopefully.

Again, she let him down, shaking her head. "No. Mary thought I should tell people whenever appropriate, so it came up now and then in company. I've been trying to recall if anyone ever showed a special interest. I knew you'd ask. But I can't think of anyone. These are usually old women I'm talking about — people sitting around over tea, trading intimate details nobody else would care about."

Again, her voice faded away, only this

time, he let her be, in part distracted by the greater impact of what she'd just told him. Up to now, Elise Howard had been the holdout in a theory voiced earlier — that in each of these three homicides, an intimate knowledge of the victim had been displayed in the manner of death.

Joe got to his feet, came around the coffee table, and squeezed Elise's frail shoulder, conscious of the fact that every time they parted ways, he left the poor woman in shambles.

"Thank you, Elise," he said softly. "This was valuable. It'll help a lot. I am so sorry to keep putting you through it, though."

She reached up and patted his hand, although speaking to her own lap. "It's all right. It has to be done."

He showed himself out.

Joe slid behind the wheel and stared out the windshield for a moment, still pondering what he'd learned and how it fit with everything else. Ahead of him, Church Street T-boned into Elliot, where he was parked — an intersection constructed like a river delta meeting the sea, wide and broad, allowing traffic ample room to negotiate.

He started the engine and nosed away from the curb, moving by instinct up

Church, around its short and gradual curve, to where it blended with Green, his own street. Two minutes later, he pulled into his driveway.

Lyn was peeling an orange in his small, low-ceilinged kitchen. "Joe," she said happily, coming into the mudroom section to give him a kiss. "What're you doing home? I didn't think I'd see you till crack of dawn."

Lyn had the shift at her bar tonight, and would have been gone in half an hour, until probably two or three in the morning.

"I took a shot and got lucky," he admitted. "I never know which house you'll be at, but I was around the corner and thought, what the hell."

She kissed him again. "Well, I'm glad you did. You want an orange? Or something hot to drink? I just took the kettle off the stove."

He accepted a cocoa and shucked his coat, moving to one of the stools lining the counter between the kitchen and the living room. There, he watched her move around, preparing his drink, taking in her body language as he had a few years ago, when he'd first seen her tending bar in Gloucester. Who would've guessed?

"What were you doing around the corner?" she asked without turning around.

"I got a call from an earlier witness — the

roommate of the woman we found hanging at the school. She had something to add to what she'd told me back then."

Lyn faced him briefly. "Really? Something she forgot?"

"Something she held back," he admitted, and then told her what had just transpired.

Lyn listened carefully, interrupting rarely, and only for small clarifications, as he detailed how each victim had been accompanied by a bit of theater designed, it seemed, to show that these had not been crimes of chance.

Finally, seated opposite him, she suggested, "You've been trying to connect all three killings. Isn't this what you've been after?"

He didn't disagree. "Maybe, but what is it?"

"Well," she said simply, "if it's a message, it sure as hell wasn't for the dead. So what did it tell the living left behind?"

He merely shook his head before taking a sip of his cocoa.

"Who *was* left behind?" she then asked.

He thought about that. "Mary left Elise, obviously," he began slowly. "Bobby left . . . I don't know. I guess the closest person in his life is Candice. And Doreen . . . Well, her mom's dead."

"But she wasn't right then, correct? She committed suicide."

Joe paused a moment, considering that in a new light. "Right."

Lyn was looking at him. "Three old women," she said.

He didn't answer, the point of her revelation growing in his head.

"You ever run this by them?" she asked.

He rose in his seat enough to lean across the counter and kiss her.

"I will now," he said.

CHAPTER TWENTY-ONE

Candice Clarke had been asleep the last time Joe had visited her home in Post Mills, and he had gathered what he could from his mother.

This time, things were going to have to follow more conventional lines.

Still, Candice and he had known each other since his youth, she and his mother were best of friends, and he saw no reason not to make his return visit as supportive and friendly as possible. He therefore called ahead before he left Brattleboro and, ninety minutes later, collected his mom before arriving at Candice's.

They found her subdued but composed — a small, friendly, gentle woman, as fresh and tidy in appearance as the home around her. She'd laid out little sandwiches and a choice of tea in preparation, and had dressed for the occasion.

To Joe, however, who knew her so well,

Candice's bravery was all in the wrapping. In her eyes, he could see the bafflement, the loss, and the irredeemable pain.

Ushering them in from the cold outdoors, she took their coats, asked for their preferences in food and drink, and made sure they were seated according to their comfort. The small talk went back and forth for a quarter hour, a few safe memories were revisited, and the first few bites of sandwich were complimented.

But the inevitable hung in the air like a mist, and when he felt he could do so with decorum, Joe fixed their hostess with a steady gaze.

"Candice?" he began.

She smiled sadly. "I know. This is not a social call."

"Well, not entirely."

His mother, whose wheelchair had been placed beside her, reached out and silently slid her hand into Candice's.

"What would you like to know, Joseph?"

"It's actually not much to do with Bobby," Joe reassured her. "At least, we don't think it is. Have you been listening to the news at all lately?"

"No," she admitted quietly, her voice barely floating across the utterly still room. "I haven't had the heart."

"I totally understand," he told her. "It has come out, though, that Bob was one of three people killed by the same person."

Her eyes widened. "What? But why? He was just a boy."

"It may have had nothing to do with him," Joe repeated. "We're thinking that Bobby could have been a means to an end."

Candice was shaking her head. "An end? What end? Revenge against Taco Bell? It's crazy."

Joe leaned forward for emphasis. Here, he had to be careful. The emotions were high enough, along with her sense of lapsed responsibility. Candice had taken over Bob's upbringing; she had made it her mission to set things right by doing so. To tell her now that the boy had possibly been killed to get to her — with no proof — would be careless and destructive.

"The three people I'm talking about," he explained slowly, "are Bobby, of course, a woman named Mary Fish, and another named Doreen Ferenc. Are either of those last names familiar?"

Candice paused to think, her head slightly bent as if in prayer. "No," she finally said.

"How about Elise Howard and Maggie Agostini?" he asked.

She gasped and raised her eyes to meet

his. The sadness he saw there caused a skip in his chest.

He reached out at her sudden pallor and touched her shoulder. "Are you all right?" he asked as his mother leaned in from the other side and murmured, "Candice, Candice."

She blinked a couple of times and held her hand up shakily, patting Joe's fingers. "Yes, yes. It's okay. I'm sorry."

"Don't apologize," Joe's mother said, adding without a glance at her son, "and we can stop this immediately if you'd like."

"Absolutely," he echoed.

"No," Candice said. "I'm fine. It was just a shock, hearing those names from so long ago. That horrible time. I did all I could to forget it . . ."

Joe remained silent, the obvious nature of his next question making the phrasing of it superfluous.

Candice didn't move for a few moments, collecting her thoughts.

"We were all on a bus trip," she eventually began. "It was one of those social things — the garden club. Something like fifteen women and a few family members, all packed together for a weekend to Burlington — two days of plays and museums and a boat ride out on Lake Champlain. It was supposed to be the highlight of the summer . . ."

"How long ago was this?" Joe asked in barely a whisper.

"Seventeen years this past August," she answered without hesitation.

"Something went wrong," he suggested.

She nodded. "Oh, yes. One of the women, Gini Coursen, had brought her son along, a crude and swaggering boy named Ben. An awful person, it turned out later, but at the time just someone who seemed like so many other boys who are careless and a little stupid. He'd gotten in trouble with the police — nothing very serious, according to Gini — and she'd brought him for the change of scenery. I remember her using that phrase. He was eighteen."

"Was his last name Coursen, too?"

This had come from Joe's mother, who was intently studying her friend's profile. Joe smiled at the question, and considered how many times he'd felt her influence upon him in how he conducted his job.

"Miller," Candice said. "Benjamin Steven Miller. Lord knows, I heard that often enough."

"What did he do?" Joe asked.

"He raped a girl," she told them simply. "One of the other children on the bus. Actually, it was Betty Frasier's niece — a sweet, frail girl named Alice. On the morning of the second day — we'd been put up in a motel south of Burlington — Betty found Alice crying in her room but couldn't find out why. The poor girl was a wreck and we were terribly concerned. Betty came to us — that is, me, Maggie, and Elise — and asked for our help. The four of us met with Alice, telling the bus tour to go on without us, and we spent hours with the child, trying to get her to open up."

Candice sighed heavily. "She did at last," she continued, "and told us everything. Benjamin had become friendly the night before, and had tried to get fresh. She'd told him no, and had gone to her room to go to bed. Of course, he followed her, and forced his way in when she opened the door . . ." Her voice trailed off.

Joe exchanged glances with his mother and raised his eyebrows wonderingly, but she minutely nodded, encouraging him to keep going.

"What did you do next?" he asked.

"We went to the police," she said. "We talked and talked, and did our best to involve Alice. We were hoping that it might help her, at least a little. We knew it could never be taken away, but maybe it might start getting her back on her feet."

Joe's mother looped her arm awkwardly across Candice's trembling shoulders and murmured, "Keep going, Sweetie. Get it out."

Candice nodded and spoke, her voice broken and weak. Her eyes once more bore into Joe's. "I am so sorry, Joseph, but I think it was the worst thing we could have done. And now, with what you've told me, I think that even more."

"What happened, Candice? Did they drop the ball?"

She shook her head emphatically. "Oh, no. I wish they had. They pulled over the bus, they questioned everybody, they arrested Ben. The motel room was searched and evidence found. Ben eventually confessed. He went to jail for the rest of his life, as things turned out."

Joe frowned. "What? I'm not sure . . ."

"He died in prison," she explained. "That was years later. I don't know the details. I heard it by accident and never pursued it."

Joe's mom had been rubbing Candice's back with her open palm, and now offered her a Kleenex from her purse.

"Candice . . ." Joe began, but again, she interrupted him.

"She killed herself. Alice did. All the attention — the police, the prosecutor, the lawyers, the judge. She had to explain again and again what had happened, reliving it every time. It was too much. And Betty followed a few months later, of a heart attack, although we all knew what caused that. She'd never been sick a day in her life."

She paused to dab at her eyes and blow her nose. "I understand that things are better now," she then said. "That there are special police officers and laws to handle these things better. But back then . . ."

He was already nodding. "I know. I understand, Candice."

"And now you tell me," she resumed, "that Bobby was killed for the same reason." She spread her hands, the tears flowing once more. "How could that be? How could something so long ago . . . ? We were all trying to do the right thing, to help a poor girl in trouble. And now, so many people dead; so many broken hearts . . . What happened, Joseph? How did it all happen?"

He was starting to have a pretty good idea. The thread they'd all been searching for, from the moment Doreen's murder had been linked to Mary Fish's, and from there to Bobby Clarke's, was beginning to emerge in his mind like a shape looming out of the fog. The problem all along, of course, had been a simple matter of focus — they'd been analyzing the victims, trying to establish a common link, and missing the second rank of walking wounded. These were the people who'd been left alive to suffer, and presumably the intended targets all along.

Just as someone else had been left to suffer in the course of Candice's story.

"What happened to Benjamin Miller's mother?" he asked. "What was her name? Gini Coursen?"

Candice straightened, stopped her crying, and stared at him wide-eyed. "Oh, my God."

"What?" her best friend asked.

"Do you think she had anything to do with this?" Candice asked.

He shook his head cautiously. "I don't know what to think right now," he stressed. "I'm hearing this for the first time. For all I know, Gini Coursen's dead. Do you know otherwise?"

Candice blew her nose again. "No. I'm sorry. The last time I saw her, I'll never forget. It was in the courtroom, right after the sentencing. She was screaming at us — Elise, Maggie, Betty, and me. She called us terrible things, and said awful things about poor Alice. How Alice had lured her son into a trap; how Betty had trained her to do so; how we'd all conspired to put him in jail and ruin her life. It was insane. They finally pulled her out of the room."

In the brief silence that followed, Candice passed her hand across her forehead, as if wishing for the removal of all that was pressing against it from within.

When she spoke again, her voice, though still soft, was clear and direct. "Gini said she'd make us pay. I think she was true to her word."

Joe wasn't about to argue.

"Can you hear me?" Joe took the cell phone away from his ear and stared at it, as if he'd find a wire dangling loose or a gerbil in need of food.

"God damn it," he muttered and watched the small screen for the appearance of any tiny bars. They cropped into view at the crest of the hill, where he gave up and pulled over into the interstate's breakdown lane.

"You still there?" he asked Sammie. He'd found her at the office in Brattleboro, where he knew she and Spinney had been combing through an ever-growing pile of employee and customer rosters.

"Loud and clear now," she answered. "What was that name? Gini what?"

"Coursen." He spelled it out. "You'll have

332

to run it through Spillman to get her DOB, but look for an elderly woman. More to the point is the next name: Benjamin Steven Miller. He's definitely in the system — died in jail a while back; I don't know when. He was inside probably for aggravated sexual assault. Those names are mother and son, by the way, which means that if you can't find her normally, she might be listed with him as a person of interest."

"Got it," Sam responded. He could hear in the background both her typing and her restrained note of impatience.

"Sorry," he responded to the latter. "I know you know all that. Anyhow, they're the ones we've been looking for. Ben raped a girl on a bus tour outing to Burlington almost twenty years ago. Most of the other passengers were old ladies blowing off steam, and three of them — Elise Howard, Candice Clarke, and Maggie Agostini — helped to put Benny in the slammer."

"Which pissed off Mom big time," Sam guessed.

"Right. Whether she killed our vics or not, I don't know, but whoever did apparently wanted the three ladies to suffer as Gini Coursen had suffered — by losing a loved one and living with the pain."

"Jesus," Sam said softly.

"So you know what to do: Tear apart that family and find out who fits the profile we've got with the oak wood, the gunpowder, the acetylene, access to blood samples, and everything else. At least one name's got to surface on those lists you've been building."

"Roger that, boss. By the way, you might want to check your phone messages. David Hawke's been trying to get in touch. He wouldn't tell me why."

"Okay. Thanks."

Joe snapped the phone shut and then reopened it to navigate through the commands to his voice mailbox, hitting several wrong buttons and cursing along the way. He saw the purpose of all these computers, PDAs, and electronic gadgetry, and used them as best he could, which he knew wasn't all that well. But in his heart, he didn't like them. They offered too much access, and deprived him of the silence and privacy that he used to enjoy to simply think. He'd tried playing the game of limiting his availability, but after a chorus of "Turn on your cell phone," he'd finally given in to the fate of always being a call away.

Which, of course, also had its advantages. Smiling ironically, he dialed David Hawke's number.

"Joe," answered the scientist happily, his tone betraying no sense of intrusion whatsoever. "Thanks for calling back."

From his point on the crest of the hill, Joe could see southward down several miles of gently winding Connecticut River. Near Ascutney Mountain, the Connecticut Valley opened up to offer some of the best that this region had to offer photogenically — rolling farms, silvery ponds, the occasional proud church spire, gleaming white. He'd always thought that if this wasn't balm for the soul in all of us, the species was indeed in dire shape.

"No problem, David," he answered his friend. "What's up?"

"It's that little assignment you requested when you were up here — the familial DNA search, using the three drops of blood? It takes a while, as you can imagine. We're trying to locate at best something like twenty-five percent matches, rather than the perfect fits we're usually after, but we got lucky."

"How so?"

"It's called an off-lateral allele," Hawke explained. "I won't bore you with the technical details, but it's like an aberration in the DNA profile, and it's pretty rare. If we find one, like we did, then instead of going through thousands of comparison profiles, we only look for ones that also have off-lateral alleles."

"And you found one?"

"We did," he admitted. "It lines up very nicely with the blood drop that the Brookhaven folks thought might fit a black man with cancer."

Joe fumbled to pull his notepad and pen out of his pocket. "What's the name?" he asked.

"Peter Hildreth," was the answer. "He was put in the system eight years ago for aggravated assault. He maxed out his jail time, from what I was told, so Parole and Probation has nothing current on him, but he was last known living in your neck of the woods, which isn't too surprising."

"You have an address?" Joe asked.

Hawke gave him a number on Sak Road in Vernon, a town south of Brattleboro most famous for its power plant.

"This is great, David. You have anything else on this guy?"

"I both faxed it to your office and sent you an e-mail attachment," Hawke told him. "I thought you'd prefer that over scribbling down notes on the phone."

Joe stopped doing just that, remembering his thoughts on the world of electronics moments earlier. "Point taken," he said with a laugh. "I'm heading south right now. I owe you big time."

"Always a pleasure," was the response. "It's nice when the planets line up."

Joe snapped the phone shut again and nosed into traffic once more, musing about how often good celestial alignments for some could spell bad luck for others.

That was certainly what he was hoping for now. They were long overdue for a break.

Chapter Twenty-Two

Vernon was a curious town. Lacking a traditional town center, and substituting a bland hodgepodge of buildings to house its police, library, and town offices, it had a power plant to give it identity. But this was no pestilence-belching, ancient coal burner — dark, sooty, and brooding. This was the same Vermont Yankee with its headquarters in Brattleboro — a huge, looming, concrete-hued nuclear facility with the obligatory cooling towers looking like outer space transplants. Yankee had made of its host town an odd contradiction of model community and hotbed of controversy.

The first badge had come from an early Big Brother benevolence, typical of the largesse of many newcomer capitalist endeavors. In the early 1970s, Yankee had invaded southeastern Vermont with its pockets bulging. Schools were helped, local ambulances purchased, sports fields built, hospital wings funded, and dozens of floundering community projects assisted. There seemed to be no end to the gravy train. In some respects, being Vermont Yankee's home base was like having — out of the blue — an ice cream–loving, Rolls Royce–riding child maharaja arrive in the neighborhood with a passion for distributing his family's assets among the local folk. In ever-widening concentric circles, starting with Vernon, people and struggling organizations throughout the county — governmental, altruistic, and entrepreneurial — began looking at Vermont Yankee as a cash cow of unimaginable dimensions.

Which is precisely what froze the hearts of local outspoken environmentalists. Over the ensuing decades, in busloads and parades, carrying placards and bags of fake blood, yelling, chanting, and being dragged off in handcuffs, this ragtag army of protesters brought varying degrees of attention to their cause and their source of ire. As a result, Vermont Yankee either saved your life or threatened to end your world, but it was rarely held in neutral regard.

And Vernon was stuck, hapless in the middle, between the wooing of the early days and the dread of a gloomy future, for it turned out that benevolence and nuclear plants have life expectancies. And VY's was nearing expiration, making of Vernon an erstwhile smudge on the map that might soon be facing the fate of the dodo bird.

Willy, of course, had his own take on it all. "They should've told those assholes to shove their millions and slammed the door in their faces — stayed the goat fuckers they were to start with."

He and Joe were driving to the Sak Road home of Peter Hildreth, whose blood was genetically tied to the drop they'd found decorating Doreen's forehead.

"A lot of people were helped with that money," Joe commented.

Willy twisted in the passenger seat to stare at him. "Oh, my God. Is this the man who used to sleep with our future governor? A closet toady of capitalist pigs? No wonder Miss Hug-the-Trees threw you out. And you told us she couldn't live with the stress of your job. What a crock."

Joe smiled at the outburst. "Are you done?"

Willy pulled out his phone. "Done? I'm calling the media."

"She's not the governor yet," Joe said obliquely.

Willy pocketed the phone, his smile widening. "Oh, oh. Don't tell me you're voting for the other guy."

Joe rolled his eyes. "I'm just saying it'll be close. And you should talk. Why're you bashing Big Business? I thought you'd be delighted with what they've done."

Willy snorted. "I don't give a rat's ass about the environmental crap. That's all he-said, she-said to me. I am suspicious of anyone who buys affection, and I hate people who trade their self-respect. As far as I'm concerned, both the town and the plant deserve each other."

Joe didn't respond, knowing better than to feed such a conversation. Willy was many things, including a man of integrity and strength. But he'd come to it the hard way, and harbored some rigid, close-minded principles as a result.

The bland countryside drifted by. The hilly terrain making Vermont famous was considerably diminished in Vernon, being close to the Massachusetts border and the banks of the Connecticut River. That's what had made it so attractive to the state's first settlers, when they built Fort Dummer on the water's edge in the early 1700s.

On the other hand, the irony of Vernon's current plight — being at the mercy of the now aging and endangered enterprise that had made it rich beyond its means — could be glimpsed in the fate of that original fort. The actual historic site was underwater today, a victim of the Vernon Dam, built around 1910.

And so it goes, Joe thought, turning off the main artery of Route 142 and onto Pond Road. Call it progress if you will.

In some ways, he mused, taking in surroundings so rural as to defy the suburban label some Brattleboro residents applied to Vernon, it was an odd magnet for so much heated attention. It wasn't surprising that Vermont Yankee was always pictured when this town was featured in the news — there wasn't that much else to photograph.

They took two turns off of Pond to finally enter Sak Road, and up to a modest but well-maintained trailer, about two hundred yards along.

"What do we know about Peter Hildreth?" Willy suddenly asked as Joe pulled over to the side of the road, clear of the house's narrow dirt driveway. There was an old Chevy sedan beside the trailer.

"I ran him through Spillman," Joe began, killing the engine. "He did time five years ago for aggravated assault — some bar brawl in Bellows Falls. That's how we got his blood on file. Other than that, he's pretty run-of-the-mill — a couple of domestics, some neighbor complaints now and then, a DUI."

"Married?"

Joe opened his door. "The computer said he wasn't; he may have been, considering the two domestics."

"I saw a woman's face looking out at us," Willy told him over the roof of the car.

They crossed to the trailer as its flimsy front door opened to reveal an angular blond woman with a hollowed-out, tired face.

"Who're you?" she asked without preamble or real show of interest.

"Police," Willy answered, flashing his badge.

"Great," she said. "He rob a bank or something? That would be a laugh."

"Why?" Joe asked.

" 'Cause he can barely move. What do you want?"

Joe gave her a sympathetic smile. "Must be tough. What happened?"

"Has its moments. Dumb bastard broke his leg. You didn't answer my question."

Willy laughed. "I like that."

"Good for you," she said, still looking at Joe.

"We'd like to talk with him, ma'am," he said, adding, "Assuming we're talking about

Peter Hildreth."

This time, she smiled, if barely. "Right. That would be embarrassing, wouldn't it?"

He nodded. "A bit."

She glanced at Willy. "You gonna threaten me or something? You look like the type."

Willy was enjoying himself. "Nope. I'm like him. You don't want to know why we're here, we'll just take off."

That got her interest. "You want to hassle him for something?"

"We need his help," Willy admitted. "A drop of blood led us here."

That disturbed her demeanor. It also caused a voice to slip by her. A man asked, "What the hell's that mean?"

"Mr. Hildreth," Joe spoke to the shadow now looming behind the woman. "We're in a jam and we need your help. We think a family member of yours may be in trouble."

A tall black man appeared beside the woman, his right leg in a cast. "What family member?"

"That's what we'd like to find out."

The couple exchanged looks. The blond shrugged. "You have to admit, at least they're original."

They stepped back as the man said, "Come in."

Willy and Joe climbed the metal steps in

single file and entered a neat, spare living room with a large, muted television facing a couch banked with a pile of carefully placed pillows, obviously designed to support Hildreth's leg as he watched the set. Football players were running across a field bordered with stands jammed with silently cheering people.

"Good game?" Joe asked.

"College," Hildreth answered. "I like it better than pro ball. You want coffee?"

Both cops shook their heads.

"Sit," the blond woman instructed them.

They complied, choosing armchairs, as Peter Hildreth settled back onto his couch and raised his leg with a wince.

"What happened?" Willy asked.

Hildreth grimaced. "Fell off those god-damned steps. Stupid as hell. So, what about this family member of mine?"

"Let me start over," Joe began. "I'm Joe Gunther and this is William Kunkle. We're from the VBI, which as you probably know only takes on major cases, so why we're here is pretty important. I hope you'll understand, therefore, if I ask you for some form of identification."

Without comment, Hildreth extracted a wallet and tossed it to Joe, who opened it to the driver's license tucked behind a scratched plastic protector. Joe half rose and returned it to him. "Thanks. Sorry for the formality."

"It's okay," he said, replacing the wallet.

"Ma'am?" Willy addressed the woman.

She smirked at him. "I don't think so."

"I'm sorry?" he said.

"You may be, but you can't have my ID. I'm in my own house here, and you're guests. Live with it."

Joe was impressed by Willy's self-restraint.

He shrugged and said, "You got it."

Joe addressed Hildreth's earlier question. "We're investigating a crime where a drop of blood surfaced that didn't make any sense to us. We had to find out who it belonged to and so we ran it through the state data bank. We didn't get a direct hit, but enough of one to discover that it belongs to a male relative of yours. Mr. Hildreth, do you have a brother?"

Hildreth let out a little snort. "Call me Peter. I used to have a brother — not much left of him now."

"Cancer?" Joe asked.

Hildreth's eyebrows rose. "How'd you know that?"

"That was in the blood, too, duh," answered the woman, her scorn undisguised.

Joe nodded. "It looked pretty serious."

"Leukemia," Hildreth conceded. "He doesn't have much time left."

"You two close?" Joe asked.

But the woman overrode his answer. "How the hell does Robert's blood get at a crime scene? He's been sick a long time."

"We don't know," Joe told her. "That's part of the puzzle. We would sure like to talk with him to find out, though, in case someone's trying to frame him."

"To hell with 'em, Peter," the woman urged her companion. "Robert's in enough trouble anyhow. Who cares about a drop of blood?"

But Peter was smiling. "You shitting me? He'd love this. It's right up his alley."

"That is *so* not true," she countered. "The man's paranoid about his privacy. You think he's gonna like the cops telling him they traced his blood all the way to his bedside? That'll flip him out totally."

"It'll do him good," Peter argued and addressed Joe. "He's at BMH, in Bratt — under Robert Jones. It's really Hildreth, but like she says, he's a little paranoid."

The woman, who'd been leaning against the wall throughout the conversation, straightened and glared at Peter. "You are such a shit sometimes." She began walking down the length of the trailer, talking angrily as she went, "The poor dumb slob is dying, and you still have to fuck with him. No wonder he never liked you."

The door at the far end of the room slammed behind her.

In the stillness following her departure, Joe muttered, "Sorry about that."

Hildreth let out a short laugh. "You kidding? That was nothing. I fell off the steps because she pushed me."

"I'll be damned," Lester said under his breath.

"What'd you find?" Sam asked from across the office. Each of them was sandbagged by a semicircle of piled folders, making their desks look like machine-gun nests. They were the clearing house for every officer in the field combing establishments that could have produced Brookhaven's trace evidence. New folders containing lists of customers, clients, subscribers, practitioners, employees, and patients seemed to arrive hourly.

He held up a sheet of paper. "This one. He's on a list of somebody named Schuyler Thurber's customers."

"Yeah," she said. "Friend of mine; runs an oil undercoating shop. What's the name?"

Les held up another page. "He's on this

one, too. Part-time hospital employees, as a per diem janitor. And I talked to him at the Back Stop gun store. I met the man. I think we got a winner."

"Sky?" Sammie asked, looking confused.

"No." He shook his head emphatically. "The one on both lists and who works around gunpowder all day — Ike Miller."

He gave her a broad smile. "We just earned a field trip."

Robert "Jones" Hildreth was in a hospice room at the hospital, although it proved difficult to get in to see him. Apparently, his thirst for privacy had been all but injected into his caregivers. Instead of simply poking his head in the door, as planned, Joe had to work through legal channels to even approach the man.

That, as it turned out hours later, proved less than worth the effort.

Hildreth's back was propped against a snowbank of pillows, much as his brother's leg had been perched on one earlier, but where Peter had offered the world a sort of weary amusement, Robert's energies were wholly given over to anger.

"What do you want?" he demanded testily as soon as Joe came into view.

Joe had left Willy in the hallway, for obvious reasons.

"I'm the police officer I think your lawyers told you about, Mr. Hildreth," he said.

That, of course, was his first mistake.

"How do you know my name? And where the hell *are* my lawyers?"

Hildreth was so thin, he barely made a lump under the sheet. His gaunt face was skintight and bony, his dark cheekbones flushed with fury.

Joe sat on the windowsill by the bed, choosing to get straight to the point. "Sir, that's what I'm here to tell you. We found a sample of your blood at a crime scene recently. Understandably, we're trying to find out how it got there."

Hildreth's reaction caught him off guard. He seemed to levitate, if slightly, with rage, and poked a skeletal finger at Joe. "How did you trace that blood to me?"

Joe's eyes widened slightly. "Ahh, we ran it through the state data bank. Found your brother, and through him, we found you."

"Peter?" he screamed faintly, suddenly grabbing his chest. "That son of a bitch."

A nurse stepped into the room. "Is everything all right?"

"No, it is not," Hildreth yelled at her, and began to cough.

The nurse looked at Joe apologetically.

350

"I'm sorry, sir, but . . ."

Joe was already standing. "Not to worry. I understand. Mr. Hildreth, I'm sorry to have upset you."

But Hildreth was coughing too harshly to care any longer.

Willy was slouching in the hallway outside, his good elbow propped on the nurse's counter. "Shoulda had me in there with you, boss."

Joe was still shaking his head slightly. "Why's that?"

"I woulda given him a good slap."

Joe paused to admire his colleague. "You're just saying that 'cause you know I love it so much, right?"

Willy straightened and raised an eyebrow. "I take it he didn't say anything the whole hospital didn't hear."

"You got that right."

They walked down the hall together, by a janitor holding a mop standing off to one side, half hidden by a wheeled crash cart parked against the wall.

The janitor waited until they'd passed and then, abandoning his mop, strolled down to where a group of nurses was standing just outside Hildreth's room.

"Wow," he said to the first one as he approached, "that was some blow-out."

The nurse shook her head angrily. "What was the point? Goddamn cops. They come in like storm troopers and get what? Nothing. The man's dying, for God's sake. Let him be."

"They were cops?" the man asked.

"Yeah. Vermont Bureau of Investigation," another chimed in. "Big frigging deal. Think they're the FBI or something."

"They're not that bad," a third said. "They used to be Bratt cops. Jones is a pain — you know that. He screams at us all the time. I felt sorry for Joe."

"Joe who?" the janitor asked.

"Gunther," she volunteered. "He's the older one. The one with the gimpy arm actually is a jerk. That's Kunkle. But Joe's a sweetheart."

"Why would they want to talk to someone on this floor?" the janitor persisted. "Aren't they all dying?"

"They are that," the first nurse agreed. "They wanted to talk to him about a drop of blood or something. I didn't hear everything, but it sounded weird to me."

"A drop of blood?" the man repeated.

"Yeah. Funny, huh? Given the pints we've extracted from that man for one test or another, a single drop is like a joke."

The janitor began retreating down the hallway, looking grim and distracted.

"Where're you going, Ike?" one of the women asked. "You want to have lunch with us? It's almost noon."

"No thanks," he said, not looking back. "There's something I gotta do."

CHAPTER TWENTY-THREE

Gail Zigman smiled broadly, waved both hands in the air in a broad farewell, and stepped back from the speaker's podium. Before her, the assembled audience was seated around a scattering of dinner tables, clapping enthusiastically, but making her think of frogs clinging to lily pads.

"What's next?" she asked the young woman perpetually at her elbow. She was named Sally, had been supplied by a Democratic organization from outside the state, and had never even been to Vermont before joining the campaign. But she was enthusiastic, bright, and highly organized. She was also both Gail's scheduler and primary late-night chauffeur. Gail kept forgetting her last name.

"This is almost it for tonight," Sally told her, guiding her off to the left of the stage and toward a door on the north wall of the banquet room. Gail was pretty sure they were at the Sheraton in Burlington, but was wondering if it wasn't actually the Rutland Holiday Inn. She didn't bother asking. In a few minutes, they would be back on the road anyhow.

"We have a small press conference just outside," Sally was saying. "After that, it's a two-hour drive to St. J. You have an early-morning Rotary there tomorrow. We thought it would be better to travel tonight and let you sleep till five-thirty. Keep you fresh."

Gail laughed. "Right. You guys are spoiling me rotten."

They stepped through the side door, into a small semicircle of journalists. A couple of lights had been set up by the hotel to help the photographers, but they made it hard for Gail to see the faces opposite her.

"How's your confidence level, Ms. Zigman?" came an anonymous voice.

Gail resisted shielding her eyes, hearing the cameras clicking and knowing how she'd look in the morning papers.

She smiled brightly. "My opponent's latest comments about teacher/student ratios made pretty clear how out of touch he's become with the true interests of Vermont voters. I think even *he's* begun to realize that it's time for a change."

There were several chuckles, accompanied

by, "Gail, the Woodchuck Blogger wrote this morning that a member of the Brattleboro Women First organization was complaining how you, as a rape victim, weren't making sexual abuse of women a big enough issue in your campaign. How do you respond?"

"The Woodchuck Blogger won't even identify himself," she reacted. "And now he's — or she's — supposedly reporting on the basis of another anonymous source. Is this guy afraid to leave the house, or what?" She allowed for more titters before resuming. "I am a survivor of rape. That is a fact. It is not a personality trait. I have addressed the subject of sexual violence against women, and children, and the elderly, and the mentally challenged, just as I have addressed many other crucial issues in our culture. But I will not be a single issue candidate because of a personal misfortune. I owe the voters of this great state more than that, and I think they have come to expect more of me."

"What about the bill currently being considered banning cell phone use by drivers?"

Gail reached into her jacket pocket and extracted her own phone. "I darn near live by this thing. I text on it, speak on it, access my e-mail on it. I told it to do my laundry the other day, with mixed results. But I do not drive while using it. I think that's dangerous, and I think doing so should be against the law."

"You're wearing pants suits a lot lately. Are you trying to imitate Hillary Clinton?"

"They're comfortable in cold weather. I'll start wearing skirts when you do, Jim."

"Jyll Ivory says you're a Republican in Democratic clothing and that you've compromised away your principles."

Gail forcefully responded, "Jyll Ivory is a smart, ambitious, take-no-prisoners poster child of the Progressive Party. I admire and respect her intellect. She's not a college professor for nothing. But she's never held elective office, never had to haggle to get anything done, never worked for an hourly wage, and never understood the value in occasionally settling for a seventy-five percent victory instead of pridefully walking away from the table, her head held high, with a one hundred percent failure. Vermonters are practical people; they like getting things done, even if the results aren't always neat and shiny and pure as the driven snow."

"A dying man named Robert Hildreth filed an invasion of privacy suit today against the Department of Public Safety," a male voice said from the back. "He said that the crime lab, by request of the VBI, had ordered a familial DNA search done of a blood sample within the state's criminal DNA database. Mr. Hildreth says that he's on his deathbed with cancer, cherishing what little time he has left, and that he's being harassed by the police simply because his brother's biological information is on file."

Gail cast Sally a quick look, who murmured, "I don't know anything about this."

"What's your question?" Gail asked, trying not to squint into the glare. She was now pretty sure she recognized the Fox News reporter assigned to cover the campaign.

The answer wasn't what she wanted to hear. "The police officer behind it all was VBI field force commander Joe Gunther, with whom you once had a long-term romance. Is there any chance this old relationship has influenced your silence on what is clearly an invasion of privacy issue?"

"My silence, as you put it," she countered, "has nothing to do with anyone's influence, Mr. Granierre. This happens to be the first I've heard of this issue. I'll look into it immediately and share my thoughts with all of you tomorrow."

Sally stepped up beside her and leaned into the microphones. "The future governor has a long drive ahead of her . . ."

"Surely you have an opinion," Granierre shouted over her. "Invasion of privacy is just that. It is what it is."

Gail put her hand on Sally's shoulder to show command. "But what, precisely, is this, Mr. Granierre? Everyone who stands before a judge pleads innocence. Does that mean it's true? Sometimes yes, and some-times no. Let's get all the facts here first, before leaping to conclusions. You may want a quick and thoughtless knee-jerk reaction, good for one of your famous sound bites. The voters of Vermont deserve better. Thank you for your questions. I'll see you all tomorrow. Drive safely on your way home."

She stepped back and swung in behind Sally to quickly march down the hallway toward the rear exit into the parking lot.

Outside, braced by a wall of cold night air, she waited until she heard the door slam behind them before pulling out her phone and sighing, "I guess I better call Joe."

Gini Coursen watched her son hurriedly coming in and out of the kitchen, carrying items from various parts of the house and dumping them onto the breakfast table.

"Tell me what's happening, Ike."

"Nothing, Ma. I just have to go for a while."

Her voice climbed a note. "For a while? What am I supposed to do? I need you."

Ike froze in midmotion for a second, his hands trembling with frustration. He didn't want to tell her that only his part of the plan had gone wrong. "Call Louise. I don't know. She'll take care of you."

"She will not. She's a lazy bitch who steals my stuff."

Ike turned on her and yelled into her face. "I don't know, Ma. I'm not your nurse."

She grabbed his arm and froze him with a hard, calculating look. "What went wrong? Something went wrong."

"The cops're getting wise."

"What's that mean?"

"I almost bumped into a couple of them at the hospital," he answered vaguely.

"So what? They don't know about you."

Ike pulled away violently. "That's easy for you to say," he screamed, red-faced. "You're not the one whose butt's in a sling."

Almost as quickly, his mother changed back to the needy supplicant. "Honey, honey. You're my reason for living. You don't think I know what you've done for me? You turned my life around, righting the wrong that was done to Benny."

She caught up one of his hands in her own. "You gave me hope that there was justice in the world. How else was I going to get back at those bitches — do unto them as they did unto me? Stuck in this damn house . . ."

Almost reluctantly, he squeezed her hand in turn. "I know, Ma."

"So," she tried again. "Why do you think those cops were interested in you?"

"One of them came by the gun shop earlier," he admitted, feeling on slightly safer ground. "I don't know why. He was looking for customer lists. But he was definitely working on the murders; he got all vague when I asked him."

"That may not mean much," she said thoughtfully, gazing off. "They're looking at everything right now. They're confused. And that call to the paper you made was a stroke of genius, putting even more pressure on them."

He paused a moment, as if doubting himself, and then rallied, crossing to the living-room section of the room, opening the drawer to the small table by the couch, and extracting an old Colt .45 he kept there.

"Still, I gotta get out of here, just in case."

He held up his hand to interrupt his mother, whose mouth had opened in protest.

"Ma, damn it all. The two places where I work, they show up. That's more than coincidence. If they come by here for some reason, I better be gone. You just tell 'em you haven't seen me. I'll take one of the beaters outside they can't trace to me. They got no bone to pick with you. And I know what you think about Louise. Maybe I'll try to drop in now and then, when I know the coast is clear."

He reached for a duffel bag he'd previously dumped on the floor and began stuffing it full, adding a short, semiautomatic assault rifle that he'd placed on the table previously, along with several boxes of ammunition.

"Don't you worry, Ma. This'll blow over soon enough. We can get back to life as usual, and you'll know that the whole thing with Benny was set right."

She smiled for his sake and nodded complacently. He was correct about the last part. Her firstborn, the only living creature she'd ever truly loved, had at least been avenged, even if he'd never return to her. But Ike was living in a dream world if he thought this would blow over. She knew cops. They didn't quit.

And this bunch sounded like they were on to something.

She watched her son finishing his packing, heading for God knew where. She didn't want to know. Nor would she truly miss him, except for his general usefulness. He was as much a bore as he was handy to have around.

Well, she thought, you take the bitter with the sweet. That's what they say.

Joe and Willy pulled up next to Sam's car in the parking lot. Lester was beside her in the passenger seat. They were outside a convenience store in West Brattleboro, where they'd decided to meet by phone, partway between Brattleboro and Wilmington, which Sam and Les had just left. It was dark, and unseasonably cold, but at least with no more snow in the forecast.

They'd parked cop-style, driver's door to driver's door, so that Joe and Sam were inches apart. In the sodium lamplight flooding the gas pumps beyond, Joe was struck by Sammie's appearance.

"You okay?"

She shook her head. "Fine. I got a bug, is all. It'll pass."

"Don't breathe on me," Willy told her across Joe.

"Nice," Joe commented, before returning to Sam. "What've you got?"

"Ike Miller," Spinney said. "I met him at the Back Stop when I was checking out gunpowder suppliers. He gave me a crash course on reloading and sent me out to the front office for a list of customers. Nothing went off in my head. We just got back from there; he's gone. My contact, Ed Silverstein, said he called in and quit, just like that, and to mail him his last paycheck."

"He lives with his mother off of Augur Hole Road," Sam chimed in. "Somewhere in the boonies. Also has a part-time job at BMH as a janitor, which gives him access to both blood and the basement morgue, and he had his car oil-undercoated by Sky Thurber. So far, he's the only one to fit so much of the Brookhaven profile."

"BMH," Willy repeated tellingly.

"What?" Sam asked, reading into his tone of voice.

Joe told her, "We just left the owner of one of those three blood drops — he's in a hospice room at BMH. The nurses told us they used to draw blood from him all the time, because of his leukemia."

"That's the other thing we found out," Lester chimed in. "Once we made the BMH connection, I got hold of its morgue records.

A week before Dory was killed, both a male and a female were in cold storage at the same time. The woman was a blond with blue eyes and the guy had been dead longer than her by a couple of days."

"I'm guessing you ran Ike through the computer?" Joe asked.

"Six ways toward the middle," Les admitted. "Standard bad boy stuff — disorderly, DUI, petit larceny, minor possession, simple assault, lots of person-of-interest references. No jail time and no felonies."

"We also put the word out to all our people," Sam added, "to run the name Ike Miller through any lists they haven't submitted yet. We haven't heard back, but that just happened. He's clearly on the lam, though, for what that's worth."

"Because of the Back Stop?" Joe asked.

"And BMH," Les said. "I called them about him specifically. He was there today and pulled a vanishing act without a word. The supervisor I talked to was pissed."

"You go by the Augur Hole Road address?"

Both Sam and Les shook their heads. "Figured we better talk with you first," Sam explained. "We have enough for a search warrant, don't you think?"

Joe shook his head. "Not yet. I want one

last totally concrete connection between Miller and that address, specifically."

He stared out the front window for a moment, watching some customers go in and out of the convenience store.

"How many people-of-interest entries were listed in Ike's involvements? You said lots."

"About ten," Lester said.

"Let's split them out," Joe told them. "We'll go back to the office, divide them up, and make a family tree of Ike's friends. I want to find out how things function at that address. What happens there, who comes and goes, what the layout is, the works."

He looked over at Sam, who was wiping her forehead. "That'll give us enough for a warrant, I bet, and it might give you time for a nap or something, 'cause I have the feeling you're not going to head for bed or the ER like you should."

She smiled broadly, despite her pallor. "You got that right, boss."

Lyn heard the knock on the front door downstairs over the sound of the television news. She quickly finished dressing for her upcoming late-evening shift, buttoning a pair of tight jeans, and ran downstairs shouting, "Coming."

She pulled open the door to reveal a woman older than herself, well groomed and stylishly dressed, who disguised her own obvious surprise with a polite smile and an outstretched hand. Behind her, in the driveway, a car was idling with a driver at the wheel.

"Oh, my God," Lyn blurted out, ignoring the hand for a moment. "You're Gail."

The smile widened. Gail said, "And you're Lyn, from what I've heard. I'm sorry we haven't met until now."

Lyn clumsily took the handshake and stepped back. "Do you want to come in?"

"That would be great. It's cold tonight."

Lyn paused. "Is your driver okay out there?"

Gail walked by her. "She's fine. She can listen to her own radio station for a while."

Lyn blinked at the now empty doorway, shut out the cold, and turned around to take Gail's long, elegant coat and hang it on one of the hallway pegs.

"Have a seat," she offered. "Would you like a drink? Or some coffee? I have a fresh pot."

Gail settled into an armchair, looking around Joe's living room. "Coffee would be great. So, you and Joe are living together?"

Ouch, Lyn thought, entering the kitchen. "No, no," she said over the counter partition. "We visit each other's place . . . Or not, depending. We have pretty crazy schedules."

"That, I remember," Gail said pleasantly. "This doesn't look any different. That's for sure."

Lyn turned her back to pour two cups. Try not to read anything into anything, she counseled herself. "Well, like I said, neither one of us is home much. You take cream or sugar or anything?"

"No thanks. Joe's the one who turns decent coffee into a hot milkshake. I'm guessing he's not here."

Lyn took the two cups into the living room. "No. I actually don't know where he is. He has a big murder case —" she interrupted herself as Gail took one of the coffees.

"I guess you know that," she ended.

Gail placed the cup on the wooden arm of the chair, where Lyn expected it would sit untouched.

"I certainly remember the rhythm," Gail said. "Does running a bar make his schedule more bearable?"

Lyn sat opposite her and took a sip of her own beverage. She's letting me know she's researched me, she thought.

"I wouldn't know," she told her guest. "I have nothing to compare it to. I don't mind it, though. We seem to see enough of each other."

"I guess he hasn't landed himself in the hospital yet," Gail said, her voice neutral. "You'll get to see a lot of him when that happens."

Lyn nodded, and tried to change the subject. "I see you on TV almost every day now. How's it going?"

"Well enough," Gail answered dully. The next words out of her mouth came in a hurried, almost irritated fashion. "Is he even in the area, or is he upstate? I called his cell, but of course he didn't pick up. It would be just my luck if he was in St. J."

Lyn frowned slightly. This was weird. "As far as I know, he's around. I think he was at the office earlier. He might still be, if you want to call."

Gail cupped her cheek in her hand. Suddenly she looked tired, almost exhausted. "I just wanted this to be simple," she said softly, as if to herself.

Lyn put down her cup and sat forward. "Are you okay? What's wrong?"

Gail closed her eyes briefly, trying to rally. "I was told some bad news tonight, at a press conference. It might put me and Joe at odds — politically, I mean." She sighed deeply. "God, I hate some of this shit sometimes."

"Is it this case?" Lyn asked.

Gail nodded. "It sure is. I should've known that something would come up. I thought it would be our past together — the cop and the liberal. I didn't think of an ongoing case . . . It's always what you aren't expecting."

Lyn nodded politely, half wondering if she shouldn't just leave this woman alone with her thoughts.

She reached for the phone by her side, instead. "Want me to call his office? Just to see if he's in?"

"That would be great. Thank you," Gail said, showing a warm and disarming smile.

Lyn placed the call, identified herself, and asked if Joe was there. She then followed by saying that there was no reason to put him on the phone; she was just curious. And then she hung up.

"He's there," she said unnecessarily.

Gail stood up, the coffee forgotten. "I better go then. I have to be in St. J later tonight."

Lyn's eyes widened. "Jesus. That's two hours from here."

Again, the tired smile greeted her. "I know. I have a sunrise Rotary in the morning. I'd sooner travel tonight than at the crack of dawn."

Lyn rose also and escorted her to the door, helping her on with her coat. "I don't know how you do it," she said.

Gail turned to face her. "Why I'm doing it makes the how easier. If I didn't believe all the stuff most people think is political crap, I wouldn't last a week."

"I'll be voting for you," Lyn said simply.

Gail gave her a hug at the door. "Our Joe is a lucky man," she said, and left.

CHAPTER TWENTY-FOUR

Ike dropped his duffel bag on the floor of the motel room and looked around. The clerk had taken cash, hadn't asked for a credit card or an ID, and hadn't made eye contact. A well-trained man for a certified, hole-in-the-wall dump. It was a worthwhile exchange for a room that could have been improved only with a can of gas and a match.

The one thing it did have, however — the one thing he'd made sure of — was wireless access to the Internet.

Ike locked the door, drew the curtains against the night, turned the TV on with the sound off, and pulled a battered laptop out of the duffel. The chair near the door looked too fragile for occupancy, so he bunched up the two small flat pillows for a backrest, and sat on the bed.

He turned on the computer, opened up to

Google, and typed in, "Joseph Gunther, VBI."

Joe glanced up to see Gail standing in the doorway, looking awkward.

"Gail?" he asked, immediately feeling foolish.

Everyone in the office followed suit.

"Holy shit," Willy muttered.

Sam moved first, crossing over quickly to give her a hug. "Gail, my God. What a treat. How are you?"

Gail smiled wanly, patting Sam on the arm. "I'm doing well. A little tired."

Lester was next, stepping up for a handshake. "You're doing great work out there." He laughed, adding, "You keep it up, I might have to vote for you, if you don't tell anybody."

Gail patted her heart. "Swear to God, Les. Between you and me."

But Joe knew this wasn't a casual drop-by. He rose from his desk, crossed the small office, and gave her a warm embrace. "Hey," he said simply.

Without waiting for her to explain her presence, he told his crew, "Be right back," and escorted Gail back into the central hallway.

It was after hours in the Municipal Building, so he took them down to where the selectmen normally met — familiar territory for Gail, who used to number among their ranks, although many years ago by now.

She smiled as they entered the room and Joe hit the lights to reveal the semicircular row of desks facing the assembled chairs for the audience.

"Wow," she said. "Memory lane."

She moved along the wall, as if trying not to disturb the ghosts, and took in the scene from the far corner.

Joe stayed by the front door. "Good to see you," he said.

"I met Lyn at the house," she answered, not looking at him. "She's very pretty."

Joe chuckled. "That's what I thought of Don. That was his name, right?"

That made her turn toward him. "Donald. Please," she corrected with a smile, adding whimsically, "Yeah, he was pretty, too. I think your Lyn is a lot brighter, though."

"I take it that means Donald's in the past?"

She nodded, her attention taken by the traffic moving outside, far below. "Oh, yes. Not much time for that sort of thing these days."

"They running you ragged?"

She finally stepped away from the wall and sat on the nearest chair, still in her coat. "I am never not totally exhausted. I think it's going well, though."

"Except for . . ." he suggested.

"What?" she asked.

He sat as well, across the room. "Well, you're here for some reason. I'm assuming you hit a hiccup involving me."

She laughed shortly but without humor. "You should be a detective. Yeah — I was asked a question at a press conference tonight. Apparently, you just used the criminal DNA data bank for a familial search."

Joe's slight smile slipped away. "True. David Hawke ran it by his lawyers beforehand, just so you know."

"I do know," she said. "I spoke to him on the phone on my way here."

"So, what's the problem?"

"The person you located that way is suing the state for invasion of privacy."

Joe laughed incredulously. "Robert Hildreth? No shit. The man's on his deathbed. That's feisty."

Gail's response was more restrained. "It's also a little awkward. I happen to agree with him."

Joe shrugged. "That's okay. I'm not surprised. How's this going to cause you trouble?"

"People will try to tar me with your actions, saying our past relationship is affecting my judgment."

He looked confused. "But you just said you didn't agree with it."

"I haven't made that official yet."

A silence fell between them, as each considered her meaning.

"What are you asking for?" Joe finally asked.

"Nothing," she said quickly. "I just felt so badly, calling you earlier about Felix Knowles."

"Felix . . ."

"Reynolds's chauffeur," she interrupted.

"I know," he said, repeating more softly, "I know."

She suddenly looked as tired as she sounded. "I am so sorry, Joe. I hate to hit you with all this. I know what you're up against."

He left his seat and walked through the assembled chairs to take the one beside her. He grabbed one of her hands.

"Gail, not to worry. I won't deny, I was disappointed by that, but only for a moment. I know what it's like for you, too, running for office. I've seen it in others. You can get turned around. I'm half amazed any politician can figure out which end's up after a while. You guys are surrounded by people interpreting reality for you."

He squeezed her hand. "Say what you have to say, Gail. Goddamn cops are trying to steal our civil liberties. People've been saying that forever. It's part of the process. We did what the lawyers said we could do when we went after that DNA, and between you and me and nobody else, I'm glad we did. I don't mind if after you become governor, you try to make it all illegal. Just don't be surprised if I testify in the State House against you."

She looked at him more closely. "So you think you got something?"

"I shouldn't tell you that, should I?" he asked her.

She shook her head mournfully. "No, you're right. I did like it when we could talk about what you were working on. I guess Lyn gets that privilege now."

"I don't know if she considers it that," he conceded.

"But she is good for you, isn't she?"

He smiled. One of the things he cherished most about his connection to Gail was that at its foundation was a friendship, undisturbed by whether they were a romantic couple or not. It was this, he knew, that made Lyn uncomfortable on occasion.

"She is," he admitted, thinking back over the short time he and Lyn had been together, some of it quite action-filled. "She does things I wouldn't dream of doing sometimes, but that can be good, too, assuming everybody survives."

Gail laughed softly. "I think I heard a little about that. Got a little hairy in Maine?"

He nodded, smiling. "Oh, yeah."

Outside, through the bank of windows, the passing traffic circling the district courthouse could be heard across the street.

"I better go," she finally said, not moving.

"Where to now?" he asked.

"St. J for a breakfast meeting."

He looked surprised. "You were down here doing something? I didn't know."

But she was shaking her head. "No, I was up north. I just wanted to talk to you about this."

"My God, Gail," he said. "That's hours out of your way. You can't afford that."

She stood up and gathered her coat around her. "I'll sleep in the car. I do that a lot. I've gotten good at it."

He rose with her and she laid a hand on his forearm. "I needed to do this, Joe. I hated the way we left things with that last phone call." She looked away, still speaking. "And now with this new thing, I didn't want you thinking I'd changed . . ."

He reached out and touched her hair, smiling, bringing her eye back to his. "Hey, not to worry. But thanks for coming. I know what I said about it all being okay, but your doing this counts a lot."

She nodded.

He added, "And don't worry too much on how politics is going to change you. You'll stay in control. You're tired, you're under an incredible amount of pressure, and you don't like hurting people's feelings. Things are tougher now than they'll probably ever be, unless you choose to run for something higher up the food chain. You'll get to feeling better."

He took her elbow and began guiding her through the chairs.

"Thanks, Joe," she said. "Maybe I wanted to hear that more than I wanted to tell you about this man's lawsuit."

He laughed. "Oh, right. Crazy Hildreth. What a way to wrap up your life — suing someone. Yeah, don't worry about that. I've already had a few people remind me that you're going to be my boss once this is over."

"Oh," she groaned. "Don't go there." But

then she stopped at the door and turned toward him, her expression serious once more.

"Do you really think I'll win?"

He tilted his head thoughtfully. "I'm probably the last one to answer that. You know what a political Slick Willy I am. Still, I think people are tired of Reynolds, and while Jyll Ivory is definitely going to eat into your votes, you're doing well."

He shook his head and added, "Who knows? You make a big enough stink about how we violated this poor bastard's last days on this earth, it could make you a populist poster child."

She frowned, but he could see she appreciated his releasing her. "Don't even joke about that."

They were walking down the hallway and reached the door to his office. "Joking is all I have left sometimes," he told her.

He gave her a warm hug and asked, "Is it improper to say, 'Break a leg'?"

She kissed his cheek. "Hell, what goes for the theater should go for what I'm doing, so thanks. Same to you."

He stepped back. "Guess we'll both find out in the headlines."

She laughed one last time and retreated down the hall, waving backward as she went. "Say good night, Joe."

"Good night, Joe," he answered, and returned to work.

By the time they all met up off the Augur Hole Road, a dirt track meandering through the woods between Marlboro and South Newfane, dawn was just graying the starless sky above the trees.

Joe and his three colleagues were all in one van, wearing ballistic vests and heavy clothing against the cold, and carrying shotguns. Except Willy, who preferred a specially shortened semiautomatic carbine for such outings — something he could operate with one hand.

They weren't alone. Positioned along the road near Gini Coursen's address were additional VBI agents, members of the Vermont State Police, and, farther back, a couple of ambulances, just in case.

Joe had his highly detailed search warrant, after spending the night dissecting Ike Miller's life, trolling for what they'd found at last — a bad boy colleague of Ike's whom they'd bounced out of bed and grilled for what they needed.

Now, they knew the layout of the three buildings — the house, a pole barn garage, and a storage shack; the usual inhabitants

— Ike and his mother Gini; and they'd compiled a list that included an acetylene torching rig, reloading equipment, woodworking tools, a stockpile of oak planks, blood and syringes, a computer and printer — all elements of what the Brookhaven scientists had linked to the killer of Ferenc, Fish, and Clarke — and any and all relevant documents. Ike's buddy had also told them that he regularly fooled with cars, which included changing engine oil inside the garage, where he also had his office.

The police radio mumbled inside the van. Joe left Sam to coordinate the last units to get into place while he gazed outside at the slowly emerging countryside. He could just discern the outline of the mostly bare tree limbs from the night sky behind them.

It was a conflicting time of year for local residents. The coming winter, the dying vegetation, the shortening hours of daylight, all contributed to a hibernating mood — and sharpened the conflict between it and humanity's self-imposed obligation to keep functioning. Joe often pondered, especially in the fall, how much his species had disconnected itself from its natural environment. At more leisurely moments, he was curious where it might all end up, and who would win.

"All set, boss," Sam said softly, aware of his thoughts being elsewhere.

He turned away from the window and studied the intense trio of faces beside him.

"Let's go, then," he said, and opened the door.

His team had taken his daydreaming in stride. In fact, they each had their own method of preparing for what might be coming — trying to anticipate everything. Sammie's forte; getting into a purely martial mental state, which spoke to Willy's style; or simply trying to control the adrenaline rush, which is where Les usually went. Joe, they knew, tended toward a quiet place first, as if he could achieve a balance between calm and violence when stock was taken at the end of the day.

As it turned out, none of them need have worried. Approaching from all angles, including through the woods, where several teams had been positioned ahead of time, they found no dogs, no booby traps, no snipers, and no Ike Miller.

They did get a snarling, half-crippled old lady out of bed.

"What the fuck do you want?" she demanded, having wrenched at the door after Lester pounded on it for ten minutes.

Lester produced his warrant and began

his speech, as Sam and others squeezed by the old woman and fanned out through the house. Joe stayed outside, taking in the entire compound, and eventually slipped inside the garage, Willy in tow.

They located a light switch by the sliding door and found themselves in a crude, high-ceilinged, dirt-floored workroom. It was jammed with spare parts, tools, woodworking and metal-cutting equipment, piles of lumber, slabs of steel, and accessorized with an assortment of indistinguishable trash. A partially disassembled car sat in its midst, a long, cluttered work table lined one wall, near an enormous and threatening-looking cold woodstove. And a computer was located on a table in one corner, surrounded by some much abused, dust-covered, electronic paraphernalia, including a printer.

It was the cave of a messy man with multiple interests.

Or, as Willy put it, "This place is a shit hole."

But Joe was smiling, looking around. "This," he corrected him, "is a gold mine, and we're going to be here for a very long time."

By the time Joe got to meet Gini Coursen, they had in fact been there for a long time.

Foliage season being by now a thing of the past, the surrounding skeletal trees threw angular shadows across the property as Joe crossed from the garage to the house. He had been told of the search results of both trailer and storage shed, just as he and Willy and half a dozen others had stayed in the garage to catalog its gifts. He knew that Coursen had not been dealing well with her uninvited guests, mostly because those watching her kept cycling out to trade places with their colleagues, shaking their heads at her relentless hostility.

But her being left to rage alone now had been intentional. Not only did Gunther want to learn all he could from his surroundings; he wanted her to stew in her own impotence.

Joe found her in the back bedroom, parked in an armchair that looked built around her considerable bulk. A spindly aluminum walker stood nearby, frail and puny in light of what might be expected of it.

Joe closed the door behind him as he entered.

"Who're you?" she demanded.

He located an upright chair in a corner, piled with clothes. These he unceremoniously dumped onto her bed, before placing the chair opposite her and sitting down.

"My name's Joe Gunther," he told her. "I work for the Vermont Bureau of Investigation."

She smiled bitterly. "Good for you. Now you can get the hell out of my house."

"We will in a while. We're close to getting done, and I'd like you to know right up front that if you don't want to talk with me, you don't have to. You're not under arrest. You can just sit here until we're finished and then return to your life."

"Fine," she said, her eyes narrowed. "I don't want to talk to you. You can go crap in your hat."

He nodded slowly, as if mulling over some inner debate. "Problem being," he said to her, "that your life will no longer include your son, Ike. I thought you should know that."

"What do you mean?" she asked, the eyes widening somewhat. "You don't have Ike."

"Nor do you," he said, adding, "and nor will you — ever again." He gestured outside the door, where they could hear people moving about. "What do you think we're doing out there?"

"Tearing my house apart," she ventured. "I'm going to sue your asses about that, too. Don't you doubt it."

But Joe was looking at her pityingly.

"We're collecting what makes Ike, Ike," he explained. "Believe it or not, that's one thing the TV shows get right — we can go through someone's personal belongings and find out everything about them. How they dress, what they like to eat, how they think, who their friends are. By the time we're finished, we'll know more about your son than you do."

"Well, isn't that neat?" she challenged him.

But he pretended to take it literally, sitting back and crossing his legs. "It is, actually," he conceded. "This forensics stuff has given us tools I never would have dreamed of in the old days."

He suddenly sat forward, as if confiding a secret in a crowded room. "I mean, after all," he said softly, "neither one of us is getting any younger, right? You and I have seen more than half the young puppies out there put together."

She stared at him, at sea on how to respond to someone this dense.

Joe suddenly frowned, and then cast his eyes down sorrowfully. "Damn."

"What?" she asked.

"Well, I'm just starting to worry, is all. I mean, about your situation."

She was becoming increasingly baffled. "My situation?"

Joe pointed to the walker. "My mom's in a wheelchair. Of course, my brother lives with her, so she's all set. Every time there's a problem, small or big, he's there to help."

Joe paused, as if moved to silence. "You're going to be in a real bind. There aren't many people in your life, are there? And not much money. It's going to be tough without Ike."

She tried rallying her anger. "You bastard."

"It's going to be like losing Ben all over again, but worse," he added, almost as an afterthought.

That brought her up short. "Ben?"

He rubbed his forehead. "God, that must've been hard. Your firstborn. Locked away for the rest of his life. Dying surrounded by jailbirds. Like a nightmare."

Her fists were working, opening and closing with fury. "You are a monster."

He looked at her sympathetically. "I know I seem that way. You've had so many monsters in your life, screwing things up."

He let that sink in before resuming. "Those three meddling women, for example — Elise and Candice and Maggie."

She froze, her eyes locked on to his.

"You know?" she finally whispered.

He tilted his head quizzically. "Of course we do." He waved a hand around. "Why else do you think we're here?" Again, he dropped his voice conspiratorially. "Not that we didn't have to work a bit. You two were clever — I'll give you that. Making those three suffer, just as you did? Amazing. Most people just lash out. But you thought about this, didn't you?"

She glowered. "You have no idea."

"But I do," he protested. "Spending all that time watching the apple of your eye slowly rot to death. You wanted someone to pay. A fast clean death? Forget about it." He clenched his own fist and held it up, his voice rising slightly. "The point is to make it hurt, to make the pain last and last, to crush their hearts but not kill them. What inspired you?" he asked abruptly. "Was it Betty dying of a heart attack after Alice committed suicide?"

Gini was disgusted by the suggestion. "That little bitch. She was a worm."

"Alice? But she got what she deserved," he suggested.

"Hardly."

Joe slapped his forehead gently. "Well, of course," he exclaimed. "What a dope. She took the easy way out. I see what you mean. Betty must've been a little more satisfying, though, dying of a broken heart."

She shook her head. "She had no heart. She was all high and holy; she and her friends." Coursen pointed her finger for emphasis as she asked, "Do you know anything at all about that little slut of a niece she had?"

"I know she was very young," Joe admitted.

"My *son* was young," she seethed. "That little whore spread her legs like a hooker and took him in just like that." She snapped her fingers. "*He* was the one who was raped, mister."

"Still," Joe suggested, "there are all sorts of justice."

Gini furrowed her brow. "What do you mean?"

Joe looked surprised. "You settled the score," he said. "Those three threw your son to the wolves; you returned the favor, one at a time." He dropped his voice again, as if in confidence. "And pretty elegantly, too, I have to admit," he added.

"Elegantly?" she queried.

"Yeah — it was like a perfect math puzzle. That's what scientists call a solution when it's damn near perfect: 'Elegant.' Has a neat ring to it. That's what you did. You researched your old pals —"

"They weren't pals," she interrupted.

"Okay," he retreated. "But that's what happened. You found out what made them tick — who was dearest to each one of them."

Coursen settled against the pillows stuffed behind her and smiled slightly, her expression self-satisfied.

Joe let her bask in her victory for a couple of seconds before saying, "Of course, that just means that Ike was your tool, like a hammer or something. So, even if the judge gets soft-hearted and only gives you twenty years, it means you die in jail."

He got to his feet as she stiffened and declared, "You can't stick that on me. Look at me. I'm almost in a wheelchair, too. I didn't kill anybody."

He looked down at her, filling her armchair like poured lava, the layout of the room betraying that she quite obviously could get around, if uncomfortably. "Doesn't matter. You came up with the idea; Ike carried it out. Makes you one and the same."

Her face reddened. "That is bullshit. It was his idea. I had enough on my plate just trying to stay alive with all that's troubling me. You should see the pills I take. Ike kept bugging me about Ben — he idolized his older brother. He was so angry at all of you for taking him away. He pumped me for information about Elise and the others. I hadn't thought about them for years."

Joe watched her carefully, studying how she was formulating her defense in front of him, hearing herself talk and modulating her argument, almost like a novelist, editing on the fly.

"I'd be sitting here," she kept going. "Night after night, my soul dead and my body broken, and Ike would just keep after me, asking me for details like a crazy man. Did you find his notebooks? Maybe he burned them. He would write in them every night, after talking to me. He had them divided into sections, one for each of the three women, getting all their details down. And then he'd go for trips, since what I knew was old and out-of-date, and he'd get fresh information about them. He'd tell me what he'd learned."

Joe had replaced the clothes onto the chair he'd borrowed and was standing by the door now. He couldn't resist adding a little fuel to the fire before him. "Must've been terrible, watching him go around the bend like that."

She caught his drift immediately and ran with it. "It was. It was. He was crazy, and he made me a little crazy. I saw the whole horrible thing with Ben repeating itself."

Joe opened the door and stepped almost

out of sight into the hallway, before looking back at her one last time. Caught off guard, she was staring, stone-faced and calculating, the despair of seconds earlier vaporized.

"Good luck, Gini," he said. "You'll need it."

He closed the door and encountered Lester near the kitchen. "Have a nice chat?" he asked.

Joe smiled. "Right. You didn't find any notebooks, did you, filled with personal intel about Clarke, Ferenc, and Howard? It would've been in Ike's handwriting."

Les frowned. "A notebook? Nope. Not so far."

Joe nodded. "I didn't think so."

CHAPTER TWENTY-FIVE

The morning paper's front page had little room for anything beyond Ike Miller and his doings, directly and otherwise. In a late-night conference call between Joe, Bill Allard, Neal Kirkland of the VSP, and the commissioner of public safety, David Stanton — and a lawyer from the AG's office — the decision was made to release Ike's name to the press as the man accused of the three murders. His photo was prominently displayed, along with advice that should he be spotted, 911 should be called and extreme caution taken. Also mentioned in the press release was that a familial DNA search had played a role linking evidence to the suspect.

This last tidbit was deemed necessary to at least attempt to head off trouble, based on what Joe reported from his meeting with Gail. And sure enough, sharing the banner headlines was an announcement that candidate Gail Zigman had roundly condemned this invasion of privacy by "elements of the police community." Last but not least, of course, was the news announcing Robert Hildreth's suit concerning that very topic.

"Wow," Lyn said, looking over the top of her newspaper as Joe poured himself orange juice at the kitchen counter. "I thought you guys were friends."

This was the first that they'd seen of each other for over a day, and even now, Joe had merely dropped by to shave, shower, and change his clothes. He hadn't slept in a long time, and it looked unlikely that he'd get to soon.

"Gail and I?" he asked. "We are. That's why she dropped by last night. She wanted to give me the heads-up." He changed his voice to make it sound more theatrical. "There's tension in the air. It's November, after all — only days to the election."

Lyn was still reading, largely ignoring him. "You're mentioned here."

"Well, VBI is the lead agency," he said, taking a deep swallow.

"It's not that," she informed him. "Your name's in the editorial."

He walked over and sat opposite her at the counter. "Really?" He didn't like the sound of that, and suspected Stan Katz lurking in the background.

"Yeah." Lyn quoted, " 'Zigman's stance on this issue shouldn't come as a surprise, even given the fact that VBI field commander Joseph Gunther and she used to be romantically involved. Those readers who recall Zigman's days on the Selectboard will remember her occasionally criticizing the very police department that employed her companion.' "

"Jesus," Joe muttered.

"It goes on about integrity and whatever, but your name doesn't come up again. That's a little tacky, isn't it?"

Joe laughed. "I suppose. It's not untrue, and to be honest, I told her to scream and yell all she wanted, if it would help her cause." He pointed to the paper. "Precisely because I thought people might make the connection between us and give her marks for disagreeing with me."

Lyn put the newspaper aside and gave him a thoughtful look. "It doesn't piss you off, even a little bit?"

He shook his head. "Nope. I'm not even totally sure she and I are at odds. I had a crook to identify; the law, or at least the lawyers, gave me the thumbs-up to go down this road. I did it and we got a name. But do I think it was morally right to poke into an innocent man's life because he just happened to be related to a crook?"

Joe rubbed his eyes before continuing. "I think so in this case. I didn't cause any harm; I just ticked the guy off, and he happened to be a privacy freak. But I suppose I could've caused real damage to his reputation had circumstances been different."

He checked his watch and took a last swig of juice before standing up and coming around the counter. "The older I get, the less worked up I become with all this babble. You do what you do in life. You try to make integrity and honesty and respect for others your key words, but it can get tricky sometimes, and things don't always turn out the way you expect."

He wrapped his arms around her and kissed her. "Back to the trenches," he said, breaking away and heading toward the coat rack near the door, saying further, "I'll let you know what's up as the day goes. You at the bar tonight?"

"Not tonight," she said, following him and helping him on with his overcoat. "I'll try to be here to give you a back rub when you get home."

He laughed and kissed her one last time. "Now *that'll* be something to look forward to."

She waved through the window to him as

he backed out of the driveway, and then returned to the kitchen counter and the newspaper, flipping it open to page three. There, in a bordered box, was a listing of Gail Zigman's upcoming planned appearances for the week.

Ike Miller pulled down the bill of his dirty baseball cap and dropped his chin onto his chest so that he could barely see to walk straight, choosing to look silly over possibly being recognized. He'd been inside a gas station convenience store, near White River Junction, when he'd noticed the pile of newspapers on the counter, along with his own face staring out at him — dead center, right under the headlines. Now he was trying to get outside the building without walking into a wall.

Back in the cold, he crossed the parking apron, forgetting the hunger that had driven him here for breakfast, and fast-tracked toward the road and the motel squatting untidily on its far side. At the road's edge, he tilted his head quickly from side to side, to check for traffic, and of course saw a patrol car heading east in his direction.

"Shit," he muttered, and dropped to one knee, pretending to tie one of his boot laces. After the cruiser had passed by, he repeated his traffic check and then ran for cover at full tilt.

Inside his room, he didn't bother removing his coat, but immediately went to his stolen, battered laptop and got on the Internet to feverishly read the news. He flicked from site to site, reading too fast to fully comprehend any one article completely, but getting enough in the end to gather what he needed, including the mention that his mother had been arrested following a search of their home, and that some anonymous "informed source" had reported hearing her loudly protesting that she had nothing to do with anything and that her son had clearly lost his mind, poor boy.

At that, Ike straightened and glared at the screen. "You fucking cow."

He remained that way for a couple of minutes, lost first in panic, then confusion, and finally deep in thought.

He'd done good work until now. Planned everything out. Taken his time. Something had messed up. He hadn't figured out what from the articles, but it probably had something to do with the other big news, which had caught his eye because of the mention of blood.

He frowned angrily. He'd screwed up. He knew that now. He'd just wanted to mess with their heads, leaving those drops of blood. He'd also wanted to do something extra that his mom knew nothing about, just to prove that he could. She was always ranting about what an idiot he was, how all the brains had gone to Ben. He was sick of it — and of playing second fiddle to a fag who'd died of AIDS in prison. *That* was the winner he was being compared to? Ike was the one who paid for her medicines and the groceries, hustled to come up with the rent, took care of the laundry and even helped bathe her, for Christ's sake. And now the bitch had thrown him under the bus.

No surprise there.

It made him mad. He'd figured that by doing all this shit with the two women and the kid in the truck, at least he'd gain his mother's respect, and that Ben might be finally put in his grave.

But not a chance.

He kept staring at his own photograph, floating in the center of the screen. Fucking cops.

He leaned forward and scrolled down a little. What had he noticed earlier but not really read? Something weird. He stopped and studied the words more carefully.

"No shit," he barely said aloud.

He'd just understood the connection

between the head cop and the loudmouthed politician.

"Damn," he added, his earlier confusion yielding to a renewed sense of purpose. "He thinks he can grab my mom? Guess what I can do to his old girlfriend?"

Lyn stood with her back against the wall of the so-called Governors' Ballroom, in Montpelier's Capitol Plaza Hotel. It was a vast, resonant, brightly lighted room, reminiscent of a documentary she'd once seen about aircraft carriers and their below-deck hangar spaces. And the sound was deafening — ten times the noisiest bar she might ever have tended in the old days. There had to be over three hundred people here, shouting, chanting, moving around holding signs and singing inane ditties like "Gail for Gov," and "Make Zigman the Top Woman."

To Lyn's jaded eye, it was all faintly juvenile and even a little scary, when she considered the experience and education level of some of these wannabe cheerleaders.

She began to question why she'd bothered making the trip at all. She wasn't politically inclined, sometimes had no real knowledge of the people running, and found most politicians to be contemptible hypocrites.

Of course, this one was a little different. At least, she hoped so.

As she was considering all this, the wall right next to her cracked open a couple of inches, revealing an inset door and half the face of a youthful man.

"Miss Silva?"

Startled, she stepped away from the wall and stared at what she could see of him. "Yes?"

"Gail would like to see you, if that's okay."

Feeling instantly like an idiot, she pointed to herself. "Me?"

"Sure." Two beckoning fingers appeared through the crack. "Come on in."

Thinking of Alice in Wonderland, Lyn stepped forward and was absorbed by the door quickly yawning open and instantly closing behind her, cutting down the deafening noise like a guillotine. She found herself in a dark and empty corridor, facing a thin young man, probably still in college, wearing a white dress shirt and a narrow tie, loosened at the throat, who stuck out his hand in greeting.

"Hi," he said. "I'm Phil."

She shook the hand distractedly, looking around. "How did you know I was here?"

He gave a broad, toothy grin. "We peek out at the crowd before every one of these,

checking who's there. It helps a lot sometimes. You never know, right?"

He turned and began leading her down
the hallway. "Come with me. Gail's got a
couple of minutes yet. She was really tickled
to see you."

Lyn followed at a quick pace, impressed
that Gail had even remembered what she
looked like.

They entered another side door, traveled
fast through a room filled with more people,
all working at anything from stapling signs
to wooden stakes and stuffing envelopes to
typing on laptops, and stepped into what
seemed to be an improvised office and green
room, combined.

Lyn was trying to take it all in when she
heard a familiar voice call out. "Lyn. My
God. A sight for sore eyes."

She turned to see Gail come at her, arms
wide, and gather her into a close embrace.
"I can't believe you came to one of these."

Lyn smiled awkwardly. "Well, I did say I
was going to vote for you. I guess I had to
see you in action."

Gail stepped back and took her hand. She
called over to Phil. "How much time?"

He didn't have to check his watch. "Three
minutes."

She pulled Lyn along after her, muttering,

"I'll take it."

She led them through yet another door, and into an even smaller room with a few chairs and a card table covered with paperwork.

There, she paused a couple of seconds, collecting her thoughts as Lyn watched, and then laid a hand on the younger woman's shoulder.

"I am *so* sorry for all this fuss and bother," she began. "But I just couldn't believe it when I saw you in the ballroom. It was like the answer to a prayer."

"Really?" Lyn said, baffled. "Why?"

Gail looked her directly in the eyes. "Because I was distracted and tired and a bit of a jerk when we met the other night, and I wanted you to know that I admire and appreciate you and think you've been great for Joe in ways I never was or could be."

She waved her hand in the air a couple of times as if warding off black flies, and added, "I know I'm sounding like an idiot right now, but I just had to get that off my chest, and I don't have any time anymore to simply think things through."

"You weren't a jerk the other night," Lyn assured her.

"I was," Gail protested. "Or at least I felt like one inside. I didn't expect you to open

Joe's front door, and when you did, I had a completely different speech in my head, and felt terrible that I never got to tell you how I felt. It was like having a golden opportunity to speak your mind and then discovering you have laryngitis."

She laughed and scratched her head. "And now," she continued, "I sound like I'm on speed."

This time, it was Lyn who took her hand and led her to one of the chairs, sitting opposite her, commenting, "You must be exhausted."

Gail merely sighed, smiled, and nodded.

"Gail," Lyn told her, "I really appreciate what you said. I mean, I know I don't need anyone's blessing to fall in love with someone, but you two had years and years together, and it means a lot to me that this is okay with you."

Gail suddenly leaned forward and kissed the other woman's cheek. She looked on the verge of crying. "You have no idea, Lyn," she admitted. "I felt terrible when we broke up, but I just couldn't do it anymore."

There was a knock on the door and Phil stuck his head in. "Sorry, Gail. Time's up."

Both women stood and hugged one last time.

Gail suddenly laughed. "You want to be

onstage with me? You don't have to do anything, and there'll be lots of other people. It'll give you my view of this circus."

"It is kinda cool," Phil pitched in, opening the door wider to escort them out.

Lyn looked from one to the other. "Really? I wouldn't be in the way?"

They both laughed as Gail told her, "I'm the only one they all want to run over, for one reason or another."

Lyn was swept along, self-conscious of the clothes she'd chosen that morning and feeling completely out of her element. But Phil and Gail had spoken the truth — the stage on which she soon found herself was vast and crowded, filled with yelling, cheering, waving people, and she quickly found a spot, again against the wall, from where she could see past Gail's back as she stood at the podium and addressed a throng of upturned, enthusiastic faces. It was an amazing moment, very much at odds with the barroom crowds she knew so well, and she instantly sensed the appeal it must have for so many office seekers.

She didn't hear the speech; didn't even pay attention. Her thoughts were lost in the conversation just past, and on the surreal surroundings of the moment. She was therefore caught off guard when everyone began moving around her, the noise crescendoed into wild cheers, and Gail turned around, extended her hand, and asked, "You want to walk out with me?"

Without a second thought, she took the hand and joined the triumphant march toward the front door of the hotel and the street outside, side by side with Gail.

Ollie Peterson saw the crowd shifting in front of the Capitol Plaza Hotel and knew it was time. He swung out of the driver's seat, where he'd been enjoying the heater and the radio, and expertly hopped onto the hood of his battered car, which was already prepped with a tripod. He'd parked here two hours earlier, when choosing just the right camera angle was easy, and had slowly witnessed the sidewalks fill with people.

It had been a hell of a campaign year, and he'd seen his share. As the primary newswire photographer for the state, he hadn't missed much when it came to headline grabbers — or ribbon cuttings, bake sales, and farm fairs, for that matter. But this election had created its own form of energy. An incumbent governor, wounded but still popular; a well-spoken, good-looking, Democratic challenger with the quirky extra wrinkle of being a high-profile rape victim; and the standard spoiler from the Progressives, totally lacking a majority, but attracting enough votes to once again potentially cripple the prominent left-winger.

In itself, not an unheard of recipe, either nationally or in backwater rural Vermont. But this time, because of the sheer eloquence and liveliness the three candidates had brought to it, the campaign had blossomed with time, until now, just a couple of days shy of the election, it had attracted national attention. Standing on his car, attaching his camera to the tripod, Ollie saw TV trucks stationed to both sides of the street, bristling with dishes and antennae. Leave it to Vermont, he thought ruefully. Always stirring up trouble.

He bent slightly and peered through his camera lens, adjusting it so that the hotel's steps could clearly be seen in the shot. The Capitol Plaza had a canopy he'd dealt with before — a visual eyesore that took most newbie news photographers by surprise. That's why he'd parked here and chosen this spot. He knew from experience how the sun would angle in just right and give him the shot most others would only be hoping for.

Not that this would result in anything

other than the standard cheesy picture of a candidate waving to her supporters. Still, Ollie was a professional, and had his pride.

A flash of sunlight off the glass doors alerted him to people exiting. He half held his breath, put all his concentration into the tiny rectangle before his right eye, and waited.

People fanned out to both sides, nicely making an opening among those on the sidewalk, and then, in a flurry of waving hands and broad smiles, Gail Zigman and her retinue stepped into view, pausing briefly. Ollie hit the button on his camera, which began taking a picture every half second.

He knew it was a cliché, but even much later, Ollie could only describe it as having sounded like firecrackers — a series of closely spaced pops, almost joyful in nature, and totally in context with the festive mood. He saw unexpected movement through his lens — people twisting and ducking; some falling from view — but nothing that truly registered in his head until the visual hole he'd been complimenting himself for finding was suddenly filled in with rushing, screaming, gesticulating people in a panic.

He straightened and looked around, his camera on autopilot. The firecrackers had stopped. More and more people were beginning to rush toward the hotel. His car rocked a couple of times slightly from being jarred in passing.

But for that one moment, there was no context, no logic to the story, no explanation for what had just occurred.

Until a voice cut across the street and brought it all together. "She's been shot."

Ollie dropped his eyes to the still chattering camera before him. "Shit," he said softly. "I hope I got it."

CHAPTER TWENTY-SIX

Joe walked into Barre's Central Vermont Medical Center's emergency room in a fog, steered there by Lester Spinney, who had a firm grip on his upper arm.

"You okay, boss?" Lester asked, not for the first time.

Joe didn't respond, as he hadn't bothered doing since getting the news eighty minutes earlier.

The lobby was jammed with people, crying, shouting, hugging in groups. Some wore colorful hats, others had ribbons hanging from their clothes. There were posters and bumper stickers and more hats scattered underfoot, crushed and smeared with dirt and blood. It was a scene from an old Fellini movie — an absurd commingling of jarring images.

Lester held his badge ahead of him and muscled through the crowd, muttering, "Police, please move," to whoever needed prodding. At the front of the room, they came to a uniformed officer with a clipboard and an anxious expression, who stared at them without comment for a second, as if attempting to catalog what species they fit.

"Joe Gunther," Lester said simply, tilting his head toward his companion.

"Oh, damn," the officer said, standing aside. "I'm sorry."

They entered a hallway, still crowded but less chaotic, and filled mostly with either uniforms or scrubs and white lab coats.

A nurse confronted them there, quickly read the letters on Lester's badge and asked, "Gunther?"

Les nodded. The nurse turned and led them to a curtain halfway down the corridor.

"She's in here," she said simply and faded away.

Both men stood at the curtain for a moment, simply staring at it.

"You want company, Joe?" Lester asked.

Joe seemed to think that over. "No," he finally said. "I'm good."

Lester released his arm, thinking that was the last word he would have used, and told his friend. "I'll be right here. One word, and I'll come."

Not answering, Joe pushed through the

curtain and entered the room.

It was a typical examination cubicle — a counter, cabinets, free-standing equipment parked in odd corners, ready for use. And, of course, the table in the center.

Someone had placed a sheet over her, neat and wrinkle-free. It was startlingly white and unblemished, and it showed off her body's profile as fresh fallen snow sets off the hills and slopes beneath it.

He approached the head of the table and paused, watching the surface of the white cotton as if for signs of life.

But of course, there were none.

Slowly, reluctantly, he took the edge of the sheet in his hand and drew it back to reveal her face, thinking of how many times in his life he'd done the same thing with complete strangers.

She was naked, of course. He could tell from her bare shoulders. They cut all the clothes off in cases like this, for free and complete access to the body. No discretion or delicacy when it comes to saving a life.

Or trying to.

Thankfully, they'd extracted the endotracheal tube from her mouth, although he knew they weren't supposed to. He wondered if that had been for him, or just an oversight. It happened now and then. The medical examiner liked everything kept in place, but understood when things went awry.

He bent over and kissed her cheek. It was still slightly warm, despite its pallor.

Instinctively, he pulled the sheet lower, exposing her breasts and the bullet hole between them. They hadn't bothered with any surgical intervention. She'd been dead on arrival. And so she was intact, aside from the hole. They'd even wiped the blood off her torso, leaving her skin pale and unblemished.

He pulled the sheet back up to her chin. Beverly Hillstrom would probably do the autopsy the law required. He shook his head at the thought — another woman with whom he'd slept, if for a single night. Such a tight circle, he thought — Beverly, Lyn, and Gail.

And Ellen, of course — the only one he'd married. Taken by cancer so many years ago.

Jesus, he thought. What the hell is happening?

The curtain rustled to admit a new visitor.

Joe turned to take her in, her hair a mess and her blouse stained with blood.

Gail crossed the room and wrapped her arms around him. "Oh, Joe," she wept. "I'm so sorry."

He rubbed her back and stared at the wall behind her, not seeing a thing.

"Are you okay?" he heard her ask in his ear.

"Oh, sure," he said quietly.

She pulled back slightly to study his face. "She came up to find out more about me." She smiled wanly. "Maybe to check out the old competition. I was so happy to see her there. I wanted her close." Her eyes filled with tears. "I was holding her hand when it happened."

She buried her face in his shoulder again, her body wracked with sobbing, and he rubbed her back some more.

What happens now? he wondered.

Ike Miller adjusted the radio. Goddamned thing kept fading out. Typical. You steal a car 'cause it's got good tires, not too much rust, and looks like it'll fade into traffic, and the stupid radio is busted.

He fiddled with it some more, drifting off the road slightly and kicking up gravel.

And he liked noise — TV, radio, CD — he didn't care what. Anything to fill the air and give his mind a place to park itself. Not the news, though. He was sick of that. All about the shooting and the manhunt. Ike here, Ike there, everywhere an Ike, Ike. He was up to his ears in it. You'd think the crazy bastards would give it a rest.

He liked country-western. That and talk radio. Like that Limbaugh guy — crazy son of a bitch. Ike had no idea what the hell he was talking about most of the time, but the man had style.

The car swerved again and he straightened it out. Shit. He twirled the knob off the station he'd been on and searched for another. More news. One dead, five wounded. Ike seen fleeing the scene, gun in hand. But he hadn't hit the one he'd aimed for. What a pisser. It had been like shooting fish in a barrel, except for either the sight had been off a bit, or the rifle a little sloppy. He wasn't the greatest shot in the world. He knew that much. And assault rifles were what they were — not made for target shooting. Still.

He had really liked the idea of whacking that cop's main squeeze. Ike had to give his mom that much — she'd hit a home run there, making people suffer by killing their loved ones. That was genius.

He shook his head, not for the first time. Too bad.

He looked up sharply, attracted first by the siren, and only then saw the blue lights in his mirror.

"Fuck," he said to himself.

He kept on driving. In the old days, he would've pulled over and tried bullshitting the guy, but not today. His picture was probably taped to every cruiser dashboard in New England.

What to do?

The cop didn't know who was ahead of him. Ike was pretty sure about that. He'd stolen one car in Montpelier, just before the shooting, and this one some time later, south of Burlington. No way anyone could have connected the two. It must have been his swerving earlier, when he'd been fussing with the radio.

Not that it mattered. Word was out on him, and he was betting that every cop out there was hoping to get lucky. Even Ike had figured out that it was only a matter of time.

He placed his hands more firmly on the wheel and stomped on the accelerator.

What the hell.

Briefly, he saw the cruiser fall back. I'll be damned, he thought, and concentrated on the curve ahead. He was on Route 7, below Rutland and heading south, and knew the road would start narrowing soon. He placed his car right over the center line, so he could pass any cars ahead, right or left, with equal ease.

"Come on, baby," he murmured to the engine.

Behind him, the cruiser closed the gap just a little, applying pressure without putting itself at risk. The sound of the siren was becoming annoying.

They passed several cars, went over a few hills, and then came to a straight stretch where the road not only finally narrowed, but was marked at its far end by a group of twinkling blue lights, arrayed in a row.

Roadblock.

Instinctively, Ike's foot came off the gas pedal a little.

Now what?

It was still too far away for details, but the cars looked pretty solidly arranged. There was a gap, though, near the middle . . .

Ike reapplied his speed, not noticing how the cruiser behind once more dropped back a bit.

He aimed at the weak spot and pushed the engine for all it was worth, enjoying seeing the roadblock looming up as if he were in a plane, approaching a landing.

Only too late did he notice the strip of spikes laid across the narrow opening purposefully left for him. He blew by the roadblock, seeing no one to either side — only empty police cars — felt the double thud beneath his tires. He braced himself for a sudden loss of control, not knowing that the spikes were actually hollow, and bled tires instead of blowing them up as in the movies. As a result, he just felt his steering go mushy, and the car begin to struggle to maintain speed.

He looked in the mirror and saw the roadblock come alive with activity. Ahead, more cars appeared out of nowhere, all flashing those damned blue lights.

"Damn," he said, and pulled over.

For a moment, he studied his hands still gripping the steering wheel. He wasn't truly considering his options. He pretty much knew what they were. More likely, he was just looking at what he could see of himself, thinking briefly of all the things those hands had done.

One last time.

Then he reached for the .45 beside him and placed its barrel into his mouth.

Willy Kunkle knew enough of Joe's habits to simply let himself in. Most cops had double locks on their doors and guns hidden in every cranny. Not Joe. The man was a dinosaur, galumphing around like he'd live forever, despite all the hell breaking loose around him.

Willy shook his head as he stepped into the warm living room. Not me, he thought. Anyone comes into my place uninvited, he gets to leave limping. If he's lucky.

He heard a noise from the back, toward the woodworking shop. This was Joe's meditation room, filled with ancient equipment that had once belonged to his father. Table saws, drills, lathes, hundreds of tools. Willy had no clue what most of them were. But the Old Man could spend hours in there, puttering.

Especially now.

He opened the door to the shop quietly and leaned against the jamb, watching his boss dry-fitting two sides of a cherry wood box together, making sure they were perfect before he applied any glue.

"Hey," Willy said gently.

Joe looked up and gave him a tired half smile. "Hey, yourself."

"How're you holding up?"

Joe slowly replaced the two pieces of wood onto his workbench. "Not sure I am."

Willy left his station by the door and crossed over to a guest stool Joe had available for visitors. A lot of conversations had taken place in this retreat from the world, and at one time or another, every member of his team had been here.

"It's not the same," Willy began, "but I remember what it felt like when my ex-wife was killed. Kind of like a grenade going off nearby. Stunning."

Both men had been in combat, although at different times and in different places. The allusion was apt.

Joe nodded, remembering. "Yeah. Kind of. 'Cept that wore off."

"You heard what our new governor-elect did?"

Joe looked at him. He knew of the election result, but nothing more. "What?"

"She got the Legislature to recognize Lyn as a hero or some damn thing. I didn't really read it, but it sounded nice, and it put Lyn in a nice light. She was a good lady."

Joe was back to studying his hands in his lap. "That she was."

Willy glanced around the shop, taking in its orderly and focused aura. "What're you going to do?" he asked.

Joe sighed. "I don't know."

"You must have about six years of leave built up."

Joe nodded without response.

"Of course," Willy mused, "getting back to work might be the best thing to do."

Joe didn't react.

Willy studied his bowed head. He had

never seen his unacknowledged mentor so low, and had never felt so utterly useless.

"You are coming back, aren't you?" he asked, a sense of dread rising in his chest.

Joe looked up gradually, until his eyes were fixed on Willy's. "I don't know."

Joe's gaze shifted to a window on the far wall, overlooking the small backyard.

Willy got the message. He rose from his seat and returned to the door. He paused on the threshold and commented, "I know this isn't the time or the place, but I can't not tell you. Sam's pregnant."

Joe faced him at that and smiled. He rose and crossed the room, moving slowly like an old man. When he drew near, Willy saw that there were tears in his eyes.

Joe stopped before him, nodded a couple of times, and then touched Willy's cheek with his fingertips.

"I love you guys," he said, and turned away.

ABOUT THE AUTHOR

Archer Mayor it a death investigator, a sheriff's deputy, and a volunteer firefighter and EMT in addition to being a novelist. He lives in Newfane, Vermont.

The employees of Thorndike Press hope you have enjoyed this Large Print book. All our Thorndike, Wheeler, and Kennebec Large Print titles are designed for easy reading, and all our books are made to last. Other Thorndike Press Large Print books are available at your library, through selected bookstores, or directly from us.

For information about titles, please call:
   (800) 223-1244

or visit our Web site at:
   http://gale.cengage.com/thorndike

To share your comments, please write:
   Publisher
   Thorndike Press
   295 Kennedy Memorial Drive
   Waterville, ME 04901